Praise for Elmer Kelton

"*Cloudy in the West* will be read and reread by adults and children. Elmer Kelton is a Texas treasure, as important for his state as Willa Cather is for Nebraska and Badger Clark for South Dakota. Kelton truly deserves to be made one of the immortals of literature."

—*El Paso Herald-Post*

"A story of murder and greed set in Texas in 1885 features Elmer Kelton's most endearing character yet, a twelve-year-old boy named Joey Shipman. . . . A wonderfully humorous book with just enough evil in a few of the characters to keep realism alive and well. All this, and the most delightful narrator since Huck Finn."

—*Amarillo News-Globe*

"The fast-moving *Cloudy in the West* succeeds as a young adult novel, traditional Western, and an all-around good read."

—*Fort Worth Star-Telegram*

"If you like a good Western, know that nobody rekindles the old fires like Kelton."

—*The Austin American-Statesman*

"This latest Kelton masterpiece is difficult to put down. The story was more important to finish than sleep. . . . I could easily summarize Kelton's story, but it is too good and too entertaining to take away the surprises that await readers. . . . It is a great story from a superb storyteller."

—*San Angelo Standard Times*

D0036417

Other Books by Elmer Kelton

Elmer Kelton

CLOUDY IN THE WEST

FORGE®

A TOM DOHERTY ASSOCIATES BOOK
NEW YORK

This is a work of fiction. All the characters and events portrayed in this novel are either fictitious or are used fictitiously.

CLOUDY IN THE WEST

Copyright © 1997 by Elmer Kelton

A Forge Book
Published by Tom Doherty Associates, Inc.
175 Fifth Avenue
New York, NY 10010

Forge® is a registered trademark of Tom Doherty Associates, Inc.

ISBN: 0-812-57594-6
Library of Congress Card Catalog Number: 96-30704

First edition: April 1997
First mass market edition: January 1999

Printed in the United States of America

0 9 8 7 6 5 4 3 2 1

To
Debbie and Darrell, Shane and Shea,
our grandchildren

Cloudy in the west, and it looks like rain,
My danged old slicker's in the wagon again . . .

"The Old Chisholm Trail," TRADITIONAL

CHAPTER

1

Henderson County, East Texas, 1885

All afternoon Joey Shipman had been killing his stepmother with the hoe, chopping her to pieces an inch at a time. His small hands were raw from his angry grip on the wooden handle. A water blister was rising on his right palm. Sweat from beneath the band of his floppy felt hat burned his blue eyes and fueled the banked coals of his resentment.

Two rows away in the shin-high corn, an aging black man paused in his own labor to wipe his brow and dry a sweaty hand against stained old trousers that bore new patches on top of old. He studied Joey with a bemused gaze. "Young'un, you goin' to blunt that hoe plumb down to the handle. You could chop them weeds without bein' half so fiercesome."

"I wouldn't enjoy it half as much."

"Don't look like enjoyment to me." Reuben shook his head. "It's Miz Dulcie, ain't it? She sharp to you again at dinnertime?"

From as far back down his twelve years as Joey could remember, Old Reuben had been able to see through him like

he was store-window glass. "All I done was tell her I thought
Pa was lookin' worse. She taken it to mean she wasn't carin' for
him proper, and she flew all over me. She's held a grudge
against me ever since Pa brought her here to live."

Reuben tamped tobacco into the bowl of a foul old black
pipe and lighted it. Joey had often wondered how it kept from
poisoning him, but Reuben seemed to take pleasure in it. Life
didn't afford him many material pleasures.

"She is a grudgin' woman, right enough. She takes hold of a
grudge and nurses and coddles and feeds it like it was a baby."
That was as near criticism as Reuben was likely to get. It was
his custom to tread lightly on dangerous ground. "Just the
same, she's your pa's wife. He'd want you to show her proper
respect."

"If it wasn't for Pa, I might just light out . . . leave this place
and nary once look back."

The old man shook his head. "Boy, you'd be like a cottontail
rabbit amongst a pack of wolves. The world out yonder'd eat
you alive."

"I can run pretty fast."

"So can a rabbit. But theys mighty few wolves ever starve to
death."

A peacock began a shrill cry of alarm, as it always did when
someone approached on the town road. A movement caught
Joey's eye. "Buggy yonder. Doctor again, I expect."

Reuben made no comment, but Joey caught a grave look in
his eyes before the old man covered it up. Reuben's edge-
sitting station as a hired man, and a black one at that, had made
him skilled at concealing what was on his mind. He turned
away from Joey and went back to his hoeing.

Joey said, "Pa did look awful bad at dinnertime. You don't
reckon he's fixin' to die?"

"The Lord's got everybody's future wrote down in the book
of reckonin', but ain't nobody can read it except Him."

By rights, Pa could as well already be dead, bad as the accident had been. He had been coming home from Athens by himself with a load of staple goods in the wagon when, the best
anybody could tell, something had spooked the team. They had

run away, flipping the wagon over on top of Pa at a fence-corner bend in the road. Doctor had said his ribs were busted bad, and one had evidently punched a hole in his lung. Now, on top of his injuries, Pa had pneumonia so bad he could barely breathe.

Joey watched the buggy pull to a stop in front of the white frame house Pa had built for Mama before Joey was born. Fear clutched at his throat. "Doctor says pneumonia's the old folks' friend. Takes their pain away and puts them at rest. But Pa ain't old, not by a long ways."

"It ain't for us to question the Lord's will." Reuben pointed with the stem of his pipe. "You'd best get back to your job. Miz Dulcie steps out onto the porch and sees you not workin', she's apt to serve you a cold supper."

Joey felt a stirring of rebellion. "Ain't hungry noway." However, he put the hoe back into motion. "Looks like somebody came with the doctor. I believe it's Dulcie's cousin, Mr. Meacham."

Reuben squinted, trying to see. He had lamented often that his eyesight was no longer what it used to be. But his eyes betrayed disapproval.

Joey said, "I don't know what you got against Mr. Meacham. He's always smilin', always got somethin' funny to say."

He had sensed that Pa didn't care much for Blair Meacham either. Pa had never been much for stories and idle gossip and such. Easy laughter was not in his makeup. But Dulcie's cousin had always been friendly to Joey, telling him jokes and riddles, even bringing him stick candy from town occasionally. Not many folks were that thoughtful.

Joey worked his way to the end of the row and hearing an angry snort, glanced across the fence. A dark, tight-hided bull ran up to the wire, stopping inches short of the barbs. It pawed dirt and bellowed a challenge at him, its bulging brown eyes belligerent.

Joey took that as a personal insult. This bull had been trying to get at him for five or six years. He walked past the turnrow, picked up a rock, and hurled it, striking the bull just above one eye. The animal slung its head, another angry bellow rising from deep in its throat.

Reuben shouted, "You'd best not agitate that old bull. One of these days he'll come right through the fence at you. Ain't nothin' on this earth meaner than a bad Jersey bull."

"He ain't got any horns, hardly."

"But he could get you down and tromp on you and bust your bones with that head of his. I don't know what it is makes a cow brute hate young'uns so."

It was true that the bull seemed to vent its hostility most strongly against youngsters. Being smaller, they probably appeared weaker, Joey guessed. The animal would threaten men but turn away if they stood their ground. Pa or Reuben had only to raise a hand and the bull would back off, its bluster gone. But it had put Joey up and over a fence several times. Joey knew that in his case it was not a bluff, that the bull would kill him if it could. It also pawed dirt and threatened darkly whenever it saw Dulcie. He supposed it classified women and children as natural prey.

Somebody ventured out onto the front porch and waved an arm. It wasn't Dulcie or the doctor, so it had to be Blair Meacham, who seemed to be shouting. Joey said, "We better go see what he's hollerin' about."

The grave look returned to Reuben's black-button eyes. "You run on. These old knees can't move as fast as yours, but I'll be comin' along behind you."

Mindful of Pa's ruling about taking proper care of tools, Joey held onto the hoe instead of dropping it in the dirt. He carried it down to the barn and set it just inside the door before he trotted the last fifty yards to the house.

The doctor had stepped out onto the porch with Meacham. His voice was like a minister's at benediction. "Your daddy's asking for you, boy. If you've got anything you want to tell him, you'd best be doin' it."

Blair Meacham placed a gentle hand on top of Joey's head. He offered no joke this time, nor was he smiling. "Don't look like there's much time."

Joey's throat felt as if he had swallowed a knife with its blade open. He walked into the house, struggling not to cry. He was too big for that, he thought. But his resolve came near falling apart as he entered the bedroom and looked through the iron bars of the bedstead. His father lay thin and drawn, his face flushed with the fever that was taking him. His breathing sounded like a rasp filing a horse's hoof.

Dulcie Shipman stood beside the upper end of the bed, arms folded. In Joey's mind she was already getting pretty old, somewhere in her mid-to-late thirties. He had heard men refer to her as handsome, but he supposed they hadn't seen the severe side of her face like he had. Compared to his memories of his own mother, she was skinny and thin-lipped, and he had never heard her sing to herself.

No tears showed in her gray eyes. Instead Joey saw a pinched look he had always interpreted as resentment. He assumed he was a constant reminder that Pa had loved another woman before her and that she was jealous of the attention Pa paid to him. But Pa had always had a great capacity for love. He could give it generously to Joey without taking anything away from Dulcie. Why couldn't she see that?

"Pa . . ." Joey said.

Pa seemed to have trouble seeing. "Joey? You there, Joey? Come here to me."

Joey moved closer, on the opposite side of the bed from Dulcie. His father had always had large, strong farmer hands. It seemed a supreme effort for him to extend one of them to Joey. Time was when Pa could have crushed Joey's hand like an eggshell. Now waning strength barely allowed him to close his fingers around the boy's. The hand was hot with fever.

"Son . . . I'm sorry."

Joey was puzzled. He didn't see any reason for Pa to be apologizing. It wasn't his fault the fool mules had stampeded, that he lay here helpless, his life ebbing away. It was Joey who should be sorry. Pa had offered him a chance to ride with him to town that day, but Joey had wanted to go down to the creek and try to catch a catfish. Maybe if he had been along he could have done something. At least he would have been there when Pa got hurt. As it was, Pa had lain out on the road for hours before Reuben got worried and went looking for him.

Pa tried to speak but broke into coughing. When he recouped

enough, his strained voice bespoke pain. "You're a good boy. I want you to grow up . . . and be a good man."

Reuben appeared in the doorway, breathing heavily from the hurrying. Pa beckoned weakly. The old man glanced apprehensively at Dulcie, then moved around to Joey's side of the bed, dragging his feet a little.

"Reuben . . . you help Dulcie look out for Joey."

"I'll do that, Mr. John. I sure will do that."

Pa's eyes closed. His rough breathing trailed away, then stopped. The doctor laid the flat of his hand across Pa's chest. "He's gone."

Dulcie blinked, looking a moment at the man who had been her husband, then across the bed at Joey. She spoke bitterly, "I'm his wife. You'd think the last words out of his mouth could've been for *me*."

Blair Meacham said, "Don't take it to heart. He probably meant to say more but time ran out on him."

"Another woman's son, and he expected me to raise the boy like he was my own."

The doctor said, "He's left you this good farm to do it with. Many a widow has been left with far less."

Joey could no longer hold back the tears. He leaned over his father and let them all go. He felt hands on his shoulders and knew by the feel of them that they were Reuben's. They should have been Dulcie's, perhaps, but she had left the room with Mr. Meacham's arm around her shoulder.

In a little while Dulcie called from the kitchen. "Reuben!"

The old man gave Joey's arm a squeeze and left the room. Joey took a lingering look at his father's face, then followed.

In the kitchen, Dulcie stared through the window toward the barn. She seemed to be trying not to look at anyone. "Doctor said he'll notify the preacher to come out in the mornin'. You'd best get started diggin' the grave, Reuben. You know where."

"Next to Miz Molly?"

Joey's mother was buried along with three of her babies in a small family plot up on a gentle hill that overlooked the field. Joey had been the only child to survive beyond the first days.

Dulcie did not answer the question directly. "Take Joey with you. He needs to be out of this house, not in here where his daddy just died."

Reuben nodded solemn assent. "Sunshine and fresh air will help ease his grievin'."

Dulcie turned her back. "Tell Mr. Meacham I want him to come in here."

Meacham was on the narrow front porch, watching the doctor leave. Joey sensed that Reuben was disturbed over Meacham's staying behind. Dulcie would need kinfolks around her now, and she did not recognize Joey as kin; he was painfully aware of that. But that was all right; he didn't see her that way, either.

Reuben said with a curtness unusual for him, "Miz Dulcie wants you."

Meacham seemed to overlook the attitude. His voice carried some comfort. "Too bad about your daddy, boy."

Joey did not know what to say. He grunted acknowledgment and followed Reuben to the barn. Reuben fetched out a pick and shovel and started up the gentle slope toward the tiny cemetery. "Doctor'll tell the neighbors on his way to town. There'll be some of them over here later to help with layin' out your daddy."

"Now that he's gone, am I goin' to have to live with Dulcie?"

"Young'uns got to live with somebody."

"I don't think I'll want to live in that house. I'd rather come out and stay with you."

Reuben lived in a twelve-by-twelve box-and-strip shack beside the barn and windmill. Most of the time he cooked his own meals on a small cast-iron stove and toted his water by the bucketful from a cistern filled by runoff rain funneled down from the roof of the larger house. The water always seemed to carry a flavor of cypress shingles, but it was better than the mineral-laden stuff brought up by the windmill.

Reuben said, "Ain't room in that shack for a mouse-catchin' cat, much less a half-grown boy. Besides, ain't much tellin' how long I may still be here."

Ever since she had come to the farm, Dulcie had been agitating Pa to fire Reuben and hire somebody white, like her cousin Blair Meacham. "I don't like livin' this close to a nigger man, not even an old one," she had complained. But Pa had held firm. Back in slave times, Reuben had belonged to Joey's mother's folks, and Mama had promised that he had a home here for the rest of his days. A promise from Mama had been like gospel to Pa.

Now that Pa was gone, though, and Dulcie was in charge, old promises might wind up buried in this cemetery like the folks who had made them. Joey suspected that thought was tracking through Reuben's mind.

"You promised Pa you'd look after me. How you goin' to do that without you keep livin' here?"

"We'll have to trust in the Lord."

Joey had often thought Reuben would have been a good preacher if he had turned his mind to it and if he had been able to read. Growing up a slave, he had been denied any book learning. What he knew of the Word he had absorbed from listening to other people and to the inner voices of his own gentle soul. He kept a copy of the Bible on a wooden box beside his cot. He often studied the pictures, and he claimed he could sometimes feel the power of the book warming his rough old hands.

Reuben took off his hat and stood a moment before the gravestone that marked the resting place of Joey's mother. "There was a blessed woman."

Time had faded and blurred Joey's memories of her. More than what she had looked like, he remembered the warm comfort of her arms and the soft music of her voice. He remembered the pain of losing her, a pain that returned to him now in the loss of Pa.

Reuben said, "Her and your pa, they're probably huggin' one another right now in heaven."

Joey's eyes burned. "I wish I was there with them."

"Don't say that. Remember that your mama went through some mighty sad times to bring you into this world." He motioned toward the three small stones that bore the names of the lost babies. "You were a glory to her. She'd want you to live long and happy."

"How can I be happy livin' with Dulcie, without Pa?"

The old man offered no answer. Joey turned away from him, seated himself on the stone fence, and wept quietly while Reuben dug a grave in the soft ground.

When Reuben stopped to rest and smoke his pipe, Joey took up the pick and shovel. The physical exertion helped ease, or at least mask, his pain. The hole was almost as deep as he was tall when he heard Reuben say, "Somebody comin' down the road."

Joey climbed out of the hole and made a halfhearted attempt at dusting himself off. He heard the peacock and saw a wagon. "Looks like Mr. Hayworth and his wife, come to help. Maybe I better go tell Dulcie so she can get the coffee started."

He ran more than he walked, so that he was gasping by the time he reached the house. He leaned against the wall, trying to regain his breath. Through the window he heard Dulcie's voice, and her cousin's. Meacham was saying, "You can't run this farm by yourself, Dulcie. You was always a town girl. You don't know the first thing about cotton and corn. You don't even know how to milk a cow."

"I don't figure on stayin' out here very long. Soon's the lawyer reads John's will and gets the papers fixed up, I'm sellin' this place. It ought to fetch a pretty price. I'll move to Waco or Dallas or someplace where there's life and people."

"What about the kid?"

"What *about* him? He's not mine."

"The law'll say you've got to take care of him."

"By the time the law finds out I'm gone, I'll be so far away they won't know where to look for me."

"John'll turn over in his grave."

"I don't see where I owe him anything. He married me just to have a mother for that kid. Made me all kinds of promises to get me out here, but there never was a day he ever stopped grievin' over his first wife. So whatever I can get out of this place, I've got it comin'."

Joey felt as if a mule had kicked all the wind out of him. Dulcie never seemed to lack for excuses to whip him when Pa wasn't around, but this was worse than any whipping she had ever given him. He put aside his intention of telling her that company was coming. If he went into the house now she was likely to suspect that he had overheard. He ducked down so she would not see him through the window, then retreated. He tried not to cry, but a few sobs escaped him unbidden as he made his way back to the cemetery.

Maybe Reuben would know what he should do.

The old man had made considerable progress. He stood shoulder deep in the hole. Wiping a patched sleeve across his face, he climbed out and relighted his pipe. His eyes narrowed. "By the looks of you, Miz Dulcie must've give you what-for again."

"She didn't see me." Joey found it painful to speak. He gathered up what strength he could muster and blurted, "She's fixin' to run off and leave me."

Reuben almost lost his pipe.

Joey went on, "I heard them talkin', her and her cousin. She figures on sellin' the place and takin' the money and goin' off where they can't find her."

Reuben chewed hard on the pipe stem. "First place, boy, he ain't really her cousin."

"She always said he was."

"Sayin' and bein' ain't the same thing. Your pa, he knowed."

"Then why . . ."

"There's man-and-woman stuff a boy your age wouldn't understand, nor need to know about." Reuben took the pipe from his mouth and pointed the stem at Joey. "Your pa and Miz Dulcie, they was both expectin' more from one another than they had any right to. After your mama died, your pa done his best at raisin' you, but it's almighty hard in a house where there ain't no woman. He probably told Miz Dulcie he loved her, and all that, but in tryin' to do right by you he done wrong by her.

"And Miz Dulcie, she never had much in the way of decent fixin's. She was raised dirt poor, scratchin' like a banty hen for whatever little she got. To a woman hungry as her, your pa must've looked mighty well off. So when he offered her his name and a place in his home, she grabbed at the chance. They both wound up holdin' a sack with a hole in it."

*   *   *

Joey knew it was customary for friends and relatives to take turns sitting up with the body through the night prior to the burial. He tried to sleep but found he could not. He judged that it was after midnight when he arose from bed, slipped into his overalls, and went out into the modest parlor where Pa lay in a pine box a couple of the neighbors had fashioned. The box had been placed across two wooden chairs. A lamp burned dimly, its wick turned down as low as possible without snuffing out the flame.

Overhead, suspended just below the ceiling, was Mama's old quilting frame on which she had sewn bedcovers for her family as well as for neighbors and friends. Dulcie had never used it. She did not favor that kind of meticulous, artistic work.

Blair Meacham slept on a pallet on the wooden floor. Reuben sat in a rocking chair that Pa had always favored.

"You oughtn't to be up," he whispered. "What you need most right now is sleep."

"I kept thinkin' about Pa." Joey studied the still figure in the box. A desperate hope touched him for a moment. "Maybe he's just unconscious. He looks like he could raise up any minute, wide awake."

"No, boy, he's gone to a better life. Ain't nothin' in that box but the empty shell he used to live in." Reuben arose from the rocker and put an arm around Joey. "It's a hard thing and a test of our faith, sayin' goodbye to folks we love. You'll see your pa again someday when your own time comes. Your mama too."

The wooden floor creaked. Looking up through his tears, Joey saw Dulcie standing in the door that led to the bedroom she had shared with Pa. Her voice was severe. "Joey, you've got no business bein' up. You get yourself back in bed."

Joey shrank away from her. "I just had to come and see Pa again, while I still can."

"You can see him in the mornin'. Now get to bed."

She turned away. Reuben silently indicated that Joey should obey his stepmother. Joey started to comply but paused again beside his father. Anger welled up in him at the injustice of it all. "We ought to shoot those fool mules!"

Dulcie faced around. "You'd just as well know, Joey. Your

daddy left town dead drunk, like he'd been doin' for a long time. Chances are he did some fool thing that made them mules run."

"No!" Joey shouted. "That's a lie!" He ran at her and pummeled her with his fists. "Don't you be tellin' lies about my pa."

Reuben grabbed him. Through his own anger Joey could see fury in Dulcie's eyes. She drew back a hand to slap him, but Reuben pulled him away.

"Whoa there, you've got no call to act-thataway." He turned to Dulcie. "The boy ain't hisself."

"He's himself, all right. But I ain't puttin' up with no more of it."

The commotion had awakened Meacham. He cast a blanket aside and arose. He had been sleeping in his clothes, except for his shoes. "Now, Dulcie, you calm yourself down before you say somethin' you hadn't ought to. And Reuben, you better take Joey out to your house. I'll sit up with John the rest of the night."

Reuben held firmly to Joey. "Yes sir, Mr. Meacham. Sorry, Miz Dulcie. I'll get the boy calmed down. His thinkin' just ain't straight right now."

Joey glanced behind him as they walked toward the shack beside the barn. Through the window, in the dim lamplight, he saw Meacham put his arms around Dulcie.

"It ain't true what she said about Pa."

Reuben opened the door. He fumbled in the darkness until he struck a match and lighted a lamp. The cooped-up smell of sweat and tobacco and grease from Reuben's cooking hit Joey in the face like a wet saddle blanket.

Reuben said, "You lay down on my cot and try to get some sleep. I figured on settin' up the rest of the night anyway."

Joey knew his father had been drinking some lately; the evidence of it had been on his breath, and sometimes he stumbled in his walking. But he wasn't a drunk.

"Why would she tell a big lie like that?"

Reuben took the pipe from his pocket and lighted it, staring toward a picture of Jesus on the wall. "Your pa was carryin' a heavy load of grief. He tried to lift it off with whiskey, but whiskey is the devil's snare. Him and Miz Dulcie never had the true feelins of a man and wife, sure not the feelins him and your mama had. He was just lookin' for a new mama for you. Miz Dulcie was lookin' for a home and an easier row to hoe. They didn't neither one of them find what they was lookin' for."

"So now she figures on sellin' the place and runnin' off and leavin' me. What am I goin' to do, Reuben?"

"When the time comes, the Lord always shows us the way."

"He'd better show us pretty quick."

CHAPTER
2

The funeral was like a bad dream from which Joey hoped he would awaken and find had never happened. But it was all real. He had never realized how many friends Pa had. All of them came by to shake Joey's hand or to hug him and tell him everything would be all right and he would understand it by and by.

He understood well enough. Pa was gone, like Mama before him, and Dulcie was fixing to leave him to shift for himself the best he could.

Preacher Johnson's calm voice gave him some comfort, though part of what he said went past Joey like the soft west wind that moved across the cemetery during the services. He had always found pleasure in listening to ministers, even when he didn't understand them. Reuben had told him that God spoke directly to men who preached the Bible, so listening to a man of the cloth was almost the same as listening to the Lord Himself.

Johnson labored for wages during the week but did battle for the Lord on Sundays and between times when there was a funeral to be preached or a sinner to be prayed for.

Just before giving a final prayer, the minister read a small poem:

"The glass is dashed.
The wine is spilt.
The sword is broke,
And left the hilt.
The powder's burnt,
That spent the ball.
The soldier's gone
To his recall.
May Him whose will
Controls the whole
Call the body,
Receive the soul."

The visitors began trailing away in buggies and wagons and on horseback. The lawyer Wilson, an old friend of Pa's, had ridden out from Athens with the doctor. As they started to climb into the physician's black buggy, Dulcie and Meacham caught up to them.

Dulcie said, "Mr. Wilson, could you stay a little longer? I'd like to talk to you about John's will."

The attorney seemed surprised. "I'd think you'd want to wait a few days to compose yourself."

"I am composed, Mr. Wilson."

Blair Meacham smiled easily. "It's just that it's a ways out here from town, and she wants to save you an extra trip."

The attorney seemed a little put off, but he said, "Very well." He sought out the old man with his eyes. "Reuben, you'd best bring Joey."

Dulcie gave Joey a hard glance. "He's just a boy. He wouldn't understand."

"This will concern him."

Reuben deferentially touched blunt fingertips to the brim of his hat. "I'll fetch him along, Mr. Wilson."

Dulcie and Meacham climbed into Pa's wagon, which Reuben had repaired after the wreck. Dulcie jerked her head, and Meacham put the team into motion behind the black buggy. They left Joey and Reuben to walk. Joey thought he saw a ripple of resentment flit across the black man's wrinkled face, but it was gone in an instant, covered as he always covered any ill feelings.

Joey could easily have outdistanced the old man, but he held to an untaxing pace. The former slave wore his black go-to-meeting suit, older than Joey. The cuffs of the coat were fraying, and the knees had been patched, for Reuben knelt often when he felt the presence of the Lord.

Joey asked, "What do you reckon Mr. Wilson wants with me?"

"I got a feelin' he's fixin' to dump a load of disappointment on Miz Dulcie."

Meacham stood on the porch, waiting. He gave Joey a thin smile.

In the house, Dulcie pointed to the two chairs across which the casket had so recently rested. "Have a seat, Mr. Wilson. I want to talk to you about this farm."

"A mighty good farm it is. John knew how to run it properly."

"Somebody around here ought to be willin' to pay me what it's worth. I want you to take care of the lawyer work so I can sell it."

Wilson and the doctor frowned at one another. "Dulcie, did you ever see John's will?"

"No. He just told me him and you wrote one up."

"We did. And the way it's written, the farm belongs to Joey."

Dulcie's eyes flashed dismay, then a rising anger. "To Joey? But he's just a kid."

"He won't always be. John wanted to make sure the farm would be secure for him when he comes of age. He stipulated that you have a home here until Joey is grown, provided you remain and take proper care of him."

Dulcie's face reddened. She stared at Meacham. He seemed as surprised as she was. "You're sayin' I can't sell?"

"Not without Joey's consent. And Joey can't legally give that consent until he comes of age."

"You're a lawyer, Mr. Wilson. You could find some way around all that."

"I might, if I so chose, but I won't. John Shipman was my friend."

Joey felt the old man's fingers tighten on his arm. Reuben was trying hard not to smile. Joey was not certain there was much to smile about. "You mean I got to keep livin' here with Dulcie?"

The lawyer said, "She is your legal guardian."

Meacham considered the proposition. "Sounds logical to me, as far as it goes. But what if somethin' was to happen to Joey before he comes of age? Where would that leave Dulcie?"

"She is the secondary heir. But nothing is going to happen to Joey, not if he is properly cared for."

"And he will be. Dulcie'll see to that. But we've all seen sickness carry kids away . . . typhoid fever and diphtheria and such. I was just thinkin' about what'd come of Dulcie."

The doctor said, "It'll be my job to see that none of that ever happens. John was a friend of mine too."

Joey asked, "What about Reuben? Did Pa say anything in his will about Reuben?"

"He said Reuben is to have a home here the rest of his life."

Joey looked hard at Dulcie. "And nobody can run him off?"

"It's in the will."

Reuben squeezed Joey's arm again. "I told you. The Lord will provide."

"With help from Pa."

Dulcie turned her back and faced the window. Her fists were clenched. "Damn that man! Even in the grave, he's got a chain around my neck. Why didn't he just sentence me to life in prison?"

Wilson said, "There's not a better farm within twenty miles. It will make you a living."

"If a livin' was all I wanted, I'd've left here a long time ago."

The lawyer shrugged. "Life usually gives us whatever we need. It doesn't guarantee us all we *want*."

"I can't run this farm with just Reuben and the boy. I'll have to hire a man."

"I'll see if I can find someone for you."

"No need. I'm hirin' Blair Meacham."

Wilson gave a nod of approval. Folks in town seemed to regard Meacham as a hail-fellow-well-met. People were always offering to buy him drinks so they could listen to his jokes and stories. "A good choice. Being your kin, he will take an extra interest in doing things properly."

The doctor jerked his head at Wilson. "We'd best be leaving. I have a sick woman to visit on our way back to town."

Dulcie stalked into her bedroom and slammed the door. Joey and Reuben and Meacham followed the two townsmen out onto the porch. Wilson turned to Meacham. "I hope you will stress to her that she must take *proper* care of the boy. The doctor and I will be the ones who define proper care."

"I'll see to it, or you can call Blair Meacham a liar."

Wilson turned to Reuben. "And I'll be depending upon you, just as John always did."

"I been watchin' the boy ever since the day his mama give birth to him."

As the two men rode away, Meacham walked back into the house to join Dulcie.

Joey said, "Of course Mr. Meacham ain't nothin' like Pa, but I feel better knowin' he'll be here."

Reuben's voice held a sharp edge. "No, boy, he sure ain't nothin' like your pa."

In light of her disappointment, Joey expected Dulcie to be hell on wheels the next few days. Her attitude was a pleasant surprise. It was not truly friendly but more or less detached, as if other matters had taken priority and she had more to do than pick on him.

Perhaps the amount of time Meacham spent with her was keeping her in a better humor than Joey could have hoped. He seemed to be in the house a lot while Joey and Reuben were working in the fields or garden or with the farm's few cattle. Dulcie had suggested that Reuben be moved into the barn, but Meacham had declined the use of the small shack. He said he didn't want to put Reuben out. Joey thought that was nice of him.

Supposedly Meacham was sleeping in the barn, but some nights Joey heard him quietly enter the house and go into the bedroom where Dulcie was. He never heard him leave, and Meacham was always at the table awaiting his breakfast when Joey got up.

Hand-pulling weeds from among the garden's young tomato plants, Joey glanced toward the house. Meacham had not left there since they had finished the noon meal an hour or so ago. Reuben was breaking out new rows with a moldboard plow and a mule.

Joey told him, "Dulcie ain't said a cross word to me in two or three days. You reckon she's sick or somethin'?"

"Not unless sick means givin' in to the ways of the flesh."

"What do you mean by that?"

Reuben's face furrowed. "When you get a little older, you'll know."

Joey already understood more about such goings-on than the old man gave him credit for. But he did not want to disillusion Reuben about his innocence. In any case, it did not matter to Joey why Dulcie seemed in a better humor; it only mattered that she was.

Meacham came to the garden fence. "Joey, that milk-pen calf has got out and joined its mama. I'd like you to go fetch it in. Else it'll take all the milk, and the cow won't give us none tonight."

"I'll saddle old Taw."

"You're young and wiry. You don't need a horse. Just walk out there and drive that calf and its mama back."

Joey was disappointed. He liked to ride horseback when he could find an excuse. As for missing out on the milk tonight, he would not have minded. The twice-a-day milking chore had been his since he was eight years old, and it had become eternally tiresome. But even walking out into the milk-cow pasture was preferable to pulling weeds.

"What about that mean Jersey bull?" he asked.

"That old gentle pet? He's shut up in a pen, snug and safe."

Pet? Maybe for a man full-grown who could run a bluff, but that bull had taken Joey's measure and found it short.

He climbed over the garden fence and jumped down, not taking time to walk to the gate. Reuben was always cautioning him that this was a good way to break his leg if he happened to slip, but youthful impatience had little time for such considerations. To be on the safe side, he made an arc around the barn to satisfy himself about the bull. The gate appeared shut. Joey whistled a happy tune as his gaze swept across the small pasture, seeking the cow and calf.

He found them no more than three hundred yards from the barn, contentedly celebrating their happy reunion. The cow was filling her paunch with spring grass while the calf punched her udder, trying to coax down more milk. It would be difficult for Joey to separate the two until he got them into a pen. He circled around them and shouted, waving his arms. The calf ignored him, and the cow gave him a blank bovine stare until he moved closer, shouting again. Reluctantly she turned and began plodding toward the barn. The calf twisted its tail over its back and hopped along after her, its muzzle white with milk foam. Joey began whistling again. It was an old church song, but he gave it a jaunty bounce that Preacher Johnson might not have approved.

A hundred yards from the barn he stopped suddenly, his attention caught by a dark movement, then a bellow. The bull was loose.

Joey's breath stopped; his heartbeat quickened. He looked toward the pasture fence. If the bull made a determined run at him, Joey would never reach the wire in time. He dropped to his knees, hoping the bull would be interested enough in the cow that it would not notice him.

His hopes were short lived. The bull circled the cow, unceremoniously bumping her calf aside, but after a moment's inspection found her not to be in heat. Its interest rapidly waned and transferred to Joey, who tried to flatten himself on the ground out of the bull's sight. The bellowing resumed. The bull began to sling its head and paw dirt back over its shoulder.

Joey saw no choice. He had to try for the fence, for any moment now the bull would make a run at him. He jumped to his feet and sprinted. From the edge of his eye he saw a blur of movement. The bull was cutting across to intercept him, snorting at every step, head low to the ground. Joey cried out in fear.

He did not reach the fence. The bull rammed into him from behind, a glancing blow that shot a bolt of pain from his legs to his head. The bull's horns had been sawed off years ago, but the stubs were still sharp at the edges. The impact sent Joey stumbling and rolling, then he flipped himself over onto his back so he could see what was coming. The bull's huge head was so close he could reach out and touch the snotty muzzle. The belligerent bellow froze him along his spine.

He shouted and waved his hands, but that only seemed to stir the bull to more of a frenzy. That brown-black head, hard as iron, connected with Joey's nose, and he nearly strangled on a sudden flow of hot blood. The bull hooked at Joey's chest, the stub horns cutting into his flesh. He felt the breath mashed out of him. One of the cloven hoofs pressed down on his leg. Pain seared him as the bull brought its full weight to bear.

In his panic he knew it would take but a moment now to crush the life from him.

He heard a cry that was not his own. Through a haze of pain he saw Reuben climbing over the fence with the alacrity of a youngster. He had never seen the old man's creaky legs move so rapidly. Reuben came running, waving his hat, shouting at the bull.

The animal raised its head at this new distraction. It pawed dirt in response to Reuben's challenge and made a threatening sound deep in its throat. It feinted as if it were about to charge, then lost courage and turned. It ran off thirty feet or so and wheeled back around, offering an empty bluff. Reuben made a run at it, throwing his arms into the air and yelling. The bull retreated.

Joey's heart pounded in the aftermath of panic. He choked, lungs ablaze for want of air. He fought to regain the breath the bull had knocked out of him. Blood and dirt burned his eyes.

His sides ached from the pounding his ribs had taken. He tried to arise, but Reuben gently pushed him back down.

"Slow, boy, slow. Get your breath first, then raise up easy. Got to be sure you ain't got no ribs caved in, less'n they punch a hole in your lungs like happened to your pa."

Gradually Joey regained his breath. Reuben pressed carefully upon his ribs, first one side and then the other, testing. "Looks like the Lord set an angel on your shoulders, else that old bull would've killed you dead."

Joey wheezed. He tried to tell Reuben that no angel would ever be half so welcome as the sight of him coming over that fence, but his breath was too ragged. He could not speak the words.

Reuben's gaze fastened on Blair Meacham, trotting out from the direction of the barn.

"How's the boy? Is he bad hurt?"

Reuben's eyes flared. "You said that bull was safe in the pen."

"I can't for the life of me figure how he got out."

"You think he unlatched the gate all by hisself?"

Joey recognized the oblique accusation, but Meacham either did not see it for what it was or did not want to acknowledge it. "We better get the boy to the house."

Reuben cautiously helped Joey to his feet and dusted him off the best he could. "You able to walk?"

Joey felt of his ribs. He could not tell if anything was broken. His lungs still ached like fury, and he worked up saliva so he could spit dirt and blood from his mouth. "Someday I'm goin' to take a shotgun to that damned bull."

Reuben chided, "The bull was just the devil's instrument. And you watch the words that come out of your mouth, boy, or the devil may claim you yet."

Meacham said, "I'll trot ahead and tell Dulcie."

Joey strongly suspected that Dulcie already knew. That bull was smart, but he doubted it was smart enough to unlatch the gate. And how was it that the calf had gotten out in the first place?

He limped a few steps but gave in to the pain. He protested

to no avail as Reuben picked him up. "You may be hurt worse than you think, young'un."

He was amazed at the old man's strength, the result of life-long heavy labor. The bull stood off at a safe distance, pawing dirt, but it made no attempt to charge. Joey could only imagine what kind of thinking process a bull had, but it probably remembered the painful outcome of some previous indiscretion with Reuben.

Meacham and Dulcie waited on the porch. Meacham showed concern, but Dulcie seemed resentful at the interruption of whatever she had been doing. She followed Reuben as he carried Joey into the tiny room where he slept. "I'll bet he's puttin' on a lot worse than it really is. Boy's been spoiled too much."

The criticism rolled off Reuben like rain. To Meacham he said, "Which a-one of us is goin' after the doctor, me or you?"

"Doctor?" Dulcie complained. "The old quack'll charge us three dollars just for comin' out here. And he won't find anything but a bruise or two. That old surly is mostly bluff."

She always spoke of the bull as a *surly*. It was not considered respectable for a woman to say the word *bull*.

"Boy could have some stove-in ribs. You can take the three dollars out of my pay." Reuben wasn't paid much, but he didn't spend much except to buy tobacco for that foul old pipe and an occasional new suit of working clothes when his old ones began falling apart. The merchants in town counted him as a nice old man but not much of an asset to business.

Meacham said, "Ain't no use arguin' when we've got a hurt boy to see after. I'll fetch the doctor."

Joey took Meacham's attitude kindly, especially when he contrasted it to Dulcie's. He figured her tears wouldn't wet one corner of a handkerchief if he died. She had controlled her grief mighty well after Pa's death.

Dulcie shrugged in resignation. "You'd best give the boy a good washin', Reuben. We wouldn't want the doctor to think we let him go around dirty as that all the time."

Dulcie left the room. That suited Joey fine. He was getting too big to let a woman see him without his clothes on, even his stepmother. Reuben fetched a wash pan and a rag and carefully gave Joey what Pa used to call a Tuesday bath, considerably short of a Saturday-night immersion. Joey flinched as Reuben's careful hands touched the torn and bruised places. He still spat up dirt and blood. Reuben was concerned about the blood, which he feared might be coming from a punctured lung. But Joey felt it was probably inner bleeding from his nose, which the bull had tried to flatten.

Reuben lamented, "I promised your pa I'd look after you, but I wasn't doin' a good job of it when I let this happen."

"Wasn't your fault."

"I'm goin' to take me a good look at that gate after a while."

Joey wondered if Reuben's thoughts ran along the same lines as his own. He asked, "You think somebody messed with it?"

"This farm is worth a right smart of money. Folks can do some awful things when there's money in it."

Most people would think this was just a foolish notion. Everybody knew that kids and old folks sometimes developed a lot of such notions. Joey doubted that anyone would listen if he and Reuben were to voice their suspicions. Reuben *was* old, but Joey could not remember many times he had been wrong.

Reuben spoke in a low voice, careful that Dulcie not overhear. "Worst comes to worst, I may have to take you away from here."

"Where would we go?"

"Your pa used to have a cousin name of Beau. Remember? He come here to visit one time. Didn't stay long because him and your pa never saw eye to eye about nothin'. Mr. Beau was heedless as a wild mule. Never did give much thought to anything past quittin' time."

"I remember him and Pa arguin'."

"Ain't heard of him gettin' killed, so I reckon he's still livin'. He's at a town called Bastrop, if they ain't run him off."

"I don't know where Bastrop is."

"A long ways southwest, down close to Austin City. If it come to that, Mr. Beau might know a place where nobody could find us."

"Why would they try to find us if all Dulcie wanted was to get me out of the way?"

"Because the farm is in your name. Only way to change that is to see you dead. *Gone* ain't enough. She'd have to show the court a dead body."

Joey remembered a story he had read about the wicked brother of a dying king trying to kill the young princes so he would be the one to inherit the throne and rule the kingdom. It had seemed unreal to him that anybody could be so mean. That had been a long time ago and a long way away. This was here and now. But the old story didn't seem so far-fetched to him anymore.

Still, this was the only home Joey had ever known. He would have to give the matter a lot of study before he went off and left it.

The doctor wrapped Joey's ribs tightly and painted his cuts and bruises with something that had a fearsome burn and a worse smell. "If it doesn't hurt, taste bad, or burn," he said, "it's not doing you any good."

Joey thought it must be mighty beneficial.

Reuben watched worriedly. When Dulcie and Meacham left the room, he quietly hinted to the doctor about his suspicions. "I checked the gate. Wasn't nothin' busted. I don't think it was latched proper in the first place."

The doctor's gray eyebrows arched. "Do you know what you're saying?"

"I ain't *sayin'*, exactly. I'm only suspicionin'."

"I would not want to pay a nickel for the difference." The man's eyes narrowed. "I'll forget what you said, Reuben, and you'd better forget it too. You know what could happen if you were to make such accusations in public? They could flay the hide off of you, and the law would not do a thing."

"I'm just fearful for the boy."

"I can't believe the boy is in any danger. But *you* might be, if what you told me should reach the wrong ears."

Meacham walked in. Joey suspected he had heard at least part of it. Meacham said, "Reuben, we'll all be better satisfied when you go down to the pen and put a stronger latch on that gate, one no animal can open for itself."

"I'll be takin' care of that right now." Avoiding Meacham's eyes, Reuben walked out of the room.

The doctor's gaze followed him with a look that bespoke pity. "You have to take his age into account."

"His old mind has commenced to drift. I don't take offense."

Joey had not noticed that Reuben's mind was drifting, but perhaps he had lost some of his old sense of caution. It was not like him to accuse people out loud, even by the vaguest implication.

Meacham said to the doctor, "You can tell the sheriff to come out and look things over . . . satisfy himself if there's any doubt."

"I'll tell him, but there's no suspicion on my part. Just in case I've missed something, you and Dulcie keep an eye on Joey for any undue rise of fever."

"Joey's tougher than a boot." Meacham gave Joey an easy smile and a wink. "Ain't you?"

"I've already quit hurtin', almost." That was a sinful stretch of the truth, but Meacham's endorsement stirred his pride. He hadn't cried no matter how bad the pain had been, and he was not going to let them know how much it still hurt.

He thought Dulcie might come and look in on him after the two men had gone out onto the porch, but she did not. She was probably disappointed that he had not been killed.

If that old bull ever knocks you down, see if I care, he thought.

He had assumed that when the initial pain faded that would be the end of it, but he had not counted on the residual soreness that set in on him hours later and intensified during the night. He was hurting in places he did not even know he had. He slept fitfully, waking each time he tried to turn over or change position in bed.

At daylight he surrendered to the soreness and sat up, swinging his legs carefully over the side of the bed. He was sure every joint in his body ached. Given the opportunity, he would gladly shoot that bull, taking him down one leg at a time and then making the final grace shot right between those two bulging, evil eyes.

Slowly he stood up, testing his weight, flinching at the soreness. He found he could walk, though not without pain. Pa had always said the best cure for soreness was to go back and do more of whatever had caused it in the first place. Joey did not care to go that far. He had had enough of the Jersey bull.

He dressed and went out into the larger room that served as kitchen, dining room, and parlor combined. He was not surprised to see Meacham eating breakfast, looking as content as a horse in an oat bin. Meacham seemed to take pleasure from many things, and mealtime was among the foremost of them. It puzzled Joey that he was not fat. Probably had worms.

"Mornin', Joey. You ready to wrestle Ol' Bully again?"

"I'm still ready to shoot him."

Dulcie stood at the stove. "You feel like eatin'?"

The bull had not injured Joey's stomach. "Yes'm." He knew he should add *please,* but that seemed like bowing down. If she were his real mother, and she treated him like a son—well, a lot of things would be different.

Meacham smiled sympathetically as the pain of walking caused Joey to wince. "Maybe you'd better lay around the house today."

Dulcie turned away from the stove. "Best thing for him is good hard work to exercise the soreness out. Last thing you want to do is give a boy an excuse to be lazy."

Maybe she would be more understanding if that old bull ever caught *her* without a place to run or a club to protect herself with, Joey thought. It was a show he would gladly give up a week of school for, to see her scramble up a fence with that bull blowing snot all over her sitting-down place. She would probably whip him for laughing, but the satisfaction would be cheap at the price.

She fried a slice of ham and scrambled a couple of eggs, setting the plate in front of him without ceremony. She acted angry, as if it had been his duty to let that old bull kill him. He managed to grab one biscuit before Meacham took the last one and swabbed up a helping of butter and molasses from his plate.

"Ain't no fresh milk," Dulcie said. "It taken all that calf left us to make biscuits. Reuben said he'd do the milkin' in your place this mornin', but we ain't seen hide nor hair of him."

Reuben had his own chores to do. He had probably forgotten about the milking because that normally was Joey's job. But Joey remembered how concerned Reuben had been yesterday. He thought it strange that Reuben had not already been to the house this morning to see about him.

"Reckon he's sick?" he asked.

Dulcie snickered. "He ain't been sick in his life. Except maybe sick of work."

The remark aroused Joey's resentment. Nobody worked harder than Reuben, considering his age. Pa had said that in his prime Reuben could pick half again more cotton than anybody he had ever seen. He must have been a sight to behold. But Dulcie wouldn't appreciate that. She had known him only as an old man who strained what little patience she had.

Joey said, "He's probably been worryin' about me. I'll go show him I'm all right."

"You finish that breakfast first," Dulcie commanded. "Your pa never gave much thought to waste, but I don't abide it."

The eggs and ham had lost their flavor. Joey put them down hurriedly anyway, then left the table. He took half the biscuit with him to eat on the way. He paused at the door of the barn to finish the final bite while he looked around. He did not see Reuben there or in the milk pen. The cow and her calf were separated by a fence. A glance at her udder told him she had not yet been milked.

"Reuben!" Hearing no answer, he walked to the old man's shack. The door was ajar. He pushed it open and stepped inside.

Reuben lay on the cot, one black arm across his chest, the other dangling off the near side. Odd, Joey thought, finding him still asleep this late in the morning. Often as not, Reuben woke up the rooster. The old man appeared peaceful, but the room did not. The patchwork quilt barely covered his feet, most of it hanging haphazardly off the far side of the cot. The wooden box beside the cot was turned over, and Reuben's Bible lay on the floor.

Alarm struck Joey like a dash of cold water in his face. "Reuben!" Three long steps brought him to the edge of the cot. He reached out to touch Reuben's hand, then hesitated. Instinctively he knew what he was going to find. He forced himself to it. The hand was cold and lifeless, like Pa's had been as he lay in his wooden coffin.

Reuben was dead.

CHAPTER

3

The doctor had made several trips to the Shipman farm in recent days. His first remark was, "It looks as if I may have to build me a room onto the Shipman house."

Sheriff Lawton rode in the buggy with him, for this was a sudden and unexpected death. Many lawmen wouldn't go to this much trouble for an old black man, Meacham said, but the sheriff accepted his duty like a religious calling. He had known and respected Reuben since his own boyhood.

Joey stood outside the door of the shack, leaning in just enough to see and hear. The adults might send him away if he called attention to himself.

The doctor was saying, "I believe he suffered a heart seizure during the night. Those can be violent sometimes. That would account for his kicking the cover around and knocking the box over."

The sheriff gravely accepted the explanation. "Not a bad way to go. Quick, anyhow."

Meacham left the shack and started back toward the house. Joey worked up his nerve and stepped through the door. He heard the doctor saying, "Looking back to Reuben's state of mind yesterday, I can readily understand. The excitement and exertion of rescuing Joey from that bull, then carrying him to the house . . . And he was considerably agitated afterward. The stress was too much for his old heart."

Joey blurted, "What if somebody killed him?"

The doctor and the sheriff turned, surprised. The sheriff said, "No one killed Reuben, son. The doctor and I both looked him over. There's no sign of a wound, nothin' like that."

Joey demanded, "What if she poisoned him? That wouldn't leave no bullet hole."

"You're lettin' your imagination run away with you. Why would anybody want to poison a good old man like Reuben?"

"Dulcie always wanted to run him off, but Pa wouldn't let her. And Lawyer Wilson told her she couldn't."

The sheriff patted Joey's shoulder. "If Dulcie poisoned everybody she didn't like, half the people in town would be dead. Me included, I expect. No, son, don't let such a notion sour your mind about your stepmother. The Lord decided He needed Reuben, so He called him home."

Joey blinked away tears. He needed Reuben worse than the Lord did.

The sheriff eased him out of the shack. "While I'm here, why don't you show me the gate where that bull got out?"

Joey did. He found a heavy chain had been added since yesterday's excitement, and a large bolt had been inserted solidly into the post to keep the chain tightly fastened. That must have been Reuben's final piece of work.

Joey lamented, "First Pa, then Reuben. I don't know how I'll get along without them."

"You'll always carry them with you in your memory, and they'll keep on pointin' your way."

Yesterday Reuben had said they might have to leave this place for Joey's own safety. Now Reuben was dead, and Joey could not feel confident in the sheriff's assurances. He could not shake off a dark suspicion that Dulcie was somehow responsible for Reuben's dying. He didn't see how she could have rigged Pa's accident, but once he was home she might have done something to make sure he never recovered from his injury.

First Pa, then Reuben. Who next?

Who else, except me? With me dead, the farm belongs to her.

Fear began to build a small, cold knot in his stomach. Dulcie didn't like him any better than she had liked Reuben. Not much, anyway.

At the edge of the barn, the sun shining through a spider web made the thin strands look like threads of silver. A freshly caught fly struggled vainly for its freedom. A black spider was moving down to devour it.

Joey had no use for flies, but the thought of a creature entrapped and doomed made a chill run along his back. He picked up a short stick and poked at the web, freeing the fly. He watched it disappear but felt only partial relief.

At least the fly had wings. Joey had none, and the black widow spider was closing in.

They buried Reuben just outside the family cemetery's stone fence. It wasn't fitting, Dulcie declared, to bury a black man inside, where white folks lay. To Joey, Reuben was family, but any argument from him would set her mind even firmer. It probably didn't matter too much anyhow. By the time all graves were opened on Judgment Day, that fence wouldn't still be here. Preacher Johnson said the ages would melt the mountains down. A little old fence like that wouldn't stand any kind of chance.

Joey watched the mourners depart, mostly a few near neighbors and a handful of people from town. As the last of them rode away, he felt abandoned, alone as he had never been. He watched Dulcie go back into the house, Meacham's arm around her shoulder. He had not seen any mourning on her part. Reuben's dying had probably been a relief to her, like pulling a thorn out of her foot.

He felt Meacham was the nearest thing to an ally he had left, and not even Meacham was likely to believe Joey's suspicions. Nothing less than Joey's death would prove them true.

Soon after Reuben was laid to rest, Joey began plotting his escape. He stole food in small amounts he didn't think Dulcie would miss—a little sugar at a time, a little flour and salt—hiding them in the barn. He did not customarily drink coffee, but he supposed that when he was on his own he would have to learn to like the stuff. Pa used to say that when he went off to the big war as a gangling boy, he had sometimes gone for days without more on his stomach than black coffee and a handful of parched corn. There was already corn enough at the barn, feed for the working stock. Joey would sneak off and try to learn how to parch it. He knew he should have listened closer to Pa, because he never could make it taste like anything but scorched horse and mule feed.

He wished he could bring Meacham in on his plans; he felt a need to confide in someone. But Meacham's first loyalty would be to Dulcie. He would probably tell her, and that would be the end of the scheme—and probably the end of Joey, because anyone wicked enough to plan the deaths of Pa and Reuben would have no compunctions when it came to eliminating a small nuisance like a boy twelve years old, going on thirteen.

Pa had never let Joey overfeed the stock, but he began slipping extra oats to his horse Taw. He figured to fatten him up a bit and give him stamina for a long trip. Taw was far from young. He had already been grown and broke to the saddle before Joey was born. He didn't know much, and half the cows on the farm could outrun him, but at least he was docile and responded well to the reins. The saddle was an old one left over from Pa's own youth. Joey considered Pa's much newer saddle but knew it was too large for him. He would bounce around in it like a ball on a string.

Pa had taken him nowhere much except to town, and never more than twenty or thirty miles from home. Joey had but little notion what lay beyond that limited range of travel. He had read books, of course, lots of them. While they aroused his curiosity, they also triggered a great deal of uncertainty. His imagination was not expansive enough to accommodate lands so distant or cities so large as those he had read about.

He had heard of people running off to Mexico, usually when they found themselves at cross purposes with the law. But it was his understanding that Mexico lay a considerable distance to the south, and that he would have to make his way through a lot of thirsty desert and stickery cactus to get there. A school friend had told him people in Mexico did not even know the American language. He had encountered Mexicans in town and marveled at their ability to understand one another even though he could not comprehend a word that passed their lips.

The world would be a simpler place, he thought, if everybody talked the same as he did.

Mexico was out.

He knew his mother had kin somewhere back in Arkansas to whom she had occasionally written, but Dulcie had long since burned up all of Mama's old family letters. Pa had originally come out of Georgia; Joey was hazy as to just where. None of those kinfolks had ever come visiting, so far as he could remember. They would be strangers to him even if he could find them. They would probably not believe when he tried to tell them about Dulcie. Chances were they would let her know where he was, and she would send some sheriff to bring him back. In handcuffs, like as not, as he had once seen them bring in a man accused of murdering a farmer for his mule.

Joey remembered that the steel cuffs had rubbed the culprit's wrists until they were raw and bleeding. Joey had heard in school later that the prisoner had beat his head against the stone wall of his cell until his brains began to seep out and he died. Folks had said it was better than hanging, but Joey hadn't seen that either choice had much to offer. He was sure of one thing: he did not want to run afoul of any sheriffs. He was glad the local one was a family friend.

But even Sheriff Lawton would not believe Joey's suspicions about Dulcie. He would just pat Joey on the head to humor him, treating him like a kid.

Joey strained his memory, trying to recall what Reuben had said about Pa's cousin Beau, living somewhere to the southwest. What was the name of the place? Bassett . . . Bastard . . . couldn't be *that*. Bastrop . . . that was it, Bastrop. He had only the vaguest idea where it was. He could not afford to ask anyone around here because when he turned up gone they would remember his asking and know where to start looking for him.

If he were in school he might find Bastrop on the Texas map tacked to the wall, but school had let out for planting time. Most farmers agreed that their children—the boys, at least—were benefitting themselves and their families more by working in the fields than by studying Webster's Blue Back Speller or practicing arithmetic. In their futures as farmers they were unlikely to have to add up large sums anyway.

Once he got away from here he could find Bastrop. It was not going to move anywhere. Nor was it likely to be more than a temporary refuge for him. From what Reuben had said, cousin Beau was not exactly a pillar of the community. But perhaps he would help Joey get a little farther down the road to some place where Dulcie could not find him.

Farther west or southwest were places with interesting names like San Antonio, San Angelo, El Paso. . . . They sounded as if they would be worth seeing. He began to itch with impatience to be on his way. But he would await the right opportunity, a fortunate combination of circumstances that would give him a good head start before anyone had time to miss him.

A couple of weeks after Reuben's death, Blair Meacham gave up any pretense about sleeping in the barn. He moved his stuff into the house and began sleeping in the same room with Dulcie, the room Pa had shared with her. It had only one bed.

Joey wondered what Preacher Johnson would say about such goings-on, and them supposed to be cousins. Reuben had said they weren't, and Joey guessed Reuben had known. Cousins or not, the whole thing was more than a little odd to him, especially considering how short a time it had been since Pa's death.

The saving feature about the arrangement was that Dulcie stayed in a better humor most of the time. She hadn't whipped Joey lately or even hounded him about being slow in doing his chores. He decided he could overlook her indiscretions if she was going to treat him decently for a change. He even began wondering if he might have been wrong about her intention of killing him. Perhaps, like the sheriff had said, his disliking for her had caused his imagination to run away with him.

One night after supper he sat down to read a book by the light of a kerosene lamp in the parlor. He tried not to notice the way Meacham and Dulcie kept looking at one another, making little signals, touching each other and trying to make it appear to be unintentional. Their faces began to flush. Joey pretended he did not see, but he was a long way from blind.

At length Dulcie said, "Joey, ain't it your bedtime?"

He glanced at the clock over the fireplace. "It's early yet."

"You look tired. You'd better go to bed anyway."

Experience had taught him not to argue with her. He took the book with him; he could light the lamp in his room and finish the chapter.

She said, "No more readin'. You go to sleep."

He wasn't just a kid anymore. He knew what they were about. He laid the book down on a table and walked toward his room. He noticed that the door was closed. He usually left it open in the evening to try to draw in fresh air. Perhaps the breeze had pulled it shut.

He opened the door. The room was dark except for a little reflected light from the lamp in the parlor. He started to unbutton his shirt when he heard a faint buzz that made the hair tickle the back of his neck. The buzz suddenly became louder, and he knew instantly what it was.

Rattlesnake!

His heart hammered frantically, his skin prickling with a thousand needles of panic. Scary as that Jersey bull had been, a rattlesnake was ten times worse. Instinct told him to run for the door, but he did not know at first where the snake was. Any direction he stepped might carry him to it. He froze in place and tried to pinpoint the deadly sound.

The snake was coiled atop his bed. It looked as big around as a tree trunk. Forked tongue darting wickedly, it was poised to strike.

Joey gave a shriek, then flung himself toward the door. From the corner of his eye he saw the snake hurl its body toward him. It was fast, but he was faster. He raced out into the parlor, shouting at the top of his voice.

He stumbled and fell headlong upon the floor. Meacham knelt beside him. "What the hell, boy?"

"Snake!" Joey managed the word in a wheezing voice. He pointed toward his room.

Meacham picked up the lamp by which Joey had been reading and cautiously made his way toward the door, holding the lamp out in front of him. Joey heard him say, "My God, that's a big one."

Dulcie didn't say anything. She stood near the eating table, hands at her sides. She didn't seem to have a great interest in snakes.

The reptile crawled out into the larger room. Meacham fetched a broom from the corner behind the stove and poked at the snake, which set up a fearsome rattling. He began hazing it toward the front door. As it finally slithered out across the threshold, he shouted, "Dulcie, bring me John's rifle."

She brought him the weapon from her bedroom.

The shot shook the wooden walls. Joey flinched. He found himself trembling as if he were freezing to death, though the night was agreeably warm.

He wanted to cry, but he had prided himself on not letting Dulcie see him do that except at Pa's deathbed, and once over Reuben.

Meacham came back into the house, carrying the rifle. The smell of burned powder clung to him. He handed the weapon to Dulcie and bent over Joey. "Are you bit?"

Joey found it difficult to summon voice. "It missed me."

Meacham frowned darkly. "Must've come from under the house. Probably a hole in the floor someplace. Come daylight, we'll find and patch it."

Dulcie had not said a word.

Joey hoped his eyes did not show what was running through his mind. He didn't know how, but he was certain Dulcie had placed that snake in his room, then had closed the door to make sure it did not get out. She had acted eager for Joey to go to bed so she and Meacham could proceed with whatever they were up to together, but what she had really wanted was to get Joey snakebit. He would die, and everybody would say what a poor, unlucky family the Shipmans were.

They would also say how lucky Dulcie was, because this farm would be hers.

"Excitement's over," she said. "You can go on to bed."

"No ma'am," he declared. He could not quite bring his trembling under control. "I'm not sleepin' in that room, not tonight. I'll go out to Reuben's shack."

"Suit yourself. But you're liable to find a rattlesnake anyplace."

Anyplace Dulcie was, he thought. But it was not likely she would try the same stunt again tonight. And he wasn't going to give her many more chances. He made up his mind he wouldn't stay around this place much longer.

His break came a couple of mornings later. Meacham finished his breakfast coffee and wiped his sleeve across his mouth. He was always given to good humor, but today he smiled as if he knew a secret and was busting to tell it. "Joey, reckon you can take care of things around here a day or two? Me and Dulcie are fixin' to make a little trip. We won't be back 'til tomorrow evenin', maybe even the next day."

Dulcie seemed in a fine mood too. She actually smiled, placing her hand on Meacham's arm. Her eyes held a sparkle Joey had not seen before. "I've cooked you an extra pan of biscuits and some salt pork so you won't go hungry. And you can always fix you some bacon and eggs."

Joey's heart leaped. He had not expected such a wide-open opportunity. He tried not to betray his enthusiasm lest she become suspicious. "I reckon I can make do."

He helped hook the mule team to the wagon and followed afoot as Meacham drove up in front of the house. Dulcie came out onto the porch, carrying a colorful carpetbag that once had been Mama's. She made no false pretenses about loving Joey. She did not hug or kiss him or anything like that, though she did give him the biggest smile he had ever received from her. "You watch out for things now, Joey."

"I've *been* watchin' out."

Meacham took her arm and helped her up onto the wagon seat. "You take care of yourself," he told Joey.

"I sure figure on doin' that."

He imagined he could feel the throbbing of his pulse as he watched them move along the town road. He turned toward the barn. The milk-pen calf stood at the fence, looking between the boards at its mother grazing a couple of hundred yards out in the pasture. It would be cruel to let the calf's belly go empty a couple or three days until Dulcie and Meacham came back. Cautiously, Joey looked around for the Jersey bull. It was grazing a considerable distance away, beyond the cow. He unlatched the gate. Tail raised high, the calf gave Joey a wide berth as it trotted away, bawling and racing toward its mother.

Joey threw out some extra grain for Dulcie's chickens, then went to the house to put his few belongings together. He spread the quilt Mama had made for him, rolling it up inside two blankets to protect it. He put his extra clothes in the war bag Pa had brought home from the fighting. It was old and thin and patched in places, but it was Pa's, and Joey wanted to carry it with him.

Hidden in a bureau drawer, rescued from a pile of things Dulcie had discarded when she came here, was a tintype of his mother and father, made at the time of their wedding. Joey took it out with reverence and tucked it inside the old Bible Reuben had never been able to read. That went into the war bag along with a few other items, including Pa's straight razor and twelve dollars Joey had saved up in small change Pa had given him. He had no use for the razor now, but folks said he already resembled Pa in many ways. A few more years and he would probably have Pa's whiskers.

Itching to be on his way, he rummaged in the kitchen, sacking up the food Dulcie had prepared for him as well as some extra flour and sugar and coffee. He left the blanket roll and war bag on the porch while he trotted to the barn to put on a pair of cheap OK spurs and throw his saddle on Taw. The old horse stood with his head down in infinite patience. It probably thought they were just going out to bring in the cows.

"Like as not, you'd run off if you knew how far we're fixin' to travel," Joey said. "But I ain't tellin' you."

He rode up to the house for the blankets and bag. The blanket roll was a long way from neat, bulging on one end and thin on the other. It was awkward when he tied it behind the cantle. He hung the war bag off one side and the sack of food off the other. They did not balance well. He imagined he and Taw looked a sight with their lopsided load, but appearance was not a major concern at the moment.

He rode up to the cemetery. He removed his hat but did not dismount because it was a struggle to throw his leg over the thick roll of blankets. He felt a catch in his throat as he stopped at Mama's grave, then the fresh mound that marked Pa's. There was no stone yet. He wondered if Dulcie would ever bother to put up one.

"I'll come back some day when I'm grown, and I'll fix things proper," he promised. A haze came before his eyes, and he decided it was time to ride on. He forded the creek, which lapped against Taw's belly. The morning sun was at his back, so he decided he was headed in the right direction.

CHAPTER

4

By midafternoon Joey had passed beyond the neighboring farms with which he was familiar. He had avoided roads and made broad detours around fields where he might encounter someone who knew him or who might remember him later when he was reported missing.

He found it difficult to sort out his conflicting emotions. On the one hand he was uplifted by a sense of escape, of being on the road to adventure, to new discoveries. On the other he harbored an unsettling doubt about the unfamiliar. Never had he ventured off alone. The little traveling he had done had always been with Pa. He had felt protected beneath Pa's long shadow.

He had no watch—he had been unable to find Pa's—so he could only guess at the time. He had begun feeling hungry long before noon, so he had dug out a couple of biscuits and sliced off a piece of the pork Dulcie had cooked for him. By the middle of the afternoon he did it again. He realized that at this rate he would empty the food sack considerably sooner than he had planned. He had not realized how traveling could stimulate the appetite. Or perhaps it was just knowing he had the food with him and could eat any time he took the notion.

He noticed that the biscuits were taking on the flavor of horse sweat. He tried shifting the food sack so that it did not rub against Taw, but it seemed to have an affinity for horse hide. He decided to eat the biscuits now, before they became inedible.

Though he had hoped to avoid people, he came upon a stranger so suddenly that he had no chance to change course. A large-bellied man in dirt-stained overalls appeared without warning from beyond an oak thicket, astride a big Missouri-looking mule built along the same generous lines as its rider. Joey checked an impulse to break and run. He thought that might look suspicious.

The stranger hauled up on the reins. He spat a stream of tobacco juice, a little of it trailing down into his gray-splotched whiskers until he rubbed a sleeve across his lantern-sized chin. He looked beyond Joey as if expecting to see someone else trailing along behind.

"Boy, you lost?"

"No sir."

The man gave him a moment's silent, critical study, a wad of tobacco pooching out his left cheek. "Ain't seen you before. You ain't from around here."

"No sir. From back yonder a ways."

"Where's the rest of your folks?"

Joey pondered a lie. He had never been good at lying. He always turned red in the face and gave himself away. But he decided he would have to learn if he intended to get plumb away from Dulcie. "Back yonder at home. I'm on my way to visit my aunt and uncle."

He felt his face warming. The man would have to be blind not to catch on, and his steady gaze indicated good eyesight. He surveyed the uneven blanket roll and the food sack. "Runnin' away from home, ain't you? Just about every boy does it, some time or other. I must've run off five or six times myself."

Joey had no idea how to reply.

The rider said, "I learned one lesson real early, though. When I found my food supply half gone, I always turned around and started back." He motioned toward the food sack. "How's yours holdin' up?"

Joey could not admit that he had already used up the biscuits and had cut heavily into the pork. "I'm all right."

A jovial smile spread across the broad face. "Well, if you're hungry on your way back, my house is over yonderway. Old missus has always got somethin' on the back of the stove."

Joey was tempted to say *I ain't comin' back,* but all that came out was, "Much obliged." He watched glumly as the man set the mule into motion again, its belly sloshing from a goodly fill of water. The stranger stirred a concern Joey had suppressed from the beginning. It was easy not to dwell upon such mundane things as food when there was plenty to eat. But hunger could change the complexion of this whole trip.

He wondered why he had not thought to take a ham or two out of the smokehouse. He considered going back for it; Dulcie and Meacham were not supposed to return for another day or two anyway. But to retreat now would mean a waste of all the miles he had put in and all the miles it would take him to get home again. He wished he had Reuben along. He could always depend upon Reuben for advice.

When Reuben didn't know a better answer, his stock reply had always been, "The Lord will provide." But Joey was not where the Lord was accustomed to seeing him. What if the Lord was looking for him somewhere else?

He was not ready for nightfall. It came much too soon and a long way from water. Reluctantly he made a dry camp, staking Taw to graze at the end of a cotton rope. He ate a little of the pork that remained and thought wistfully of the biscuits he had used up earlier. Any satisfaction they had given him at the time was long gone. He rolled out the blankets but found they did little to cushion the hard, uneven ground. Lying with eyes wide open, he studied the stars. The longer he lay there, the harder the ground seemed to get. Worse, he imagined he could feel a hundred tiny critters crawling around on his body, punishing him for usurping their piece of ground. And he could not escape the notion that somewhere out in the darkness a rattlesnake was looking for him.

It was the first time in his life he had ever spent the night completely alone. He listened to the distant yipping of coyotes and the challenging reply of a farm dog somewhere in the darkness. He had no fear of coyotes. They were harmless to people, unless one happened to be infected with hydrophobia. Folks said hydrophoby coyotes didn't howl, so as long as they were talking to each other he needn't worry about them. He worried a lot more about what he might eat tomorrow and all the other tomorrows down the road.

Sometime during the long night weariness overcame the loneliness, and he drifted off into a troubled sleep. Pa and Reuben came to him and seemed to be trying to give him advice, but he could not understand what they were saying. Their voices were muffled. When Dulcie appeared, he understood her well enough. She wanted to kill him, and stated her intentions in plain American.

Once he thought he heard some kind of rustling noise and a snort from Taw, but it was not enough to bring him all the way out of a deep sleep. Eventually the faraway crowing of a rooster summoned him to rise up from his blankets and stare into the rising sun. Taw stood with feet braced and head down, sleeping while the world awakened around him. The old horse had seen a lot more sunrises than Joey, and they held no surprises for him. Joey had slept with his clothes on, except for his boots. Those he found wet with dew. He realized he should have tucked them beneath the edge of the blankets to keep them dry.

A lesson of the road, one he would remember.

His stomach growled, reminding him of another road lesson he was rapidly learning: to stretch his food supply. He reached for the food sack to quiet the rumblings. It was not where he had left it, beside his saddle.

He walked a slow circle around the camp and found the sack ten or fifteen paces from where it should be. The smaller cloth bag holding the coffee beans lay near the larger, empty one. The sugar was scattered on the ground like a white powdering of snow, its paper sack torn open. The pork was gone. Small canine tracks indicated that a couple of coyotes had helped themselves. Sneaky little devils, they had known he was harmless. Folks claimed a coyote could smell a gun, and Joey didn't have one.

It was just as well he had eaten all the biscuits when he did, for now he would have none anyhow. Not counting the coffee, he had nothing left to eat except the corn which he had done a poor job of parching. The coyotes could have had that with his blessings.

A cottontail rabbit watched him from beneath a bush thirty feet away. It would be breakfast if he had a way to bring it down. Had he planned his trip better he would have fetched along Pa's rifle. He picked up a rock and hurled it in the rabbit's direction but missed. He saw a flash of white tail disappear down a hole.

He had a canteen, but he had drunk up the last of the water when he had made camp. He thought of a couple of times yesterday he could have refilled it but had not bothered.

More lessons of the road.

He remembered Pa saying that soldiers had sometimes survived for days without anything to eat; that they lived off of their own stored fat. Trouble was, Joey had always been on the skinny side.

He managed to roll his blankets into a neater bundle than yesterday. He hoped he would look a little better organized and less like a runaway kid. He saddled Taw and set out, the early-morning sun behind him again as he traveled in a southwesterly direction. He could not stop thinking of the breakfast table back home. If things had been different, he would be sitting there now. Whatever her shortcomings, Dulcie had been a fair-to-middling cook.

He tried to focus his mind on bigger matters, like where he was going and what he would do when he got there, but the thought of a breakfast missed kept getting in the way. At length he came upon a farmhouse that appeared to be abandoned. At least, some of the shingles were missing from the roof and the windows had all been removed, leaving wide-open holes in the weathered log walls. He approached it cautiously, for the coyotes had been about as much surprise as he wanted in one day.

He found nothing of interest or use except an open well, which reminded him that neither he nor Taw had had a drink of water since last evening. He turned the windlass and was pleased to find a bucket at the end of the rope. Though no one lived in the house anymore, they evidently used the well on occasion. He lowered the bucket until he heard a splash and felt the weight as it filled with water. He drew it up. The water looked all right. At least it didn't have a drowned bird or anything like that in it. He dipped a little of it in his cupped hand and sipped carefully. It tasted all right, so he drank what he wanted, then held the bucket for Taw.

He imagined the lecture he would get from Dulcie if she saw him letting a horse drink from a bucket meant for people. He almost wished she *could* see him. He felt a flush of independent spirit, even rebellion.

Joey filled his canteen. Only now did it occur to him that he should have done it before Taw had drunk from the bucket. Well, he didn't figure the horse had any dread disease that it could pass along to him. A traveler could not afford to be narrow-minded in such matters.

The water was only a temporary substitute for food. The abandoned log house was still in sight when hunger began gnawing at Joey again. Reuben had always said adversity helped shape a man's character. Much more of this, Joey figured, and his character ought to be in pretty good condition.

Toward noon he saw a farmer leaving his field, heading for his house. A woman stood on the front porch, banging a piece of metal against a large iron ring, tolling him in for dinner. Joey reined up, running his tongue along his lips and imagining what kind of fixings waited on the kitchen table. It would be biscuits, surely, and pork or beef roast, and probably red beans, topped off with pie that had meringue six inches deep. He watched, arguing with himself. The argument went on a while, but eventually caution won out over hunger. He rode on, looking back over his shoulder. He ate a little of the parched corn and came near gagging on it.

By evening, caution was no longer a primary consideration. He felt weak, even a little faint. When he saw a campfire flickering in the dusk, he headed toward it. By now he was hungry enough that he was almost willing to go back and take his chances with Dulcie. At least, he would risk getting caught if he could just get something to eat.

He heard children's laughter before he was able to make out any details about the creek-side camp. He saw the dim form of a wagon with a canvas top and a team of mules staked on grass nearby. As he approached, a small girl watched him a moment, then turned and ran, shrieking.

Probably thinks I'm an Indian or something, he thought. The notion gave him a momentary sense of power, until he heard a man's voice. The shout carried a hint of threat.

"Who's that out yonder?"

"It's just me," Joey shouted back. He thought afterward that they had no way of knowing who *me* was.

Nearing the wagon, he saw a man cradling a weapon in his arms. Joey could not tell whether it was a rifle or a shotgun, not that it made a nickel's worth of difference. He felt a chill. A woman and three children waited distrustfully beyond the wagontongue, barely touched by the flickering light of the campfire. The little girl who had given the alarm peeked out from behind her mother, exposing only her left eye.

The man took a few steps forward, giving Joey careful scrutiny before he lowered the weapon. He was large framed, but that frame was not fleshed out. He had probably spent a lot more time at hard labor than at the dinner table. "You ain't nothin' but a boy. Who's with you?"

"Nobody. I'm by myself."

The man moved closer. Distrust faded, and his face began to warm with a smile. "Kind of short in the britches to be travelin' alone, ain't you?"

Joey considered repeating the lie he had told the stranger yesterday about visiting an aunt and uncle. That man had seen through him immediately, and this one probably would too. Joey either had to improve his storytelling technique or quit trying to lie. "I'm runnin' away from home."

That was the last answer the man would have expected. He reacted with surprise, then a degree of pleasure. "At least you're honest. Most boys would've made up some fool yarn. By the looks of things you didn't get off very well fixed for travelin'. Bet you're hungry."

"Ain't had nothin' to eat all day."

"Well, you won't founder yourself here, but you're welcome to share in what little we got. You see, we been out west, tryin' to farm. Now we're headin' east, back to the wife's kinfolks." The man turned toward his family. "Wife, we got another hungry young'un here."

Reluctance tinged the woman's voice. "We already had three. How far do you think them two squirrels'll stretch?"

The man ignored her negative attitude. To Joey he said, "You can look at the campsite and tell which direction folks are travelin'. Goin' west, they'll leave ham bones and coffee grounds and empty airtights. Comin' back, they don't leave nothin' but rabbit skins and squirrel tails." He motioned toward the food sack hanging almost limp from Joey's saddle. "What you got in there?"

"Nothin' much but a little corn and some coffee."

"We run out of coffee a week ago. Boy like you has got no business drinkin' coffee anyway. It'll stunt your growth and turn your skin black, and then white folks won't associate with you."

Joey would trade it all for a square meal. "You folks are welcome to it." They could have the parched corn as well as the coffee. He untied the sack and handed it to the farmer before he climbed down from the saddle. The man pointed at the mules. "Stake your horse yonder and come on to the wagon. We'll be eatin' directly."

At home Joey was sometimes choosy about what he ate, but here he would ask no questions. He saw two steaming pots suspended from an iron bar over the small campfire. One held a stew of some kind, the other a plentiful supply of red beans. The woman lifted the coal-covered lid from a black Dutch oven and exposed a batch of browning cornbread. Cornmeal was the poor man's flour. Anybody who could raise a crop of corn could grind his own rough meal without having to haul it to a mill. Wheat flour was harder to come by.

The woman gave him a reluctant look, then turned to her husband. "George, the blessin'."

The big farmer bowed his head. "Lord, we'd rather it was beef and biscuits, but we thank Thee for them squirrels just the same. Bless this poor runaway boy, and show him the road to righteousness. Amen."

Badly as he wanted to dive right into the fixings, Joey managed the good grace to stand back and let the three youngsters fill their tin plates first. His stomach was talking loudly, but he imagined he could hear Reuben speaking even stronger, reminding him that no matter how hungry he thought he was, someone else was worse off. Joey remembered how hungry he often got when *he* had been a kid.

The three children shyly gave him room even as they stared at him with undisguised curiosity. He surmised that they were not used to strangers. Country kids often hid from visitors and would not reappear until the company left or it was time to eat.

He could see that the squirrel stew was badly depleted, so he took only a little of it and made up the difference in beans and cornbread. Pa had always maintained that though Texas since the big war had gained a reputation as beef country, the pioneers who settled it had subsisted largely on beans and cornbread, augmented by rabbits, squirrels, and poke salad.

Joey felt kinship to those pioneers, venturing off on his own this way.

The farmer ran some of Joey's coffee beans through a hand-cranked grinder attached to the wagon. With a look of eager anticipation, he suspended a coffeepot over the fire. Wistfully Joey watched the children divide up what was left of the stew. He could have handled a second helping, but manners prevailed over appetite. These folks looked as if they were ready to throw open the gates and declare surrender after a long siege of hard luck.

"You-all been out west," he said. "What's it really like?"

The farmer jerked his head toward the old wagon. "Just look at this used-up outfit. That about says it all."

The woman said, "That country ain't good for nothin' but heathen Indians and heathen cowboys. I'm hard put to say which one is worse."

The farmer gave her a look of reproach. "Now, wife, we never even seen an Indian. They're all on the reservation up in the Territory. And there never was a cowboy done us any harm either. There was even a couple of them brought us a quarter of beef when we needed it most. It's just that the Lord never intended that country for farmin', or He'd've let it rain once or twice. Grass is all that country's good for, and weeds. I swear, you plant one grain of corn and three weeds come up."

Joey's interest quickened. Two or three young men in town had claimed to be cowboys, but he had been unable to tell them from everyday farmers. "I've heard about cowboys. What're they like?"

"Like everybody else, only a little different."

The woman put in, "They're a hard-drinkin', hell-raisin', uncurried lot. Beyond redemption, most of them. A boy like you has got no business goin' amongst them. They'd turn you away from your mama's teachin's."

The farmer frowned. "What *about* your mama? Don't you know she's worryin' about you?"

"My mama died a long time ago. Pa died a little while back. I got nobody but a stepmother, and she don't like me." He thought about telling them the rest of it, that Dulcie had been trying to kill him, but he doubted they would believe it. They would probably take it as a sign to disbelieve everything else he said.

The farmer sympathized, "It's a hard world for orphans."

His wife motioned toward her children. "It's a hard world even for kids that've got their mama and daddy."

It took Joey a while to go to sleep, for the ground was as hard as the night before. As he lay wide awake, his mind ran back to Pa, and even farther, to Mama. The nearness of this family brought a crushing weight of loneliness down upon him. Poor though these people were, at least these children had a mother and a father. He wanted to cry a little but would not allow himself. He was getting too old for that sort of weakness.

He made up his mind not to abuse this family's hospitality by imposing further on their scanty food supply, though he stayed for a breakfast of cornmeal cakes and even drank a little of the black coffee made from his beans. Its bitterness required some forcing down but got better after the first couple of strong swallows. It warmed his stomach. With time, he thought, he might learn to like it. That would be a sign of manhood.

The farmer gravely watched him saddle Taw. "Son, I'm not your daddy, so I can't tell you what to do. But what you *ought* to do is go back. Get three or four more years on you before you set off by your lonesome again."

Joey did not want to tell him he might be three or four years dead by then. "I ain't wanted back yonder."

"I hope you find yourself wanted where you're goin'."

Joey had decided this man could be trusted not to give him away. "Do you know where there's a town called Bastrop?"

"You'll need to keep travelin' west and maybe edge south the least bit. I hope you got kin there."

Joey's eyes burned a little. "My daddy used to have a cousin in Bastrop. All the other kin I know are in the cemetery."

The farmer blinked some himself. "I wish we could take you with us, but I don't even know where *we'll* end up. Choppin' some other man's cotton, like as not." His handshake was so strong it hurt all the way to Joey's elbow.

Though the woman fretted about how to feed her own, she gave Joey what was left of the cornmeal cakes from breakfast. She also gave him ground corn with instructions for preparing rough hoecakes from meal and water. "They won't make you fat, but they'll hold you 'til you find somethin' better."

"Much obliged, ma'am."

"You got a Bible?"

"Yes'm, in my war bag. It's pretty old."

"The Word never gets old. Read a little in it every night. Feed your soul as well as your body."

The body wasn't likely to be fed very much, he thought, not unless his luck took a sharp turn for the better. The family started eastward in their wagon, and he rode westward, turning once to wave.

Remembering how Taw's sweat had flavored the biscuits, he took pains to keep the food sack hanging atop his leg. That did not present a serious challenge, for it was much smaller than the first sack he had carried.

CHAPTER

5

Joey ate a couple of the cornmeal cakes at noon to quiet the rumbling in his stomach. Shortly afterward he came upon a well-beaten east-west wagon road that paralleled a clear-running creek. He felt less nervous about meeting strangers, now that his encounter with the farm family had produced no serious effort to send him back. He and Taw had traveled a lot of miles. He felt that distance had decreased the chance of anyone getting word back to Dulcie. Perhaps he would be fortunate enough to come upon a kind soul who would invite him for supper.

Luck brought him into a freighters' camp as the sun was setting. He saw dust stirring before he came upon the big high-sided wagons and teams of mules. The drivers were unfastening the leather harness, dropping it on the ground where the mules stood. One of the young mules was acting up. The man at the singletree expressed displeasure in words that would have launched Reuben into a sermon about the perils of blasphemy.

Joey surveyed the crew, picking a tall, lanky fellow with a gray beard who appeared to be the oldest in camp and most likely to be the boss. "Mister, reckon I could help some way and earn a supper from you?"

Graybeard pointed to the youngest man Joey could see. "You'll have to ask the kid yonder. He owns the outfit this trip."

The "kid" did not look as if he would have to shave often to keep his beard in check. Joey guessed he was no older than his early twenties. He would have thought a man had to be thirty at least, and therefore middle aged, before he could own an outfit like this.

The young man said, "You can help me lead these mules down to the water." His eyes turned quizzical. "I'll bet you're not out of the fourth reader. How come you're not in school?"

Joey recognized this as an oblique way of asking why he was on the road in the first place. "School's out. Reckon how far it is to Bastrop?"

"You might make it in four or five days if that horse don't die of old age on you."

Joey felt a flare of resentment. Nobody had any call to insult a man's horse. "Taw's all right."

The young man grinned, recognizing that he had touched a raw spot. "We'll give your horse a bait of oats after a while. Looks like he could stand a good fill."

"He's come a long ways," Joey admitted.

The teamsters all gave him a suspicious looking-at while he helped water the mules. They probably had him pegged rightly enough as a runaway. There wasn't any point in trying to lie to them. But nobody asked. Some had an outlaw look, the kind of men Pa would have said weren't using the names their mothers and fathers gave them. These men wouldn't want their own pasts inspected closely, so they were given to tolerance of others who posed no threat.

Joey didn't see how he could appear a threat to anyone, except perhaps to Dulcie.

After they had fed the mules and Taw, the young boss said, "You might help Ol' Shiloh yonder start fixin' our supper." Shiloh was a big-shouldered man with rheumy eyes and red-veined face. Joey guessed him to be a heavy drinker when the opportunity presented itself. He looked as if he could wrestle a bear but had lost his last match. He had not shaved in a couple of weeks, nor was there evidence that he had washed in at least that long. Joey decided he had better not look too closely at his supper.

The cook dug a fire pit with a dull shovel and piled some dry wood into it in a haphazard manner. He poured coal oil from a can onto the wood. He tried to strike a match on the patched seat of his old cotton trousers but had to lift one foot and use the sole of a well-worn boot instead. Flames shot up with a *whoosh*. Backing away from the burst of heat, Joey noted that Shiloh recklessly held the coal-oil can in his hand while standing close to the fire.

Reuben would have said he risked burning himself up before the devil even had a chance at him.

Shiloh rigged an iron bar across the fire. On a small table lifted down from the wagon he began mixing a batch of bread dough without taking time to wash his hands. He pinched off pieces of sourdough and laid them into a greased Dutch oven, which he placed over glowing coals as soon as the fire had begun to burn down. He pointed toward the wagon. "Boy, fetch me that bucket of beans hangin' under yonder."

The bucket was suspended beneath the wagon bed. Joey found it heavier than it appeared, but he supposed it took a lot of beans to feed a freighting crew. Shiloh said, "I let a fresh pot simmer over the fire every night so it's ready by mornin'. All I got to do is heat it up for dinner and supper."

Joey feared at first that beans would be the main course, but Shiloh unwrapped a blood-stained tarp to reveal a hind quarter. "You like mule meat, boy?"

Joey had never tried it and didn't want to now. He saw a fleeting smile and realized Shiloh was teasing him. This was beef. Wielding a butcher knife, Shiloh carved off enough thick slices to go around and dropped them into a deep pan of melted lard bubbling over the fire.

He still had not washed his hands, but Joey's appetite was strong enough to overcome any squeamish reservations. Anyway, the grease was hot enough to kill anything it touched.

When Shiloh hollered that supper was ready, the freighters

crowded around, wasting no time on ceremony or manners. Joey would have thought they should defer to the boss, but some of them stiff-shouldered him aside to fill their plates first.

Standing back with Shiloh, Joey made a quiet comment about the lack of respect for authority. The cook said, "He just won the outfit a few nights ago playin' poker with Ol' Fontaine yonder." He pointed a thumb toward the older man Joey had first assumed was the head teamster. "Like as not Fontaine'll win it back before we get to where we're goin'. With this outfit, you never know from one game to the next who you'll be workin' for. Not that it makes much difference. Ain't none of them much smarter than their mules."

Joey could not imagine Pa ever risking what he owned in a poker game. Whatever he had acquired, he had held with the tenacity of a tick in a cow's ear. The main thing Joey remembered about cousin Beau was of listening to him and Pa argue over the sanctity of property, over the virtue of hard work and frugality. Pa had said Beau was improvident. Beau had declared that a shroud had no pockets—whatever that meant.

Joey watched from outside the circle of firelight as the men played poker on a blanket spread upon the ground. They were using matches instead of chips. Joey did not understand the rules of the game. Pa had never indulged in card playing, and Reuben had always maintained that cards were the devil's invention, a means of increasing the population in hell. But Joey was fascinated to watch the young boss's pile of matches shift gradually over to the gray-bearded Fontaine.

When the final hand had been played, the young man shrugged with indifference. "Well, I reckon I'm workin' for you again."

Fontaine seemed less happy over the situation than Joey might have expected. "You sure you wasn't cheatin'?"

"Naturally I was. How else do you think you won?"

The men began walking off toward their bedrolls. Joey felt he owed it to the young former boss to express his regrets over loss of the outfit.

The answer came with a smile. "This is a money-losin' operation anyway. I make more money workin' for him than ownin' the whole works."

Joey was tired enough that he quickly dropped off to sleep, feeling safe in the company of these men. They looked and talked rough, but he sensed that there was no harm in them for a boy of his age. They might even go out of their way to protect him should they see harm coming his way.

He awakened sometime during the night to the sound of snoring. He had heard snoring before, but none as harsh as this. It came from the area where the mules were tethered to picket lines. Nobody had ever told him that mules could snore.

It was amazing the lessons a person could learn on the road, though he doubted that this one would ever be of much use.

The next morning he pitched in to help feed and water the mules. He kept waiting for Fontaine to invite him to share breakfast. The man never did, so Joey quietly invited himself. He dried utensils, cups, and plates after Shiloh washed them in a tin tub. He decided the only time Shiloh ever got his hands clean was when he did the dishes.

Fontaine cracked a whip and the mules quickly found their individual places in front of the several wagons. Joey had never seen mules trained like this. Harnessing them was a relatively easy matter. One young mule's rebellion earned it a quick kick to the belly. The mule tried to retaliate with its hind foot. The teamster anticipated the move, stepped out of the way, then kicked the animal again. The rebellion was quelled.

Shiloh gave Joey the few biscuits and some thickly sliced bacon left from breakfast. "You been a right smart of help, not to be no bigger'n a watch fob. You may not run onto anybody else as generous as us down the road."

Joey drew back to avoid the dust and watched the wagons lurch into a ragged start eastward. He had not set his mind on his life's work yet, having always assumed he would remain on the farm. But he thought the mule skinners' life might not be so bad. Most of the time they rode on their wagons, and the mules carried all the heavy load. But to fit in he would have to learn to cuss, and it might be helpful if he could play poker.

He could still hear the popping of the whips and the sharp voices of the skinners as he turned Taw southwestward.

He rode through a considerable pine forest before he broke free of the timber and saw the town spread before him. He supposed this had to be Bastrop. A farmer a few miles back had paused in his plowing to tell him it was no longer far. Joey had asked if he knew Beau Shipman. Giving him a strange look, the farmer had nodded in the affirmative and had shouted for his mule to *giddyap*, biting the point of his moldboard plow into the soft ground. He left Joey standing there choking on several more questions he wanted to ask.

Pa's first stop when he went to town was usually the livery barn, where he left his horse or his mules to be fed while he took care of whatever business had taken him off of the farm. The hostler usually brought him up-to-date on whatever news there might be. It was seldom much, for not a lot happened around Athens. Joey considered it reasonable that a livery barn might be a logical place to find out something about cousin Beau. After passing a number of houses along the wagon road, he saw a red barn and a layout of corrals with horses and mules standing around several hay racks. Half a dozen wagons and buggies had been left standing outside.

Taw poked his ears forward, interest sparked by the other horses or perhaps by the smell of feed. Taw would have enjoyed a bucket of oats, but town stables were not in the habit of giving those away. Maybe Beau would have some.

A hostler came to the wide-open door, carrying a pitchfork. He gave Joey a momentary glance, then looked beyond him. "Where's the rest of your family?"

"I'm all there is."

The man's eyes said he knew: Joey was a runaway. Joey wondered how everybody seemed to know that right off.

"It'll take fifty cents to put your horse up and feed him. You got fifty cents?"

"Yes sir, but I ain't spendin' it. I'm lookin' for Beau Shipman. Know him?"

"Everybody knows Ol' Beau. What you want with him?"

"He's about all the kin I got left. Him and my Pa were cousins. Where do you reckon I can find him?"

"I can guess. You see that tall buildin' yonder, the one with the cupola standin' up so high? That's the courthouse."

"That's where Beau is at?"

"No, there's another buildin' just back of it. The jailhouse. I expect that's where he'll be."

"Is he the sheriff or the jailer or somethin'?"

The hostler made a little smile that said he knew a joke Joey didn't. "No, he's one of the reasons we *have* a sheriff and a jailer. He's one of the steadiest customers they've got."

The bottom seemed to fall out of Joey's stomach. He had counted on cousin Beau's help, but he wouldn't be much help from the wrong side of the iron bars. He grasped at a fragile thread of hope. "You sure that's where he's at right now?"

"If it ain't, just wait around."

Joey thanked the man for the information, unwelcome though it was, and reined Taw toward the courthouse. Several people on the street stopped what they were doing to look at him. They might be seeing him as a runaway, or they might somehow sense that he was kin to Beau Shipman. He wondered which they would rank the lowest.

As he approached the courthouse, he saw the jail in back of it, smaller but built of the same sort of stone. Back home, he had always regarded the jailhouse with some dread, and that feeling prevailed now. He would rather take a beating from Dulcie than approach that somber-looking building with its iron-barred second-story windows. But he had come this far. He swallowed hard and climbed down from the saddle.

He remembered from home that it was common for the jailer, or perhaps the sheriff, to live on the ground floor of the jail and keep the prisoners upstairs. Joey tied Taw to a post and walked reluctantly to the open door. He could smell food cooking inside, but he would not enter without an invitation. He rapped his knuckles against the door facing.

A woman appeared, her broad middle covered by a white apron. Her expression seemed pleasant enough, though a little reserved. She reminded him of the teacher he had had in the first and second grades, before she up and married the widowed owner of the general store and became a woman of property.

"Ma'am, can you tell me if you've got Beau Shipman in jail?"

"*I* don't."

His momentary relief was dashed when she added, "My husband does, though. He's the sheriff. Of what possible interest could Beau Shipman be to you?"

"He's my cousin, and I've rode a long ways to see him. Reckon I can talk to him?"

"You'll have to ask the sheriff about that. He's off somewhere in town right now." She frowned, studying him. "You look to me like you might be hungry."

He admitted that he was. The smell of baking bread made his stomach growl like a quarrelsome dog.

She said, "Well, then, you come right on in here. I've got my husband's supper cookin', and he weighs too much anyhow. Won't hurt him to share it."

"I'm obliged, ma'am, but I'd like to see Beau Shipman first."

"I have no authority above this floor. But here I do, and I say you're goin' to eat. A couple of hot biscuits should hold you 'til the sheriff comes for supper."

As she opened the oven, the smell of fresh bread overwhelmed any disappointment over postponing a reunion with cousin Beau. She lifted down a jar of jam from a crude cabinet that had its legs standing in cans of water to thwart the foraging ants. "Any more than this might spoil your appetite," she warned.

He doubted anything could do that. He had finished off Shiloh's sack of grub days ago. Later he had summoned the nerve to visit a farmhouse where a kindly woman had questioned him carefully before refilling the sack. Nothing remained of that food now but a warm memory.

While she bustled around the kitchen the sheriff's wife asked him the same questions everybody else was asking, either directly or by implication. He told her about losing his mother, then Pa. He did not tell her about Dulcie trying to kill him. She wouldn't believe it anyway.

The sheriff came along after a while. The woman told him he had company and that he had best watch what he said and did.

The sheriff seemed an affable sort at first. He gave Joey a quick study and declared, "Why, you ain't big enough to be an outlaw. Way she talked, I thought you might be Miller Dawson or somebody like him."

"Who's Miller Dawson?"

"One of the worst badmen that's ever left his tracks in these parts. Holds up stores and banks. Folks claim he's killed fifty men. But I can tell that you ain't him."

"No sir, my name's Joey Shipman. I come to see my cousin Beau."

The sheriff's expression changed with the abruptness of a door slamming. He bored a hole in Joey with his eyes. "You don't look anything like Beau. I hope you *ain't* anything like him, either."

Joey flinched from the look. "What's the matter with him?"

"His mama ought to've drowned him when he was a baby. Works hard when he's sober, but that ain't often enough. Soon as he gets a few dollars in his pocket he goes on a tear, and he don't stop 'til I shut the cell door on him. One of these days I'm goin' to forget to ever open it again."

Joey tried to picture Pa doing such things. The image was alien to all of his memories except the drinking part. Pa *had* taken to drinking after Mama died. Joey figured that he must not have been sober when he chose Dulcie to be his second wife.

The sheriff said gruffly, "I'll take you up to Beau, but I'm eatin' my supper first."

His wife said, "I've set a place at the table for Joey."

"We've got no responsibility for any kin of Beau Shipman."

Her voice was stern. "He's a boy, and he's hungry, and we're feedin' him."

The sheriff surrendered to the inevitable, but not in good grace. "If Beau is all the kin you've got, you're in a bad way."

The stairway to the second floor was uncomfortably dark as Joey followed the lawman. He had never been inside a jail. The atmosphere was oppressive, even hostile. He quickly resolved that he would travel miles out of his way to avoid ever getting locked up in a place like this. Because whiskey seemed to have a lot to do with people going to jail, he decided he would allow it no part in his future plans.

The sheriff declared, "Beau, got some company for you."

A voice answered from a dark cell in a back corner. "I never promised her nothin', Sheriff. If she claims I did, she's a liar."

"Got a boy here says he's your cousin."

"Second cousin," Joey said quickly. Given the sheriff's attitude toward Beau, the more distant the kinship the less prejudice there ought to be.

Obscured in semidarkness, a man arose from a cot and moved uncertainly toward the barred door. Joey recognized him despite the poor light and several days' uneven growth of whiskers. The only time he had seen Beau he had studied that face, vainly seeking some resemblance to Pa. Cousins should look at least a little alike, he had thought.

"Remember me, Beau? I'm Joey."

Beau Shipman looked as if a team of mules had dragged him across a rocky field. His voice bordered on belligerency. "I don't know no Joey."

"Joey Shipman. John Shipman was my daddy."

Beau seemed to have difficulty bringing Joey into focus. "I don't remember John havin' a boy your size."

"Last time you saw me was when we buried Mama. I wasn't this size then."

"You ain't got much size on you now. Where's your daddy at?"

"He died too. I'm all that's left. Except you."

A spark of hope lifted Beau's voice half an octave. "Did John leave me somethin'?"

"I don't remember him ever mentionin' your name again after you left."

"Then why the hell are you here pesterin' me?"

The sheriff said, "Looks like the boy's got nobody to turn to except you, Beau. That sure don't speak well for his prospects."

Beau's expression ran the gamut from fear to denial to anger. "I hope he don't expect me to finish raisin' him."

Joey flared. "I don't expect you to do anything. I wasn't stayin' noway. I just came to let you know about Pa."

"I'm sorry about John, but I ain't in no position to take on any added responsibility."

The sheriff snorted. "*Added* responsibility? When was the last time you had any responsibility at all?"

The hostility rolled off Beau without a trace. "I ain't takin' on no kid to raise."

"The boy's your kin."

"I could always choose my friends. I never had no choice in pickin' my kinfolks. Tell him to go find somebody else."

"You want out of this jail?"

"I never was crazy about the place."

"Maybe if you *did* have some responsibility, I wouldn't be havin' hell with you so often. I might be persuaded to turn you loose if you'd take this boy home with you and do right by him."

"I don't know the first thing about takin' care of a kid. That's why I never had none of my own."

"You never had any kids because no woman of a sound mind would have you. If I saw a better way out, I wouldn't be givin' you this chance, but I can't keep the boy here. Jail ain't no place for a young'un. Take him home with you for a few days 'til I get things figured out, or I swear to God I'll keep you in here 'til Christmas."

"Stayin' in this place, I could be dead by Christmas."

"Maybe even sooner if you keep grindin' on my patience. What do you say?"

Beau glared at Joey as if he had brought him this load of trouble with malice aforethought. "It's a stacked deck either way."

The sheriff smiled wickedly. "And I'm the dealer."

Beau said a few words that would have done credit to a mule skinner. "All right, then. But the first time he gives me any of that sass . . ."

Rattling the keys, the sheriff swung the door open. "You got anything to eat in that shack of yours?"

"Damned little."

The lawman considered a moment. "Well, the county would have to feed you anyway if you stayed in here. I reckon it can afford to set you up to a few groceries." He took five silver dollars out of a desk drawer and started to hand them to Beau. He thought better of it and gave them to Joey instead. "Here, boy. Don't buy anything with this but good solid grub. Beau don't need nothin' stronger to drink than coffee."

Joey started to tell him he had a few dollars of his own, but he decided he had better hang onto those for an emergency. Someday, when he had a regular paying job, he would send the sheriff's money back with maybe an extra half dollar or so for interest. Pa had always held that a man should go into debt only with great reluctance and regard that debt like a rattlesnake in his pocket until he paid it off.

Beau demanded of the sheriff, "Where'd you put my horse?"

"Turned him out on grass. County don't need the expense of keepin' him at the wagon yard."

"That means I got to walk all the way home."

"I wish it was twice as far. Come on over to my desk and I'll give you back your stuff." It did not amount to much—a pocketknife, a few coins, a couple of scraps of wadded paper.

Beau declared, "Seems to me like I still had half a pint or so of whiskey left. Where's it at?"

"Don't you remember watchin' me pour it out? You bleated like a lost sheep."

"You got a streak of cruel in you, Gardner. You'd pull the wings off of a butterfly."

"Not as cruel to you as you are to yourself. One of these days I'll probably have to drag your pickled carcass out of a muddy ditch someplace and see to your buryin'. If I don't kill you first."

"Just leave me lay. It'll be a lesson to wayward youths." Beau turned to Joey. "You comin', kid, or am I goin' to be lucky after all?"

Reluctance dragged like a heavy weight on Joey's legs. He thought he had an inkling to the reason Pa had never talked about Beau. If Beau was the best he had to show for kinfolks, he would be better off among strangers. A few days' rest for himself and Taw, a few solid meals, and he might decide to strike off on his own again. He was a free-born American. He had put Dulcie behind him. He could leave Beau the same way.

But right now it was coming on dark, and he fancied the idea of having a roof over his head after all those nights under an open black sky.

CHAPTER

6

Joey could hear the sheriff's wife arguing with her husband over the propriety of sending a little boy off with a bad example like Beau Shipman. The sheriff countered that Joey could learn from bad examples as well as from good. "Once a young'un touches a hot stove, he learns not to ever touch it again."

Joey could not help resenting being called a little boy. She must not have looked at him very closely. He *was* twelve, going on thirteen.

The sheriff said, "Beau's broke. He'll have to work a while before he can afford another binge. By then maybe somethin' better'll turn up for the boy."

Taw was still tied outside, where Joey had left him. Head drooped, he appeared to be asleep. Beau made a long, frowning study. "This the best horse you've got?"

"He's the *only* one I've got," Joey said.

"You're the next thing to bein' afoot." Beau tried to raise his leg high enough to reach Joey's left stirrup but could not. "Damned poor saddle you've got, too."

"It fits me all right."

Beau pulled himself up, dragging his leg across Joey's bedroll tied behind the cantle. His feet hung down far below the stirrups. "You're young and healthy. You can walk."

"He's my horse," Joey protested.

Beau reined Taw around and set off in a walk. Smoldering, Joey followed. He suspected that Beau would gladly ride away and leave him if he did not keep up.

Joey had never been in a saloon, but he knew what they were for. He saw a woman standing just outside the saloon door, smoking a cigarette, and he knew what she was for, too. She gave Beau a look that might cause cotton to wither and die. Beau seemed to make a concerted effort not to see her.

Joey said, "That woman don't appear to like you very much."

"She's got an odd notion that I owe her money."

Joey thought he knew, but he asked anyway. "For what?"

Beau ignored the question. "It's humiliatin', everybody seein' me ride a ewe-necked old nag like this."

The insult to his horse added fuel to Joey's anger. "Any worse than seein' you staggerin' drunk?"

"You've got a smart mouth, kid. Keep it shut, and the flies won't get in."

"The flies are all followin' *you.*"

"My way of livin' ain't none of your business."

I guess not, Joey thought, *because I ain't staying very long.*

Beau reined up at a general store and swung down from the saddle, almost falling before he got his feet under him. He held out his hand, the palm up. "Sheriff gave you some money for groceries. Hand it here."

"He said for me not to give it to you."

"Give it to me before I hoist you up by your feet and shake it out of your pocket."

Reluctantly Joey reached into his britches. His fingers played over the five coins, then brought out three of them.

"That's all there is?" Beau demanded. "I thought it was more."

"You must've been seein' double."

"Can't cut much dust with three dollars." Instead of going

into the general store as Joey expected, Beau walked two doors down to a saloon. In a few minutes he returned with a bottle of whiskey. "Ain't had my supper," he said.

After leaving the business section they passed through a nice residential area where Joey assumed the merchants lived. Most of the houses were larger and featured more gingerbread trimmings than the one Pa had built on the farm. Joey's hopes rose at the thought that Beau might have a house like this. Expectations flagged, however, as they passed smaller and plainer houses. Finally, at the edge of town, Beau reined up in front of a crude frame structure little larger than Reuben's shack. It lacked even a porch.

Beau seemed to catch the disappointment in Joey's face. "What did you expect, bay windows and a balcony?"

"I hope you didn't pay much for this place."

"Didn't pay anything. Folks that built it decided to leave. Nobody else claimed it, so I moved in."

Joey tried to make the best of a poor situation. "I guess it's dry inside."

"When it don't rain." Beau slid down from Taw and handed the reins to Joey. "He's your horse, take care of him. Ain't got no oats. He'll have to fill up on grass, same as mine."

Joey gave in to resentment. "At least he won't be fillin' up on whiskey."

Beau had to push hard on the door. It was bound against the threshold because the shack leaned slightly northward. "Just unsaddle him and turn him loose."

"What if he strays off?"

"Wouldn't be no great loss."

Joey took the precaution of hobbling Taw. From the unpromising looks of things he might be leaving here sooner than he had expected. He didn't want to have to hunt for the horse all over the town section.

Beau had lighted a lamp and sat at a small, rickety table, the bottle in front of him, its cork gone. "If you're hungry you'll have to stir up your own supper. I've got mine."

"I done ate with the sheriff and his wife." But Joey looked around, for this trip had taught him to eat whenever and wherever he got the chance. On top of the small cast-iron stove sat a blackened pot. In it he found red beans, soured and growing a coat of mold that resembled soiled velvet. In a small pan three remnant biscuits were dry and hard as stone.

He asked, "How long were you in jail?"

"This time? Three or four days, maybe five. I never kept count."

Rummaging, Joey found but little food in the cabinet: a tin container almost empty of flour, a limp burlap sack with perhaps a single potful of dry pinto beans, and a bacon rind with just enough meat left on it for half a dozen thick slices. Breakfast would finish it and leave both of them hungry.

He wondered how much the sheriff's remaining two dollars would buy. He did not intend to benefit Beau with any of the little money he had brought from home.

A steel cot in the corner was the only bed, its blankets carelessly tangled atop a lumpy-looking mattress that Joey guessed was filled with straw or corn husks. "Where do I sleep?"

"You got your own blankets. Spread them on the floor or go outside; I don't care."

Joey had seen no sign of rain. The night air was probably a lot fresher than the shack's. At least it wouldn't smell like cigarette smoke and whiskey. He spread his blankets on the ground, moving them twice but finding no spot less hard than another. He lay staring up at the stars, wondering why he had bothered to hunt down cousin Beau. He was better off without any kinfolks if this was the best he had.

The tight door was almost too much for him to push open, and the scraping of wood against wood made enough noise to stir the dead. It did not stir Beau, however. He lay asleep on the cot, snoring like a freighter's mule and still wearing all his clothes except boots and hat. The cover blanket lay on the floor. The bottle stood beside it, uncorked and two-thirds empty.

Joey studied Beau's inert form, and last night's resentment boiled up again. It didn't seem possible that Beau and Pa had come out of the same family. Pa had always put a lot of stock in bloodlines when it came to farm animals. Joey supposed that just being cousins, Pa and Beau didn't share as much blood as brothers. He was glad *he* was only a second cousin.

He had it in mind to fix a little breakfast for himself, then ride off. Beau might sleep until noon. Even then, he would probably be relieved to find Joey gone. He was unlikely to say anything to the sheriff until the lawman came out and asked him. By then Joey would be miles away.

He gave his attention again to the whiskey bottle. Last night he had noticed a knothole in the floor, near the cot. He turned the bottle over, shoving the neck of it down into the hole. The whiskey gurgled as it disappeared.

Rattlesnakes often took refuge beneath houses like this. Joey grinned wickedly as he pictured how a drunk snake might act. Probably couldn't hurt Beau. He should have enough alcohol in his system to be well fortified against snakebite.

Joey built a fire in the small stove. He was not much of a cook, but he knew how to fry bacon. He could try his hand at whipping up a batch of biscuits because he had watched Dulcie make them many a time. She always mixed milk or clabber with the flour, though, and he doubted that there had been a drop of milk in this shack since Beau had lived here. Water would have to do.

The bacon was sizzling when he heard a creaking sound behind him. Beau sat up on the edge of the cot. He hit the whiskey bottle with his foot and sent it rolling. He grabbed it up and studied it in bleary-eyed dismay. "I thought I still had some left."

Joey was tempted to tell him the truth and revel in his mischief, but he did not know Beau well enough to gauge his potential for violence. "I guess you didn't."

"Where's the coffee?"

"I didn't find any. Reckon you're out."

"No whiskey, no coffee. Ain't much use in gettin' up." Beau lay back on the cot and brought both arms up over his face. "What's that you're fixin'?"

"Bacon. Got biscuits in the oven."

"Bacon. It smells terrible. God, kid, I'm sick."

"You wouldn't be if you hadn't spent the grocery money on whiskey. Now what you goin' to do?"

"Die, if I'm lucky."

Joey had no experience in handling people with a hangover. Dulcie had sent him away when Pa was like that. "Maybe you need to eat somethin', but there ain't nothin' except bacon and biscuits. It'll take all mornin' to cook beans."

"Don't you understand, kid? I'm sick, maybe dyin'."

Joey thought he ought to feel sympathy, but it wasn't as if somebody had poked a six-shooter in Beau's ribs and made him drink. "Pa always said if you hadn't climbed up, you wouldn't have fallen down."

"Your daddy had a mean streak in him. Appears he passed it on." Beau pressed his hand against his forehead. "Feels like there's three blacksmiths beatin' out horseshoes in there."

Joey could only imagine, and he didn't really care to. "You want some bacon or not?"

Beau got up again, arms pressed tightly against his stomach, and staggered toward the door in his sock feet. Joey had left it half open at the point where the bottom dragged so heavily upon the floor that he could not move it further. Beau bumped his shoulder hard against the edge of the door. Joey thought he felt the shack tremble. He could hear his cousin outdoors, retching.

He managed to eat a biscuit and some of the bacon before he was overcome by an imagined image of Beau Shipman vomiting. His own stomach made half a turn. He sat at the table a while, waiting. Beau did not appear.

I don't care if he never comes back, Joey thought. But in spite of himself he began to worry. He peered out the half-open door. Beau lay face down on the ground, not moving. Painful images of Pa and Reuben flashed into Joey's mind. "Beau!" He rushed outside and knelt beside his cousin. To his relief he could see little puffs of dust as Beau exhaled. He tried to turn Beau over onto his back but only succeeded in getting his face a little higher from the ground.

"You've been breathin' dirt," he said. "If the whiskey don't kill you, that probably will." He realized he could not lift Beau by himself. Beau had to help him. He tugged at his cousin's arm.

"Come on, get up. Don't you be dyin' on me!"

Beau tried to fight him off but lacked the strength. Joey provoked him into rising to his knees and crawling to the shack with Joey tugging on his arm. Beau made it through the door and to the cot. With Joey's help he managed to pull himself up and flop onto the mattress.

Breathing hard from exertion, Joey felt emotions pulling him in two directions at once. He still intended to leave, but he realized he should put it off until he knew Beau was going to make it. Left alone, for all Joey knew, Beau might lie here and die. "There's still some bacon and biscuits on the table. You'd better eat somethin'."

"I don't need no snot-nosed kid tellin' me what to do."

"You need somebody. You sure don't take care of yourself."

Joey realized that if he was going to stay here a day or two and see Beau get on his feet, he had better lay in a few more groceries. He started for the door.

Beau demanded, "Where you goin'?"

Joey did not feel that Beau had any right to question him, so he did not answer. He found the hobbled Taw grazing near the shed and corral. A brown horse stood nearby, the brand GO on its hip. Joey assumed it was Beau's. He saddled Taw and rode into town, stopping in front of the general store where he had thought Beau was going to buy supplies last night. He double-checked his pocket to be sure the two dollars were still there. Wrestling around with Beau, he might easily have lost them. The feel of the coins reassured him.

The sign over the door said *Casper Tatum, Groc.* Joey assumed that the merchant who met him at the door was Tatum. He was a middle-aged man whose girth showed that he had partaken well of his own merchandise. The broad smile on his face shone almost as brightly as his bald head. "Good mornin', sonny. What can I do for you?"

"Need some groceries." Joey fished out the two dollars. "Reckon how much that'll buy?"

The grocer rubbed his chin. "Well, not enough to give you a bellyache. Just what is it you need?"

Joey told him he thought they needed some bacon, beans,

and flour, maybe a few potatoes and surely some coffee. "My cousin Beau needs lots of coffee."

"Beau Shipman? You're a cousin of Beau's?"

Joey wondered if he ought to try to lie out of it. Beau might owe the store money, and the merchant might simply keep the two dollars without giving him anything for them. But he owned up to the truth. "Yes sir. He's my daddy's cousin, anyway."

Tatum's voice softened with sympathy. "Most people like Beau, except for Sheriff Gardner and those that've had a fight with him when he's drunk. He's his own worst enemy."

"I sure couldn't argue none with that."

"Tell you what I'll do: Seein' it's for Beau, I'll give you my brother-in-law rate. We had a bad hailstorm a year or so ago. Beat my roof into splinters. Beau helped me reshingle it and wouldn't take any pay. I slip grub into his cabin now and again when he ain't lookin'."

"I didn't know he was a carpenter."

"He's a carpenter, a jackleg blacksmith, a plowman, and a pretty good hand with horses and mules. Beau can do just about anything he sets his mind to. If he just didn't like whiskey so much . . ." Tatum put the groceries into a burlap bag. It was so heavy Joey could barely lift it. The grocer carried it out for him and tied the sack to the horn of Joey's old saddle. "Now, don't you tell Beau where you got this. If he asks, just tell him you found it along the road somewhere."

"I sure do thank you, sir."

"*Sir.*" The man smiled again. "Ain't every boy says 'sir' anymore. Glad to see that there's a few of the younger generation ain't gone to hell in a handbasket."

Joey found Beau still lying on the cot, his face clabber gray. But Beau was not too sick to scold. "What do you mean runnin' off like that and not answerin' me, kid? I figured you was gone for good."

"I thought about it. I'd be better off if I'd rode plumb around Bastrop and never seen you."

"You ain't my notion of a life's companion either. Where'd you get the money to buy groceries?"

"Found it layin' in the road."

Beau hurt too much to keep up the attitude. He lay back and pressed his arm to his forehead. "Anyway, thanks for comin' back, kid. I didn't think you would."

"Don't keep callin' me kid. I'm almost thirteen years old. Name's Joey."

He decided he had better get busy fixing the coffee. Beau looked as if it might save his life. Joey said, "I got some potatoes here. I'll fry you one for dinner, along with some more bacon."

"I tasted what you fried up this mornin'. Who ever taught you to cook?"

"Nobody."

"That's what I thought. Boy your age ought to learn. Might save him and his cousin from starvation. Let me do the cookin', and you watch me." Slowly and painfully rising from the cot, Beau made his way to the little stove. He pointed to the coffee grinder. "You know how to crank that thing, don't you? I'll punch up the fire." He burned himself lifting a stove lid and muttered under his breath as he sucked on the scorched fingers.

A voice called from the doorway. "You-all alive?" The grocer Tatum stood with one hand braced on the door facing and peering around the door that was stuck half open.

Beau beckoned for him to come on in. "Just barely."

Tatum said to Joey, "The sheriff told me about his bargain with Beau. Glad to see you're still here. If you weren't, Gardner's got a cell reserved for Beau over at the jail."

Joey recalled how close he had come to leaving. That was still his intention, as soon as he and Taw rested up a little and Beau seemed able to stand squarely on both feet. "Beau's fixin' to teach me about cookin'."

"Good thing for an orphan boy to know. You did tell the sheriff you're an orphan, didn't you?"

"Yes sir."

"I thought that's what you said. Gardner seemed to have some doubt about it."

Beau said, "I was at his mama's funeral. As for his pa dyin', I don't see any reason he'd tell us a windy."

Tatum said, "I hope you two are gettin' along with one another. The sheriff might take it kind of bad if he was to ride out here and find this boy gone."

Even in his weakened condition, Beau seemed to appreciate the grocer's concern. "Much as I hated to, I gave Gardner a promise. I do keep my promises."

"I wish you'd promise to quit drinkin'."

"The shock'd kill half the people in town. I'd hate to be responsible for that."

"I'd chance it." Tatum went to the door, then turned back. "You feel up to a job of work?"

"Doin' what?"

"I've had Luke Quincy buildin' me a new barn and pens out at the farm. He fell off of the ladder and stove in some ribs. There's probably a couple weeks of work left if you want it."

"I'll be out there tomorrow."

"Bring the boy. He can earn a little by fetchin' and carryin' for you."

Joey was elated. "You mean you're goin' to pay me?"

"Your legs are too short for full wages. How about fifty cents a day?"

That was fifty cents more than anyone had ever paid him. "I reckon it'll be all right." He did not want to seem overeager, but he could not help exclaiming, "It'll sure be all right." A few extra dollars in his pocket would be helpful when he struck out on his own again.

He would probably have to hide it, though, to keep Beau from spending it on a bottle.

Tatum frowned at Beau. "I don't want you takin' whiskey out to the job. Luke was cold sober and got hurt anyway. Drinkin', you'd fall off the roof and break your neck."

Beau frowned back. "You sure know how to take all the pleasure out of hard work."

Joey watched the merchant leave. Beau turned back to the stove, his hands shaking. He appeared ready to throw up again, but Joey doubted that he had anything left in his stomach.

Joey asked, "Why do you drink when you know it's goin' to do this to you?"

"Why do you ask so many questions that ain't none of your business? A button your age wouldn't understand even if I told you."

"You probably don't understand it yourself."

"What I *don't* understand is why you ran off from a good home and came here to bother my life. You've got a stepmother. Sure, she ain't your real mama, but she'd take better care of you than I can."

"She was tryin' to take care of me, all right. She was tryin' to kill me!"

The look on Beau's face was like the look Joey had seen on everyone else he had tried to tell. Beau said, "The devil's got a special place for kids who tell stories like that, and you're knockin' on his door."

"It's the truth. I think she let Pa die, and I know she killed Reuben someway. Then there was the bull that almost got me, and the rattlesnake . . ." He stopped, for the disbelief in Beau's eyes told him it was useless to go on talking.

Beau said curtly, "I wisht you'd go out and chop some wood. Ain't enough left in here to keep the coffee hot."

Joey choked off a retort and stomped outside. They would believe him someday if Dulcie got her way. They would look at him lying in his coffin, and they would be sorry. He would like to see their faces then.

CHAPTER
7

The Tatum farm lay just across the Colorado River an hour's horseback ride from town, beyond the last of the pine trees. Beau rode the brown horse with the letters *GO* branded on its hip. Joey asked if the horse answered to "Go." Beau said that was too short a name for a horse, so he called him Git Out.

He abandoned the meandering wagon road and cut across country. "We'll save us some time," he explained.

Joey suspected it was not time Beau wanted to save, it was his badly abused innards. The whiskey and the brown horse's rough trot were keeping them riled up. Beau's shortcut missed the road's shallow ford, so they struck the river at a point wide and deep. Taw balked until Beau rode up behind him and slapped his rump right smartly with a quirt. Taw jumped into the water with an alacrity that almost threw Joey out of the saddle.

Joey shouted, "You didn't have to do that."

"Sometimes you got to show a horse who's boss. Same way with a kid."

"I'm not a horse. And I'm not a kid, either." He worried that his blankets would get wet, rolled and tied behind the cantle, and that they might not dry out before night.

Beau said, "You need a bath anyway."

"I'll bet I've had one since you did."

"Won't hurt either one of us to slip down here after dark and take off a pound or two of dirt and sweat. Now quit your belly-achin' or go back to town."

Joey quickly decided he liked the farm because of its variety of livestock: horses, cows, pigs, sheep . . . also chickens, guineas, and a couple of peafowl that screeched at every disturbance and sometimes when the only disturbance was the one they created. It reminded him of home in happier days when he had been younger, when Mama had been there, and Pa, and the sun had laid a golden glow upon the Shipman farm.

"You know somethin'?" he asked Beau that night as they soaked in the shallow water at river's edge. "I'm goin' back home someday when I'm bigger. I'm goin' to take that farm away from Dulcie and fix it up a lot like this one."

The cool water had not improved Beau's disposition. "Why wait? You ought to go back now."

"I told you about Dulcie. She's set on killin' me."

"Never saw a boy with such a wild imagination. You'd be a lot better off at home."

"I'd be dead."

Tatum came out in a well-traveled buggy the second day to see if they had settled in and started work. He seemed pleased to find Beau on the barn roof, nailing down fresh cypress shingles. He hollered up, "I brought some extra grub for Emma, since she's got two more mouths to feed."

Emma was a black cook who lived on the place with her farmer husband. She sang to herself while she worked, like Joey remembered Mama doing many times. He had found the first day that she could bake a better cobbler pie than any he had tasted since Mama died. The man, called William, reminded him a bit of Reuben, though he was younger and could read. He had a stack of newspapers Tatum had brought him and tried to talk to Beau about current affairs like the situation in Europe. That came to naught because all Beau knew about Europe was that it lay somewhere on the other side of the big water. He didn't know London from St. Petersburg. Joey knew, but his knowledge was only from schoolbooks. Those were not current enough to give him much ground for conversation. William knew who most of the kings and queens were, who was at war and who was fixing to go.

"I don't reckon you brought anything to drink," Beau said to the grocer.

"Only coffee. Emma broke William from drinkin' twenty years ago. Time you leave here, she may have you preachin' temperance too." He turned to Joey. "You doin' all right, sonny?"

"Yes, sir."

"Sheriff Gardner asked me to check on you, make sure Beau's treatin' you proper."

That rubbed Beau the wrong way. "And what if I wasn't?"

"I expect you'd be back in jail before dark."

"That Gardner's got a special rope saved up with my name on it. He'd've hung me a long time ago if he'd had an excuse."

The turn of the conversation made Joey nervous. He tried to change the subject. "I sure like your place here, sir."

"I'm glad you do. It's somethin' anybody could have if they're willin' to work hard and save their wages." He gave Beau a look that said the remark was aimed right between his eyes.

It bounced off. When the merchant moved on to the house to talk to Emma and William, Beau said, "It's somethin' anybody could have if they're careful to marry a woman whose daddy has got money. That's the secret of success: to marry into it or to pick a mama and daddy that's already got it."

"He doesn't look rich. First time I saw him, he was sweepin' out his own store. And look at that old buggy he's ridin' in. The wheels are sprung."

"The way rich people stay rich is that they don't ever spend nothin'. Their money just sets there and mildews. When I've got it, I put it to work and spread it around. I believe in havin' a good time."

"Like you were havin' the mornin' after you got out of jail?"

Beau struck his thumb with the hammer and ended the conversation. "I wisht you'd take the posthole diggers and start workin' where William put down stakes for the corral."

They had been on the job a week when Blair Meacham showed up. Joey did not see him ford the river, so he was taken by surprise when one of the peacocks screeched to announce the arrival of a stranger. Meacham drew rein behind Joey, almost close enough to reach out and touch him. Joey was holding a post in place while Beau tamped the fill-in dirt around it with the tip of the shovel handle.

He had begun to feel that there might be some chance for Beau if he could stay away from town and the tantalizing lures it dangled to trap the weak willed. During long days on the farm Beau had labored as if the place were his own and everything would be lost if he slacked off for even an hour while there was daylight to see by. The new barn was finished, its pine siding bright in the sun and waiting for paint. The new corral adjoining it lacked perhaps a couple of days' labor to be finished. Casper Tatum had estimated the job would require two weeks, but he had not taken into account Beau's nervous-energy drive when the alcohol was burned out of him.

"See?" Joey had said. "You can do a good job when you stay sober."

"The sooner done, the sooner I get paid. There's several bottles of pure happiness waitin' for me in town."

Joey was beginning to realize that a man, like a coin, could have two sides. There was heads, and then there was tails.

He stared in open-mouthed amazement at Blair Meacham, sitting on his horse and staring back. A smile slowly spread across Meacham's face, but Joey had an uncomfortable feeling it was false as a lead dollar. He saw coldness in the gray eyes, and rebuke.

Meacham said, "Well, Joey, you've caused me and Dulcie a right smart of trouble and worry."

Joey swallowed, unable to answer.

Beau wiped a sleeve across his sweaty face and let the shovel fall, the handle thumping upon the ground. He asked Joey, "You been struck dumb or somethin'?"

Joey had to clear his throat before he managed to speak. "This is Mr. Meacham. He's Dulcie's cousin."

"Not cousin," Meacham said, "husband. Me and Dulcie, we went on a little trip and got ourselves married by a preacher. Then we went home and found you'd run off without a word. Now, that wasn't no thoughtful thing to do, was it?"

His mouth was still smiling, but there was no smile in his voice or in his eyes. He didn't seem the same Mr. Meacham who used to bring Joey candy and tell him jokes and stories.

"You married Dulcie?" Joey did not understand how any man could do that after seeing the way she treated Pa.

"I did."

"Bet you wouldn't if you'd known she was tryin' to kill me."

"Kill you? Now, what ever gave you such a notion?"

The words spilled out like water through a broken dam. "There was Pa. I don't think she wanted him to live. She just stood back and let him die. And Reuben . . . I don't know how she done it, but she killed him. And she turned that bull loose on me, and she put that rattlesnake on my bed. She wants me dead so she can have the farm."

Meacham shook his head in disbelief, like everybody else Joey had tried to tell.

Joey said, "You better watch out. She'll get tired of you, and then she'll kill you too."

Meacham turned to Beau. "Poor boy went through a lot, losin' his daddy and then the old darkey that helped raise him. Unsettled his mind, it looks like. I suppose you'd be the cousin Sheriff Gardner told me about?"

"Beau Shipman." Beau reached up and shook hands.

Meacham dismounted. "We sent letters to every county sheriff in two hundred miles. I've come to take Joey home where he belongs."

Joey hoped Beau might stand up for him. They had gotten along decently well the last few days, between occasional sullen spells on Beau's part brought on by his painful withdrawal from whiskey. But Beau only shrugged. "That's the best thing to do. I can't provide no fittin' home for him."

Joey protested, "Beau . . ."

Meacham took a firm grip on Joey's arm. "Come gather up whatever stuff you have and let's get started. We can make a good many miles before dark."

Beau volunteered, "His stuff is in the old barn yonder."

Meacham said to Beau, "Sheriff Gardner told me you're a man who likes whiskey."

"I've been known to indulge a little now and then."

"I've got a full bottle here in my saddlebag. It's yours if you'll go fetch up Joey's horse."

Beau said, "It won't take any time at all."

Joey tried to jerk free of Meacham. "No! You-all listen! She'll kill me if I go back!"

He dragged his feet, pulling against Meacham, but he was no match for the man's strength. He began to cry. "Please! Please! I don't want to go."

Meacham argued, "You'll see how wrong you are when I get you home. Dulcie'll bake you the biggest cobbler pie you ever saw."

And put poison in it, Joey was certain.

"Beau," he pleaded, "please talk to him. Make him see."

But Beau had turned his back and ambled out to catch Taw. Joey would bet he was already tasting that whiskey in his imagination. Damn him for the sot that he was!

Meacham stopped at the door of the old barn and pointed inside. With Beau out of hearing, he made no pretense at the kind nature and easy humor he had shown Joey in the past. His voice was gruff. "Throw your stuff together and let's be movin'."

Joey wished the barn had a back door, but it didn't. Even if it had, he could not run fast enough to elude Meacham's horse. Beau would probably even aid in his capture. What an awful fix this was, two men working together to carry him to his death and neither of them realizing his peril.

Joey rolled his few belongings in his blankets, tied them behind the saddle, then carried saddle and bridle out the door. Beau brought up Taw, leading him along by nothing more than a gentle grip on the horse's mane. Why couldn't the fool horse have taken a notion to run away? Joey wondered. Instead he had simply stood there and let Beau walk right up to him in the edge of the pasture. Gentle as a dog, but not half as smart.

About like Beau!

Joey gritted his teeth in frustration. Well, it was a long way home. Somewhere along the road, with any luck, he would catch Meacham off guard. The man had to sleep sometime. When he did, Joey would slip away. He wasn't going to his death without putting up the struggle of his life.

Beau saddled Taw and pulled the girth up tight. "You'll realize after a while that this is the best thing for you. If you stayed with me you'd probably grow up a drunk."

"You've been sober for more than a week."

"I won't be tonight. Go back to your stepmother, kid. She'll be so happy to see you that maybe she won't even give you a whippin' for runnin' away."

"She'll be happy all right." Joey's throat was painfully tight as Beau boosted him up into the saddle. He could not control the sudden flow of tears. "I'm tryin' to tell both of you if you'd just listen. She'll kill me."

Meacham shook his head pityingly. "You've got her all wrong, boy. Come on, let's go."

They started toward the river. Beau watched them a minute, then came running, waving his arm. "Hey! What about that bottle you were goin' to give me?"

Meacham pretended not to hear him. He put the horses into a long trot and quickly outdistanced Beau.

Despite the fear that put pain in the bottom of his stomach, Joey found satisfaction in the fact that Beau had been beaten out of the promised whiskey. Mr. Meacham probably didn't have a bottle with him in the first place.

It served Beau right.

Gradually Joey began pulling himself together, trying to bring his fear under control so he could think clearly. He realized Meacham was not heading toward the shallowest spot to cross.

Joey said, "If we'll follow the wagon road it'll take us to the ford. The horses won't even have to swim."

"Shorter this way. You need a bath anyhow. Look at the dirt on you."

"Been buildin' fence." A hopeful thought struck Joey. "We're goin' by town, ain't we? Mr. Tatum owes me some wages." It wouldn't be more than four or five dollars at best, but the grocer had seemed an honorable and intelligent man. He might listen if Joey could just talk to him. It was a chance.

Meacham did not reply. He rode down the long, slanting riverbank and stopped at the edge, looking back. Joey turned to see if Beau might be following in the vain hope of getting his whiskey. The house and barn were more than half a mile back and hidden by heavy timber that fringed the river.

The water appeared sluggish, but Joey knew it could be deceptive. The undercurrent was swifter than the surface. He said, "It's real deep right here. There's shallower water upriver a ways."

"This'll do. A little swim won't hurt the horses." Meacham took hold of Taw's reins, pulling them out of Joey's grasp and over the horse's neck. When Taw showed reluctance, Meacham circled behind him and slapped him across the rump with a quirt. Taw plunged in. Soon Joey sensed that the ground had gone out from under the horse's feet. Taw was swimming, fighting the current. Joey held the horn with both hands. It was a challenge to stay in the saddle.

He shouted, "We ought to've gone to the ford."

Meacham did not reply. Joey thought he was busy with his own struggle. Something bumped his leg hard, and he saw that Meacham had drawn his horse up against him. A chilling look had come into his stepfather's eyes.

Meacham grabbed Joey's arm. Joey shouted in alarm as Meacham dragged him free of Taw and plunged him into the water. Joey clutched at Taw's mane, at the saddle strings, at the horse's tail. But Meacham held his arm, pulling him away, pushing him under.

"Mr. Meacham . . ." Joey choked as he gulped a mouthful of water. "What're you doin'?"

What he was doing came clear in a blinding flash of panic. Meacham was trying to drown him. Many other things suddenly came clear, too.

Joey struggled to break loose, but Meacham grabbed a handful of his hair and pushed his head under. Trying to hold his breath, Joey swallowed water nevertheless. He kicked and tugged and came up gasping for air. He managed a cry like the desperate bleating of a lamb.

"Quit fightin'!" Meacham shouted at him. "Ain't goin' to do you no good." He pushed Joey down and tried to hold him. But the struggle threw Meacham's horse off balance and caused its nose to go under water. Terrified, it came up fighting the river. Meacham lost his hold, and Joey began swimming away.

Meacham cursed first the horse, then Joey. He brought the mount under control, and Joey felt a hand clutching at his arm. He dove to get out of reach and sensed the current taking hold, carrying him downstream.

Coming up for air, he heard shouting. The voice was not Meacham's. Beau was swimming his brown horse, waving his arm. "Here, Joey! Come to me!"

The weight of water-filled boots and wet clothes tried to drag Joey down, but he splashed toward Beau as Beau closed the distance. Choking, gasping for air, Joey grabbed desperately at Beau's outstretched hand.

"Hang on, kid."

Joey clutched Beau's sleeve. Beau got his arm around Joey's shoulder. He shouted at Meacham, "I've got him. It's all right now!"

Joey realized Beau had mistaken Meacham's intentions. He probably thought Joey had fallen off his horse and Meacham had been trying to rescue him. Joey managed to cry, "He tried to kill me."

Beau seemed not to have heard him. "I'll get you to the river-bank, then your Mr. Meacham had better have that whiskey."

From behind them, Joey heard Meacham shout. Joey turned his head, though he had to blink the water from his burning eyes before he could see. "Beau! He's got a gun!"

Beau was too surprised to move. Meacham pulled up beside him, pistol in his hand, and swung the barrel at Beau's head. The blow was deflected by Beau's upraised arm and softened by the crown of his felt hat. Beau wheezed, "Godalmighty!" and turned Joey loose.

Meacham's horse was already spooked. Joey's splashing and threshing frightened it more. Meacham cursed the animal and tried to pull its head up. Fighting restraint, the horse plunged forward, rolling over onto its side. Meacham yelled in surprise just before he went under. He came up floundering and no longer had the pistol. The horse swam away from him. Meacham splashed around wildly.

Beau managed to take a new grip on Joey's arm. Joey felt Git Out steadying himself as he took solid footing on the riverbed. On the bank, Beau let Joey slip to the wet sand amidst several broken pieces of driftwood. Joey's heart was hammering, and he coughed up water. He saw Taw climbing out downstream, stopping to shake himself like a dog. Incongruously, Joey's immediate worry was the roll of blankets tied behind his saddle. They were strung out halfway to the ground and thoroughly soaked. He would have to sleep wet tonight.

At least it would not be the long sleep Meacham had planned for him.

Beau seemed a bit stunned, struggling to understand. "What's the matter with him, anyway? He didn't have to pistol-whip me over a bottle of whiskey."

Joey managed to quit coughing for a moment. He fought for breath. "It would've been hard to explain a bullet hole in you."

Meacham was still splashing, reaching out his hands as if he sought something solid to grasp. There was only the water. His shout was a strangled cry for help.

Joey said, "You were a witness. He had to try and drown us both."

Beau slowly began to comprehend. He eyed Meacham without sympathy. "I don't believe the son of a bitch can swim."

Joey began to regain his breath. "This is three times him and Dulcie have tried to kill me."

Beau said, "They ain't very good at it, are they?" He pushed Git Out back into the river. "It'd be a great lesson to him if we let him drown. But the sheriff wouldn't see it like me and you." He drew up next to the gasping Meacham, took a handful of the man's wet collar and dragged him to the bank. He dropped Meacham in the mud at the river's edge. Meacham spat water, his shoulders heaving.

Beau told him, "What I ought to do is stomp hell out of you and throw you back in. But when you're done spittin' up mud I'll take you to town and let the sheriff treat you like he's been treatin' me for so long."

Joey clenched his fists. He could see the plan. His dying had to look like an accident. And Meacham had to get it done as soon as possible so Joey would not have a chance to escape on the long trail home. "I'll bet he was goin' to say I ran away from him and got drowned when I tried to cross the river."

"Pity the sheriff didn't believe your story in the first place."

"You didn't either."

"It sounded like somethin' a runaway kid would make up."

Joey began to feel the warmth of gratitude. "At least you came out to help me."

"I had no such notion. I came to get the whiskey he promised me. See if you can catch his horse and look in his saddlebags."

Joey's gratitude vanished more quickly than it had come. "You'd sell your soul for a bottle of whiskey."

"I already did, a long time ago."

A blur of movement caught Joey's eye. Meacham rushed toward them, a large chunk of driftwood swung back over his shoulder. Joey cried, "Watch out, Beau!"

The warning was too late. The club smashed against the side of his cousin's head with a solid thump. Beau staggered, instinctively throwing his arms up against a blow that had already struck. Meacham raised the club again.

Joey grabbed up a piece of driftwood, smaller than the other but about as large as he could handle. Meacham struck Beau a second time. Beau's arm took the brunt.

Joey aimed for Meacham's head, but Meacham bent forward and the stick struck him in the ribcage, costing him some breath. Meacham hesitated, struggling to regain the air he had lost. Beau grappled with him for the heavy club. The two staggered and splashed back into the edge of the river. As he fought, Meacham kept swearing, his fury sweeping him out of control.

Both men had their hands on the club, the strength of one challenging the power of the other. Beau threw Meacham off balance, then thrust the club into the man's face. Blood burst from Meacham's nose. He stumbled but kept his hold on the club. Joey waded in and swung his stick again, hitting Meacham on the back of the head. Meacham faltered, and Beau jerked the club free. He brought it around hard and smashed Meacham across the jaw. Meacham staggered backward and fell. The current carried him away face down, blood streaming behind him before losing itself in the flow of the river.

Knee-deep in the water, Joey watched in shock as the body drifted downstream. Full realization set him to shaking.

"We killed him, Beau!"

"He was tryin' to kill *us*." But Beau was shivering too, and Joey knew it was not because of cold water. "Came within an inch of gettin' it done." Beau raised a hand to feel of the place on his head where the first blow had struck. It bled a little.

Meacham's body disappeared around a bend.

Joey said, "We'd better go tell the sheriff."

"Tell Gardner?" Beau vigorously shook his head. "He'll call it murder. He's been sayin' all along that I'll get on a big drunk and kill somebody someday. He wouldn't believe a word I'd tell him."

"Maybe he'll believe me."

"Remember how much good it did to tell him about your stepmother? He'll figure I got into a fight with Meacham over him takin' you home. Probably say I was tryin' to make him give me money to turn you loose."

"But Mr. Meacham tried to kill you."

"Nobody knows it but me and you, and that sheriff's been itchin' for an excuse to salt me away for good."

"What'll we do? The body is sure to wash up somewhere." From what Meacham had said, the sheriff himself had sent him here, Joey thought. When the body was found, the lawman would know where to look for answers.

"You can stay here. Sheriff'll put the blame on me anyhow. Ain't but one thing for me to do, and that's to hightail it out of here . . . get as far away as I can before the law starts lookin' for me. I'll lose myself out west someplace where they can't find me. Arizona maybe, or California, whichever one is the farthest."

Joey visualized the map on the schoolhouse wall. "That'd be California, I guess. But it's an awful long ways."

"The farther the better. Ol' Gardner's heavy on his feet. He'll get tired of travelin'. I'd better catch up my horse."

They waded out. Taw had climbed to the high bank and had his head down in the tall grass. Joey was struck by the irony. His own world had just blown itself to pieces, but his horse was peacefully grazing as if nothing had happened. Beau had difficulty in catching the skittish Git Out. The horse turned and trotted away three times before Beau managed to sweet-talk it into standing still until he could grasp a rein.

Beau said, "See Meacham's horse anyplace? I sure could use a stiff drink of that whiskey."

"I don't think he had any whiskey."

"Then he was a liar on top of everything else."

Meacham's mount had evidently run off. Well, somebody would find it, just as they would find Meacham's body.

Joey spread his wet blankets and rerolled them into a neater bundle. He wished he had time to lay them out and let them dry. As Beau rode up to him, Joey asked, "We goin' by town to pick up the rest of your stuff?"

"Ain't nothin' in that cabin worth the risk. And *we* ain't goin' no place. You're stayin' here."

That's what you think, Joey thought. After all, he had struck Meacham a staggering blow. When he told them his story—

and he wouldn't lie—they'd count him as a participant in the killing. Maybe they wouldn't hang him as they would hang Beau, but they would probably put him in a boys' reformatory until he was old enough to go to the Huntsville penitentiary and bust big rocks into little ones.

Beau rode to the old barn to gather his blankets and a few other belongings. William came in from the field, bringing his mule team. He said, "You-all look like you went fishin' and fell in the river. Thought you was buildin' a fence."

Beau frowned at Joey, who was tying his things to his old saddle. The look said for Joey to keep his mouth shut. Beau told William, "The job is all finished except a little of the corral. Tell Casper I hate to leave on short notice, but I got an emergency on my hands."

William could probably see that for himself, because blood had dried on the side of Beau's head. "What kind of emergency?"

"Best I don't tell you. What you don't know can't get you in trouble. You got any cash money you could lend me?"

William was slow to answer. "I got a little up at the house, maybe twenty, thirty dollars." Doubt insinuated itself into his eyes. Beau was notoriously unreliable. "But if you're leavin', how you goin' to pay me back?"

"Casper can pay you out of the wages I got comin'. Tell him I said it was all right."

Joey knew from past conversations that William had money, probably a lot more than any twenty–thirty dollars, stashed in various hiding places where no robber could find it all and no banker could eucher him out of it. He and Emma were of a saving nature, trusting no one else to take care of their futures. In that, they were different from Reuben, who had never shown much interest in money.

William accompanied Beau to the house, where Beau remained evasive in his reason for leaving. Joey held his silence. Emma insisted upon washing away the blood and putting something on the head wound that must have burned like hell's hinges, from the way Beau hollered. She accepted on faith that whatever mess they had gotten into, it had not been of their choice. She sacked up most of the groceries she had. "Mr. Casper'll bring us some more next time he comes," she said.

William said, "If anybody asks us where you went, Mr. Beau, what you want we should tell them?"

Beau swung up onto his horse. "Just say that the last time you seen me, I was headin' for the moon." He set the brown into a long trot.

Joey had to spur hard. Beau turned in exasperation as Joey pulled up beside him. "How many times have I got to tell you? You're stayin' here."

"No I'm not."

"You ain't ridin' with me."

"Yes I am."

"That old horse of yours travels like a sore-footed cow. Me and Git Out'll leave you behind."

"But you've got to stop and sleep sometime. When you do, me and Taw'll catch up to you."

Beau let fly some curse words Joey did not think he had heard before and set his horse into an easy lope. Joey tapped Taw with his OK spurs. He fell behind and knew Taw could not match Git Out's brisk pace. But if he could keep Beau in sight he would be able to catch up with him eventually. And if he lost sight of him, he could follow tracks.

After a couple of miles Beau stopped and waited. He pointed his thumb toward a darkening sky. "It's cloudy in the west and fixin' to rain misery. You sure you want to face that?"

"If you can stand it, I can."

"The first time you start to crybaby on me, I'm leavin' you."

Joey made a vow to himself that the sun would come up out of the west before Beau would see another tear in Joey Shipman's eye. "Are we goin' to travel, or are we just goin' to sit here and talk?"

Beau muttered under his breath and gave Joey a look meant to sting, if not actually to bring blood. He put Git Out into a trot.

After a while the rain started. Joey hunched his shoulders against the chill of it, for he had no slicker. He had only a light cotton jacket, and it was wrapped in the roll of wet blankets. He set his jaw, determined not to let Beau see the pain he felt in his body and in his soul.

CHAPTER

8

Beau said, "We'll follow the river west as far as Austin, but we won't tarry there. That town is full of lawyers and people studyin' to be lawyers. It's no place for an honest man."

Joey thought back to the nice Mr. Wilson, who had always been a friend of Pa's. "What's wrong with lawyers?"

"They rob you without a gun, and charge you for doin' it."

"We ain't got much worth stealin'."

"They'll take it anyway just to keep in practice."

Beau rode a long time in silence. Joey might as well have been talking to Taw for all the response he received. The rain had stopped, but the sun had not emerged from behind the clouds. A light wind cut through Joey's wet clothes and made him shiver. It also reminded him how long it had been since he had eaten.

He told Beau, "I'm gettin' hungry. Ain't you?"

Beau snapped, "There you go crybabyin' on me. I got a lot more to worry about than your empty belly. I'm travelin' as long as there's daylight, and maybe after there ain't. Turn back if you want to. I wish to hell you would."

"Me and Taw'll still be goin' after you quit."

Beau did not stop until at least a full hour after darkness had fallen. He halted then only after Git Out cut sharply to the right to avoid stumbling into a steep and muddy washout Beau had not seen and which almost lost him his seat. It occurred to Joey that the horse probably had the most sense.

"We'll stop," Beau said. "Can't afford to cripple an animal."

Joey thought some bacon would taste real good, broiled on the end of a stick. "I'll build us a fire."

"And have the law spot it? You ain't got a lick of sense. Besides, where you goin' to find any dry wood?"

The tone of voice stung Joey. Defensively he declared, "This mess wasn't my doin'. If you've got to blame somebody, blame Dulcie and Mr. Meacham."

"It's part your fault. I'd never laid eyes on you but once 'til you came ridin' into town and dumped all this aggravation on me. Why couldn't you have picked on somebody else?"

"There wasn't anybody else. Not kin, anyway."

"We ain't kin. Second cousin don't count. I was livin' happy and free 'til you came along."

"Not very free. You were in jail."

He had touched a raw nerve. Beau snapped, "That's a smart-aleck way to talk to a man that saved your life."

"I saved yours too. He was about to stove your head in when I hit him with that stick."

"None of it would've happened if you hadn't come here. I ought to've rode off and left you. I still got a mind to do it."

"Go ahead then. I got along by myself all the way to Bastrop."

"The law would probably have you before sundown tomorrow, and you'd tell them where I was headed."

"I don't *know* where you're headed. And I don't think you do either."

"Didn't have time to plan ahead, or I'd've done a better job of it. And I wouldn't have you hangin' on my back like a dead weight."

Joey stewed in silence, for he was weary of an argument that was not going anyplace. He ate some of the food Emma had sacked for them, then rolled himself in his blankets. They were still damp, so he never got warm. He lay thinking about the trouble he and Beau were in, more or less making up his mind that he would sneak away before daylight and leave Beau to manage by himself, and probably do a poor job of it. But he eventually dropped off to sleep, dreaming of rattlesnakes in his bed and of Mr. Meacham. He saw Meacham's blood-smeared face rising up out of the reddened water like some avenging demon, raging at him that he was fixing to die and go to hell.

When Joey opened his eyes he found himself blinking at the rising sun. For a moment, despite his own earlier intention of going off and leaving Beau, he had a momentary sinking feeling that Beau might have ridden away and left *him*. He looked around desperately.

Beau had a small fire burning and a tin bucket of coffee sitting precariously on small pieces of blazing driftwood. Joey wondered how he had ever gotten them lighted.

"You goin' to sleep all day?" Beau demanded. "Sheriff Gardner has probably been on the trail for two hours."

"I didn't sleep hardly any. Must've dropped off just before sunup."

"You snored all night." Beau had some thick slices of bacon impaled on a couple of sharpened sticks, dripping fat into the fire. The aroma awakened Joey's hunger. Beau said, "I'm figurin' to make many a mile today, so you better get yourself fortified if you're goin' with me. You sure you're old enough to drink coffee?"

Joey had been coming around to an easier tolerance of the stuff, though it was black as tar the way Beau boiled it. "You think I'm just a schoolboy?"

"Yes, and I wish you was still in school."

"School's out."

"Not here it ain't. You'd better be a fast learner."

Joey found his blankets still about as damp as when he had spread them last night. He had no choice but to roll them that way. Reuben's old Bible was damp but not soaked. It had protected the picture of Mama and Pa. For that, he was thankful.

They ate hastily, Beau's gaze going often to their back trail.

As he mounted he said, "You better keep up. I ain't waitin' for you and that burro you're ridin'."

"Taw ain't no burro."

"Ain't much of a horse, either."

"Go on and leave me if you want to. I'll be all right."

"I laid awake most of the night, studyin' on doin' just that. But I owe somethin' to John. He *was* my cousin."

Joey saw no reason to tell Beau that he had considered the same option and probably would have taken it had he not gone to sleep. He made it a point not to fall behind, though sometimes he had to spur Taw more than he liked. Beau would put the brown into a lope at intervals then slow to a trot again to avoid wearing the animal down.

By midday Taw required more spurring to make him match Beau's pace. Joey was glad when Beau said, "We've got to rest these horses a while or we'll run them into the ground."

They had been avoiding the road, following the course of the river. Joey could often see horse and wagon traffic at a distance, however. The increasing frequency indicated to him that they were nearing Austin. He knew from school that it was the capital of the state. The governor lived there, and the legislature. Pa had said most of the laws were made in Austin, so what Beau had told him about the place being infested with lawyers rang true.

They rode down off the river's high bank where they would not easily be seen. Beau staked the two horses to graze and parceled out Emma's food sparingly. Joey could easily have eaten twice as much as Beau allowed him, but he would not show weakness by complaining. He noticed that Beau took no more for himself.

Killing somebody probably dampened a man's appetite, Joey thought, though his own hunger was not noticeably diminished.

Beau said, "I didn't get much sleep last night. I'm fixin' to catch me a few minutes' nap. You keep watch."

Joey resented the order but did not want to start another argument. He had not won one with Beau yet. At best, their set-tos had come to a draw.

As Joey walked up onto the bank where he could see for

some distance, Beau hollered after him, "Don't you go to sleep."

That was just what Joey did. The shade was a pleasant refuge from the warmth of the sun, and the high-pitched singing of insects in the trees was like a lullaby.

Hoofbeats awakened him. Opening his sleepy eyes wide, he saw five horsemen approaching from the east, so close he could have thrown a rock and hit one had he not been paralyzed by surprise. He could only stare and wonder how they had slipped up on him so easily. He felt ashamed for his dereliction of duty.

He was also scared, for he saw a badge on one man's vest. It was round with a star inside. A Texas Ranger badge, he realized.

"Well, son," the rider spoke, "you're not out here all by yourself, are you?"

Joey considered lying that he was, but his throat tightened so that he could not speak.

The lawman said, "We've been followin' the tracks of two horses." He eased carefully to the high bank and looked down where Beau slept. The officer drew a pistol, motioned with it, and led his four followers down toward the water. Joey managed to find his voice. "Beau! Look out!"

Beau jumped to his feet, but it was too late for him to do anything. He saw the lawman's six-shooter and raised his hands. His jaw dropped with dismay. "I give up. Don't shoot."

Joey reached his cousin's side. Beau's eyes burned with accusation. "You went to sleep, didn't you?"

"So did you." He knew that was an empty excuse, for Beau had stated his intention of catching a nap.

The lawman gave Beau a long study, then lowered the pistol. "Sorry we gave you a scare. You're not the man we're lookin' for."

Beau swallowed. "I'm not?"

"I'm Sergeant Curtis Wheat, Texas Rangers. We're huntin' for Miller Dawson, the outlaw. We got a report he was seen over this way yesterday. Of course that may not mean much. People claim to've seen him in Dallas and El Paso both the day before. We came across your tracks and thought you might be him."

"I ain't."

The lawman holstered the pistol and leaned forward in the saddle, bracing both hands on the horn. "What *would* your name be?"

Beau's answer was quick. "John Smith."

The lawman glanced at Joey. "And you?"

Joey was surprised at the speed and ease of his own reply. "Joe Smith." St. Peter was going to call on him for a full explanation someday, but surely the good angel would consider extenuating circumstances.

The officer appeared to doubt. He extracted a small notebook from his shirt pocket and thumbed through it. "You'd be surprised how many people named Smith I've run into in seven years of rangerin'." He ran his finger down several pages. He said to Beau, "You may be in the book someplace, but I haven't got time today to read the whole thing. We've got bigger fish to catch than you and your son."

Beau said, "He ain't . . ." He caught himself. "We ain't no fish at all. We're just farmers on our way to town."

"Then we'll be about our business of catchin' Miller Dawson. Chasin' him, anyway. Should you run across him by some accident, give him plenty of room. He is a dangerous man."

"I promise you, we won't bother him none."

Joey could not stifle his curiosity. He had heard Sheriff Gardner mention Miller Dawson's name. He asked the ranger, "Ain't he some kind of a Robin Hood, or somethin'?"

"Robin Hood took from the rich and gave to the poor. Miller Dawson takes from the rich and poor alike, and I ain't heard of him givin' any of it away."

Beau said, "The boy has read too many books. Too much readin' ain't good for anybody. It clouds the mind."

The lawman agreed. "Some people make a romantic figure out of a brigand like Miller Dawson. But they're not the people that've seen him over the muzzle of a six-shooter." He put the book back into his pocket. "One piece of advice: If you *are* in the book, I would advise you to keep ridin' 'til you wear your horses' feet off to the knees. Texas law has a long memory and a long arm."

The posse rode up the riverbank and quickly disappeared. Beau turned on Joey. "You like to've got me hung that time."

"He wasn't lookin' for you."

"He could've been, for all you knew. And where'd you learn to lie like that? I'll bet you've been keepin' bad company."

"Not 'til lately."

Beau unstaked his horse and motioned for Joey to do the same. "They've rested enough, and so have you."

"Whichaway we goin'?"

"Whatever direction that ranger took, we'll take another."

Joey's pulse had not quite returned to normal. "I sure thought he had us."

"We've been travelin' faster than the news. But we'd better not slow down or it'll catch up with us."

The more Joey thought about it, the more troubled he became about their riding where no one else traveled. He said, "That ranger followed our trail easy because there was just two horses. Sheriff Gardner could do the same thing."

"That's why we're travelin' fast."

Joey pointed southward to the distant road, where he could see a freight wagon and a couple of riders. "Seems like it'd be harder for him if our tracks was all mixed up with a lot of others."

"But on the road, people would see us."

"What would they see? Like you told the ranger, just a farmer and his son on their way to town. There's probably a lot of them."

"I don't know where a boy like you comes up with such damn fool ideas." But soon Beau began edging southward and fell into the main road. They met a farm wagon going east, a man and a woman sitting on the seat. Groceries and other supplies were stacked in the bed of the wagon.

Joey was nervous about stopping to visit, but Beau told him it might look suspicious if they didn't.

"How far on in to Austin town?" Beau asked the couple.

"We been about two hours in this wagon," the farmer replied. "You'll make it some sooner a-horseback." He gave Taw a critical study. "Or maybe not."

As the wagon moved on, Joey looked back. Its wheels were obliterating part of the tracks left by his and Beau's horses. "A few more wagons and there won't be a sign we passed this way," he said, indirectly telling Beau he had been right.

Beau could not let him off free. "But if anybody asks that farmer and his wife, they'll remember us."

As they came to the top of a gentle hill, Joey saw a town spread out before them, most of it lying north of the river. A lot of the buildings were of stone or brick. It was the largest town he had seen, larger than Bastrop. He reasoned that it must be Austin.

Beau said, "We'd better lay in a few more supplies before we head off to the west." He licked his lips. "And I sure could use a drink."

"You said we weren't goin' to tarry long."

"It won't take long to buy a bottle of O Be Joyful."

Joey could visualize the outcome. "If you do, you won't get two miles down the road. I'll go and leave you where you fall."

"You're a millstone around my neck anyway."

"The millstone around your neck isn't me. It's that damned whiskey." He surprised himself, using a word like *damned*. He supposed it was the company he had been keeping.

Beau colored. "When men are talkin', children keep their mouths shut."

"I'll keep my mouth shut when you start talkin' like a man."

Beau descended into a sulking silence that he did not break until they found themselves looking northward up a wide and busy street. At the far end of it, behind scaffolding, Joey could see a large construction site. A dozen or so wagons and teams of horses and mules were clustered about it, and a couple of dozen men worked against or atop the walls.

"Must be the new capitol," Beau said. "Old one burned down. They're buildin' this one with stone."

Though only the first-story walls had been raised so far, Joey could tell that this would be a huge structure. "Looks bigger than Pa's cornfield."

"Folks'll be sorry they didn't let the thing stay burned down. Politicians bring nothin' but misery. Like Sheriff Gardner." Beau gave the capitol no more of his attention. He sought out a general store. "I'll go get us some more bacon and flour and stuff. You watch the horses. Town like this, somebody's liable to try and steal them and get a crooked lawyer to swear they were his in the first place."

Joey was relieved that Beau was going for the groceries first, before he went after any whiskey. Otherwise the groceries might never be bought. He looked uneasily in all directions, wondering if he and Beau were being watched, if someone on the street might remember them when the Bastrop sheriff came asking questions. Telegraph wires across the street reminded him that news today could outrun the best horse that ever lived.

He was startled by a voice from behind him. "Well, young man, I see you and your father made it to town all right."

Joey's mouth went dry when he saw Ranger Wheat, still on horseback. "Yes sir. He's takin' care of some business."

"And what did you say your name is?"

Joey struggled to remember. "Smith. We're both Smith. My name's the same as my daddy's." He realized he was babbling, and trembling a little too. He tried to steady himself. "Did you find the outlaw you was lookin' for?"

"Miller Dawson? No, the report was probably false. Most of them are. But we'll catch him eventually. No wanted man gets away forever."

"None of them?"

"One way or another, every guilty man pays his debt." Wheat started to leave but paused. "That's a good lesson for every boy to learn. Wanted men must always keep lookin' back. Stay out of trouble, and you can keep your eyes on the green hills ahead."

Joey watched the ranger ride up the street, then turned his head to see what might be behind him.

Coming out of the store with two sacks, Beau tied the larger to his own saddle and the smaller to Joey's. "That takes care of

luxury," he declared. "Now for the necessities." He reined in at
a brick building where a sign declared *Spiritous Liquors*. He
said, "In a town full of lawyers you'd think they'd at least
know how to spell proper. Supposed to be a *k* in *liquor*, ain't
there?"

"I don't know. The word never came up in school." Joey
knew it was useless to lecture Beau directly. He said, "You
promised we wouldn't be here long. No tellin' how near the law
is to catchin' up with us."

Beau shot back at him, "You think I've forgot? I don't need
to be lectured by a ten-year-old boy."

"Twelve. Goin' on thirteen."

Despite being ill at ease, Joey found much of interest in the
passing traffic—horseback riders, buggies, wagons, people
afoot. By Joey's standards, many of the men were dressed
expensively. Coats were much in evidence, though the weather
was warm, and necks were decorated by ties or scarves. Men
carried themselves as if they had too much business and too
little time to attend to it. Lawyering must pay better than
farming, he thought. But then, most anything did.

Beau came back sooner than Joey expected, though his
breath indicated that he had taken time for a quick drink, or
maybe two. He carried a bottle. "They say there's a lot of
snakes in that western country." He took a long drink before he
deposited the bottle in his saddlebag and mounted Git Out.
Watching him, Joey had a bad feeling. With Beau, one drink led
to another and another and another until the bottle was empty
or Beau was on his back, whichever came first.

They rode south down Congress Avenue. Followed far
enough, Beau said, the street became the San Antonio road.

Joey commented, "I've heard of San Antonio all my life. I
sure would like to see it."

"Go if you want to. I ain't stoppin' you."

"I didn't mean right now. Someday, maybe."

"I was there once. Long's you've got money to spend they've
got a glad hand stuck out for you. But go there broke and
nobody wants to know you. Except the *po*lice."

Joey wondered whether to tell him about seeing the ranger.

That might arouse Beau's cautionary instincts. On the other hand, it might just make him drink more.

Beau needed no encouragement to drink. He stopped at the edge of town and took another long drag on the bottle, then reined onto a westerly wagon road. Joey looked back. He did not expect pursuit this soon, but one never could be sure. That Ranger Wheat seemed like a man who knew his business.

In a while they were beyond the town, moving into rough limestone hills and through extensive cedarbrakes which seemed to choke off whatever wind there might have been, trapping the heat into stifling pockets.

This road appeared less beaten out than the one east of town. Joey realized that population was thinner to the west, where the land was more suited to livestock grazing than to farming. The only cultivation he saw was in narrow valleys where soil had washed down from the hillsides and left deposits deep enough for plowing. Anywhere else the limestone rocks would probably cause a farmer to spend as much time sharpening his plow point as breaking sod or planting a crop.

They met a couple of sturdily built wagons and pulled out of the road to make room. Drawn by extra spans of big mules, each wagon carried a heavy cargo of large limestone blocks, edges and corners neatly trimmed.

Beau said, "Those must be goin' into the new capitol."

A little farther on they came within sight of the quarry from which the blocks had been cut. Men with rifles guarded other men, some white but most of them black, in dirty prison garb. Beau stopped briefly to watch and to take another drink.

"Convict labor," he explained. "The whole legislature ought to be out here sweatin' in that rock pile instead of back yonder passin' laws to tax the workin' man."

Joey thought the biggest levy Beau had ever paid was probably the liquor tax, but judgment prevailed against his expressing that opinion.

A thought chilled him. If they caught and convicted him for his part in killing Mr. Meacham, he might wind up in such a place as this. He tried not to look at the quarry again, but some morbid fascination made him turn in the saddle to stare. He saw prisoners straining to hoist a large square stone onto a wagon with block and tackle. "Poor fellers."

Beau shook his head. "There's poorer ones, them that go to the rope."

They had traveled perhaps a mile when Joey heard three popping sounds in rapid succession behind them.

"Guns?" he asked.

Beau did not even turn to look back. By this time he had made heavy inroads into the bottle's contents and was not seeing well. "Somebody tryin' to get him a venison supper. Must be a poor marksman, havin' to shoot at it three times."

"I hope the deer got away."

"You'd look at it different if you was the one hungry."

Joey heard hoofbeats. Turning to look, he said, "Somebody's comin' up fast behind us."

"That damned Gardner." Beau turned out of the trail, but it was already too late to hide. The horse was in plain sight, running. "Well, we tried."

It became evident that the horse was carrying double. The man in the saddle was not Sheriff Gardner. He was a broad-shouldered, dark-complexioned man with as big and black a moustache as Joey had seen in a long time. Joey did not get a good look at the other man until the blue roan horse came to a stop. He realized that the man behind the cantle wore the work uniform he had seen on prisoners at the quarry. The man in the saddle trained a pistol on Beau. His eyes were like flint.

"We have need of your horse," he declared. "Would you kindly step down?"

Beau had a sudden burst of courage. Joey suspected it had escaped from the bottle. Stiffening, Beau declared, "Hell no! This is my horse. Go find you another one."

The man behind the saddle slipped to the ground, looking anxiously behind him. "We got no time to argue. Shoot him, and let's be gone."

The gunman said evenly, "I don't like to shoot a brave man, but a fool is somethin' else. Which are you, brother, brave or foolish?"

Joey was afraid Beau's false courage would get him killed. "He's been drinkin', mister. He don't know what he's sayin'. Please don't shoot him."

Through his whiskey fog Beau seemed suddenly to grasp the seriousness of the situation. His belligerence evaporated. "The law's after us too. If you leave me afoot, what chance have I got?"

"Better than if I have to shoot you." The man's knuckles bulged as he tightened his grip on the pistol.

Beau dismounted unsteadily. He cursed the man who held the pistol. "Maybe I'll run into you again sometime, and you won't have that six-shooter in your hand . . ."

"Perhaps when that day comes we'll have more time for pleasantries. Right now we're a little busy."

His companion in the prison garb grabbed the reins from Beau's hand and swung into the saddle. He untied the blanket roll and war bag, letting them drop to the ground, lightening the load on the brown horse.

The tall man shoved the pistol back into its holster. "There'll be some people along directly, askin' after us. Tell them we're sorry we couldn't stay and be sociable." He spurred away. The other man had no spurs, but he beat the heels of his heavy shoes against Git Out's ribs and fanned the horse's rump with his cloth cap, trying to catch up.

Beau stood swaying in the middle of the road, his arms stiff and fists clenched. "Damn, but I hate a horse thief." He stepped over to where his blanket roll and war bag lay in the dust. The saddlebags had gone with the horse. "Not only took Git Out, but they got off with my sippin' whiskey and most of our grub."

Sipping whiskey. Joey doubted that Beau had ever *sipped* whiskey in his life. Gulping it was more his fashion. Loss of the bottle was the only positive element Joey could see in what had happened. "That sure is too bad," he said, holding down a smile that he knew was badly out of place. Beau's being afoot would slow them dangerously.

Beau picked up his blankets and war bag and tied them on Taw along with Joey's stuff. It made for an unwieldy load. "I don't know if Taw can carry all this," Joey complained.

Beau was in no mood for argument or sympathy. "Walk if it bothers you. I'm havin' to." He set off down the road afoot, not looking back to see if Joey was following. Joey had little choice.

Pursuit was not long in coming. Joey and Beau drew off to the side of the road. Four horsemen rushed past, giving them no more than a glance. They appeared to be guards from the quarry.

Joey said, "I hope they don't shoot your horse."

"They're so far behind they won't even see him."

Beau was not accustomed to walking much. His shoulders began to droop, and the steady pace he had set at the beginning slowed to a painful trudging. Step by step, Beau had to force one foot to move past the other. Joey said, "You want to ride Taw a while? I'll walk."

"Your legs are too short for walkin'. They barely reach the ground."

"I can walk faster than you've been doin'." Joey tried to raise his leg high enough to clear all the belongings tied behind the cantle but could not. He had to swing it forward over Taw's neck, then jump to the ground. Beau dropped any pretense at argument. He managed to lift his right leg over the blankets, but once he was in the saddle both legs hung down halfway between the stirrups and the ground. Taw looked back reproachfully at the extra burden.

Beau grumbled, "I still say your horse is half burro."

Joey considered a response but saved his energy for walking.

The four horsemen returned, no longer running their mounts. Their dejected attitude told Joey they had not caught up to the fugitives. An older man who appeared to be in charge gave Beau a critical study.

"Ain't you ashamed of yourself, ridin' and lettin' a boy walk?"

Beau grunted. "He's younger than I am. You ever see anything of them fellers you was after?"

"Nothin' but their dust. We shot a horse out from under one of them when they left the quarry, so they were ridin' double. Now they have two again."

"They stole mine. I'll be watchin' for the gink that took it. I'll make him wish he'd never seen me."

The horseman frowned. "I don't know as I would do that, were I you."

"He's got it comin'."

"He's got a lot comin', but you wouldn't want to be the one who gives it to him. Didn't you recognize Miller Dawson?"

Beau almost choked, his Adam's apple bobbing up and down. "That was Miller Dawson?"

"Sure was. He came and busted out a confederate that we had workin' in the quarry. He's too desperate a man for any farmer to be tanglin' with. If you happen across him, I'd advise you to go around. *Way* around."

Miller Dawson. Joey was intrigued. "How many men has he really killed?"

"If all the stories are to be believed, fifty or sixty, maybe seventy. I expect there's been a little exaggeration." The horseman jerked his chin as a signal to the other three. "We'd best go make a report. Boss is goin' to be real put out about this."

Beau said hopefully, "I don't suppose you'd want to lend a man a horse?" The men rode on. Beau said, mostly to himself, "I guess not." He turned to Joey. "My God, boy, I cussed out Miller Dawson." He shook his head in disbelief. "I sure could use a drink of that whiskey."

"If you push, you might catch up to Dawson and get it back."

Beau shook his head. "I wouldn't want to hurt your horse."

CHAPTER

9

The farther west they went, the more rugged and unfamiliar the terrain to Joey, broken limestone ledges jutting out from rough hillsides, dry creek beds yearning for a rain. Dark green mottes of live-oak timber and thickets of dense cedar offered plenty of places for Miller Dawson and his fugitive friend to have evaded pursuit across the trackless ground. Joey suspected that the four who had given chase had taken care not to get too close. Some might regard that as cowardice, but Joey recognized it as a strong aversion to suicide.

Much earlier than Joey expected, Beau said, "We'll stop pretty soon. I reckon you're tired from walkin' so long."

Joey was, but he would not admit it. He did not know if Beau was genuinely concerned about him or if he was probing for weakness.

Beau said, "I've got to think about the horse, too. There's a line of timber just ahead, so maybe there's a creek. I need a cup of coffee worse than any man ever did."

Irony crept into Joey's voice. "Don't you want to catch up to

Miller Dawson? You said you intended to give him a good whippin'."

"I've thought it over. I'm a forgivin' sort of feller."

They were surprised to come upon a camp where a small creek crossed the wagon road. A buggy stood beside a pyramid-shaped tent, the canvas too new to bear much stain. A black man knelt before an economical campfire, skillet in his hand. A gray-haired, blockily built white man stepped out of the tent and walked to the edge of the road, motioning with his hand. "Welcome, friends. Come share our camp for the night."

Beau studied the place distrustfully. "We need to be makin' some more distance before dark."

The stranger gave Joey a sympathetic study. "But this boy appears to be worn out." His eyes held silent accusation, for Joey was still walking, and Beau was riding.

Beau seemed to read his mind. "We been takin' turn about on the horse."

That was true as far as it went, but in Joey's view it had been much too long since they had last traded places.

Sizzling meat in the black man's frying pan gave off an aroma that set Joey's stomach to grumbling. "You-all fixin' supper, are you?"

"Venison," the white man replied, "and plenty of it. Samuel bagged a nice fat doe."

The black man smiled, showing a row of perfect white teeth. "Everybody'd just as well eat all they want. The leavins'd just spoil."

Joey walked to the fire, leaving his cousin little choice. Dismounting, Beau had to swing his leg high to clear the rolled blankets. He took a few stiff-legged steps to ease the cramping that came from the ill fit of Joey's saddle. "The boy's doin' fine, but I expect the horse has traveled enough for one day."

The man shook Beau's hand. "Welcome, then."

"Our name's Smith," Beau offered, his eyes telling Joey not to contradict.

"That's a coincidence," said the gray-haired stranger. "So is mine. I am Henry Smith—Judge Henry Smith."

Beau swallowed. "Judge?"

"Yes, district judge. I make a circuit through this hill country. I am on my way to Austin for a conference."

Beau dropped his gaze to hide the momentary panic in his eyes. "We appreciate your hospitality, Judge, but maybe we'd better see if we can go a few more miles."

"Nonsense. Tomorrow is another day, and this boy looks tuckered, not to mention hungry. Come, lad, by the time you wash your hands and face in the creek, Samuel will have this first mess of venison ready for you."

Joey saw that he and Beau were trapped. To leave now would only arouse suspicion if suspicion did not already exist. He went on his best behavior. "I'm much obliged, sir. So is my daddy."

The judge said to Beau, "I congratulate you, sir. So many today do not coach their children in good manners."

Beau's voice was not quite steady. "I do the best I can."

The judge's easy manner assured Joey that he knew nothing about the trouble they had left behind them. The thing to do, he thought, was to play out the game the best he and Beau could, trying not to say or do anything that might later cause the jurist to put two and two together.

He wolfed down the venison.

Sticking a fork into a second slice of meat, the judge said, "I suppose you have a farm somewhere around here?"

Beau replied uneasily, "No sir, we're just sort of lookin' for a place. We ain't found the right one yet."

"These rough hills cause many prospective settlers to turn back too soon. There is good valley land around Fredericksburg suitable for cultivation. The German farmers have proven it quite productive for the man who is willing to work."

"We'll take a look at it."

"I must say, I find it strange that you have only one horse between you."

Beau said, "We had another, but a couple of outlaws stole it. One of them was Miller Dawson."

The judge's eyebrows went up. "Miller Dawson? Are you sure?"

Beau explained briefly what had happened after they passed the stone quarry.

The judge's jaw set grimly. "Those misguided souls who romanticize the likes of Miller Dawson are deluding themselves. I hope someday to have him and all his confederates stand before me. It will be a swift and terrible judgment." His eyes flashed with the zeal for vengeance. "We have been much too lenient with the criminal class. We should chop off the right hand of every thief. We should round up every man who has done murder and stretch his neck at the end of a rope—exterminate them with no more thought than we would give to burning a wasp's nest, until every last one is gone from the face of the earth!"

He slammed his tightened fist into the palm of his left hand. Beau flinched.

The judge demanded, "Do you not agree, sir?"

Beau seemed to have trouble with his voice. "What if a man done a killin' without meanin' to?"

"Murder is murder. There is no excuse and no redemption short of the gallows."

Joey wanted to ask *What about a kid?* But he remembered a saying that used to hang in a frame on the schoolhouse wall: Silence is golden. It had never meant so much to him as it did now.

He slept fitfully that night, for he kept seeing himself standing before Judge Smith, begging for mercy and finding none. After a quick sunrise breakfast Beau pleaded urgency and departed the judge's camp as if it were a den of snakes.

"Talk about a hangin' judge . . ." he said, when they were out of earshot.

Joey asked, "What do you think he'd do to a kid?"

Joey did not know which bothered him most when they stopped that evening, his weariness or his hunger. One of the items in the sack Beau had hung on Joey's saddle in Austin was a box of crackers. Joey appeased his appetite by devouring some of those while he waited for the coffee to boil over a meager campfire. He wished they had some of the leftover venison

Samuel had offered. In their haste to depart the camp they had left it behind.

Joey asked, "Where does the road lead to?"

"I've never been this far west. Judge talked about Fredericksburg, so it must be somewhere out yonder."

"Suppose we run into Indians?"

"Been years since the last Indian trouble. You're more apt to have a rattlesnake crawl into your bed."

"I already had one *on* my bed." Joey shivered at the recollection, and again as that led him to remember Blair Meacham floating down the river, trailing blood.

Taw was staked on a level spot where grass was plentiful. It had worried Joey to see the little horse carrying not only Beau's weight but all of their belongings as well. "What're we goin' to do about gettin' you a horse? Taw can't keep this up all the way to California."

"I ain't got the money to buy one, and they can hang you for stealin'. Maybe when we get far enough west to feel safe from Gardner for a while, I can get a job and earn one."

Joey spread his blankets on bushes, hoping the air would dry them before he had to crawl into them for the night. They were still damp from the soaking in the Colorado River. He seated himself beside the small campfire and opened Reuben's old Bible. He took out the photograph that he had placed between its pages.

"What you got there?" Beau asked.

"A picture of Mama and Pa." He handed it to Beau.

Beau studied it. "I never did get to know your mama much more than to say howdy to her. Me and your daddy, though, we used to run together some as kids. One way or another, we never did get along very good after we got grown. He thought we were put on this earth for nothin' but labor."

"He did believe in work," Joey agreed. "But he was always good to Mama and me." He felt his eyes begin to burn. He took the photograph back from Beau. "This is all I've got left from them, just this old picture."

"It's not all. You've got some good memories. That's more than I have from *my* folks."

"No good memories?"

"More like bad dreams. I'll bet your daddy never told you much about me, did he?"

"I don't remember that he ever did."

"My daddy wasn't married to my mother. He already had him a wife, and folks said my mother was kind of a sportin' woman. She didn't want me so she unloaded me and ran off before I was old enough to remember much about her. My daddy's wife never wanted me either, and the old man was always tellin' me I never would amount to nothin'. I reckon I showed him he was right. When he died, the family lawyers saw to it that I didn't inherit nothin'."

"You *could* amount to somethin'. You've just got to want to, is all."

"Maybe when we get to California."

In the middle of the third afternoon from Austin, Beau walking and Joey riding, they approached a small settlement. Beau said it ought to be safe enough to stop there a bit because he saw no telegraph lines and no courthouse where some sheriff without enough to do might become nosy about their business.

A farmer in dirty overalls was stacking rocks, building a fence along the edge of a field. He wore no gloves, so his huge hands were rough as sun-dried leather. Sweat rolled down his stubbled face, cutting muddy trails through the dust. He paused in his work as Beau and Joey approached. He removed a straw hat and wiped his brow with the tattered sleeve of a homespun shirt.

"Grüss Gott," he said.

Beau asked, "They got a place here where a man can get a drink?"

The farmer seemed not to comprehend. He replied in words Joey could not understand. Beau asked him to say it again. The second time was as unintelligible as the first. The man was speaking something besides American. The only other language Joey had heard was Spanish, and the farmer did not look Mexican.

Beau said, "This must be one of the German settlements the judge talked about."

Joey thought it just as well. "Maybe you won't find a drink here after all."

"I'll find it. Whiskey sounds the same in any language."

The word brought a nod of understanding from the farmer. "*Ja,* visky." He pointed and said something more.

Beau thanked him and set off at a pace slightly more brisk than he had managed most of the day. Joey followed on Taw, resigned to the probability that Beau would be dead drunk before the sun went down.

A dozen or fifteen stores and houses fronted on the road to form the settlement's main street. Several were constructed solidly of limestone blocks, smaller but otherwise similar to those being used in Austin's new state capitol. The rest were of lumber with fancy gingerbread trim decorating porches and eaves, a touch of civilization in a land still largely raw.

Joey's gaze was drawn to four horses tied to posts in front of a frame building. They switched their tails, trying to ward off flies. One was a blue roan. Another was a familiar-looking brown with a GO brand on its hip.

Trying to control his excitement, Joey said, "Looky yonder, Beau. Ain't that Ol' Git Out?"

Beau had not been looking at the horses; he had concentrated his attention on the building, for it appeared to be a saloon. He stopped dead in his tracks. "Damned if it ain't."

"Looks to me like you're not the only man who's worked up a thirst. Miller Dawson must be inside."

"I reckon so."

"You goin' to walk in there and tell him you want your horse back?"

Beau did not consider long. "I don't like to bother a man when he's busy drinkin'." He eased up to Git Out, rubbing his hand along the animal's rump, then its neck. After carefully looking around for anyone who might challenge him, he untied the reins, eased his foot into the stirrup, and swung up. He backed the horse away from the post slowly so he would not disturb the others tied nearby and attract attention. He motioned quietly to Joey and rode between the saloon and a store that stood next to it. Glancing back, he eased Git Out into a smart trot, then a lope. When they had gone a hundred yards, he put the brown into a hard run. Though Joey pushed Taw for all the speed he could get, he lagged far behind.

Beau reined the horse to a stop once he had moved into a stand of cedar dense enough to mask him from the settlement. Joey caught up, turning in the saddle to see if anyone might be coming after them.

The sack of groceries Beau had bought in Austin was missing. Ruefully he said, "They ate up the grub or lost it. My whiskey's gone, too."

Joey grinned. "Thought you were fixin' to get a drink back yonder."

Beau did not grin. "Sometimes you're not near as funny as you think you are. I doubt Miller Dawson'll laugh much either when he comes outside and finds this horse gone. We'd better put some miles behind us."

Joey had read about Robin Hood. He thought if the merry bandit of Sherwood Forest had ever found the joke turning upon himself in this way he would probably get a chuckle out of it. But Texas Ranger Custis Wheat had stressed the point that Miller Dawson was not Robin Hood.

Several miles farther on they saw another settlement, considerably larger than the last.

Joey said, "I'm awful hungry."

"And I'm thirsty." Beau turned, looking back for sign of pursuit. "But I wouldn't want a bullet in my gut."

Joey was gratified that Beau was able to put temptation aside in the interest of self-preservation. "Maybe if you wanted to bad enough, you could give up drinkin' for good."

"If I wanted to. But I *don't* want to."

Joey guessed the place was Fredericksburg. It had the solid look of a town meant to endure, more buildings of stone than of wood, and a couple of the tallest church steeples he could remember seeing. He was especially taken by a large structure fronting on the wide main street. It resembled pictures he had seen of a steamboat. The sign said *Nimitz Hotel*. Farther north, an odd-shaped hexagonal building fitted Judge Smith's description of the "coffee mill," the first church built after the early immigrants had founded their town.

All Joey knew about Germans was what he had learned in school, that they had come from a distant country across the ocean and spoke a language he probably could not understand if he worked at it until he was forty years old. But Reuben would have approved of any people who built so many churches. He would have understood them as he had understood a Bible he could not even read.

Beau dug a few coins from his pocket. "I sure am dry."

"And I'm still hungry. Don't you think the first thing you'd better do is buy us some grub?"

"Boy, when you get a notion stuck in your head, you don't let go of it." But Beau stopped in front of a store that had one small sign reading *Eisenbach Gen'l Merchandise* and a larger one with words Joey could not decipher. He said, "I don't know if they understand American, but I'll bet they understand money. You watch the horses."

When Beau came out, he hung one sack on his saddle and handed another to Joey. "You'll find some sardines in there." He dug into his pocket for a coin and nodded toward another building which had a sign reading *Bäckerei.* "Go get you some bread to eat with it. I got a little business next door."

Next door was a dramshop. Joey protested, "You been doin' real good—you don't need to be goin' in there."

"You're just a boy. You've got no idea what a man needs." He terminated the discussion by walking away. Joey's feeling of helplessness gave way to anger, which in turn gave way to his hunger. He went into the little bakery shop and found the aroma of freshly baked bread almost overpowering. He felt as if he had not eaten in a week. He showed the coin to a portly woman behind the counter. "I need to buy me some bread."

He could not understand her reply, but he pointed to a shelf of dark brown loaves. She handed him one of them and took the coin, giving him back two smaller ones in change. *"Danke,"* she said.

Walking out, he wondered why she hadn't thanked him. Most storekeepers would, just out of common courtesy.

He sat on the edge of the wooden sidewalk and hungrily set to work upon the bread and a can of sardines from the sack. He had almost finished both when he became aware of two horsemen stopping in front of him on the street. Joey skipped a breath as he saw that one horse was a blue roan. He recognized its rider by his heavy black moustache.

The other declared, "Miller, you see what I do?"

Joey dropped the little left of the sardines and pushed quickly to his feet. The can clattered on the wooden walk, spilling oil and a remnant of tiny fish. The man who had spoken got down from a fine-looking sorrel. Miller Dawson still rode the horse Joey had seen him on before. The younger man had exchanged his prison garb for a farmer's overalls and a home-spun shirt, neither of which fitted him. Joey suspected he had stolen them from somebody's clothesline without attention to size. A Mexican sombrero sat squarely on his head. Joey could only guess where he had taken that, and how.

The man declared, "That's the horse I lost yesterday."

Dawson said, "Forget it, Hull. You've got a better one now anyway."

"And come near gettin' shot over it. Somebody here needs to be taught a lesson." An ugly anger darkened Hull's face, accenting a long scar down his right cheek.

Dawson warned, "Last thing we need right now is to call attention to ourselves."

"If there's anything in this world I hate, it's a horse thief." The escapee's eyes bored into Joey. "I remember you, kid. Where's that horse-stealin' partner of yours?"

Frightened, Joey found it difficult to speak. "I ain't got no partner."

"You ain't ridin' two horses." The man walked to the door of the general store and peered inside. Not seeing Beau, he turned back, his gaze going to the door of the dramshop.

Dawson called, "Hull, if you start a ruckus . . ." The words trailed off as his confederate passed through the door.

Joey dropped the bread and ran for the dramshop. "Beau! Beau, look out!"

A strong hand grabbed the back of his shirt, and a stern voice said, "Whoa, son. A boy your age has got no business in a place like that. It ain't respectable."

Joey wiggled free from Miller Dawson and hurried through the door. He saw Beau sprawled back against the bar, blood trickling from the side of his mouth. Hull swung his heavy fist again. The blow hit so hard that Joey feared it might have broken Beau's neck.

"You stop that!" Joey shouted. He made a running leap and landed on the man's broad back, wrapping his legs around Hull's waist. "You leave Beau alone!"

Hull pitched like a horse, trying to throw Joey off, but Joey clung, clamping one arm around the man's head, covering his eyes. Hull's Mexican hat rolled across the floor. Joey was dimly aware that half-a-dozen bystanders watched in surprise, none moving either to help or to hinder him. He pounded his fist against the top of Hull's head. Hull roared and tried to dislodge Joey by slamming him against the bar.

Joey's anger crowded out reason. He bit down hard on Hull's ear, as he had seen men do to a horse they were trying to break. Hull squalled.

Beau seemed to be in a stupor. He staggered forward as if to help Joey, but Hull bumped into him and sent him reeling back.

Miller Dawson's voice was sharp. "Hull, you quit pickin' on that kid."

Joey felt strong hands take hold of him, wrenching him loose, pulling him away from the big man. Dawson spun half around, setting himself between Joey and the raging Hull. "That's enough. Enough, I say!"

"The little . . ." Hull reached for Joey, but Dawson blocked him. "I told you I wasn't goin' to stand for any ruckus. Now back off."

Hull did not back away. In a move so swift Joey barely saw it, Dawson drew a pistol from its holster on his hip and struck Hull a stern blow across the side of his head. Hull went to his hands and knees.

Dawson said, "Sometimes he won't listen 'til you talk to him kind of rough."

Joey broke free of Dawson and hurried to Beau, who was still groggy and disoriented.

Dawson caught Hull beneath the arm and helped him to a chair at a small table. "Bartender, draw him a beer. Draw us all a beer . . . except the boy, of course. You got any milk?"

Joey's blood still rushed hot. "I don't need no milk. I don't need nothin' from you, and neither does Beau." He tugged at Beau's torn sleeve, trying to lead him out of the shop.

Dawson said, "Hold on, boy. Let your partner get his feet under him first. And you better settle down a little yourself. No use leavin' here mad."

"I've got cause to be mad, him whippin' up on Beau just because Beau took back a horse that was his in the first place."

"What's your name, boy?"

"Smith."

"Funny. So's mine, sometimes." Dawson glanced at Hull to be sure he wasn't looking for more fights. "This Beau, is he your brother?"

"He's my cousin . . . second cousin, anyway."

"You-all must be pretty close, you jumpin' in on his side so fierce."

"Sometimes I've been mad enough to shoot him, but he's all the kin I've got."

"Nobody in my family ever took up for *me* like that. You've got grit, boy."

"I didn't want him hurtin' Beau any more. Me and him got too much travelin' to do."

"What's so important about travelin'?"

Joey glanced around to be sure nobody else could hear. With Dawson being hunted like he was, there shouldn't be any harm in telling him. "We're on the dodge."

Dawson smiled tolerantly. "What did you-all do, tip over somebody's outhouse?"

Dawson wasn't going to believe him any more than the others he had tried to tell. Well, he didn't owe an outlaw any explanation. He decided not to say anything else.

Dawson said, "You and your cousin had better come with us."

Joey felt a stirring of alarm. "What do you need us for?"

"Soon as he gets his feet back under him he'll want to complain to the law. We'd sooner he didn't."

"He won't go to the law. He can't. They're lookin' for us, him and me both."

Joey wanted to retreat from Dawson's probing gaze but could not take his eyes from the man. The outlaw seemed to be trying to believe him. "If that's truly the case, you'll both be better off ridin' with me and Hull."

Every lawman in this part of Texas was probably watching for Miller Dawson. To be with him would be like cuddling up to a lightning rod. Joey hedged. "I don't know what Beau would say."

"He don't look like he's in a shape to say anything right now. He don't even know which direction is up. Let's be goin' before the local law comes messin' in our business. I've never shot a Dutchman, and I don't feel like startin' today."

Hull tried to put on his hat but took it off again, flinching from pain. Blood was matted in his hair where Dawson's pistol had struck him. In his bleeding ear was a clear impression of Joey's teeth. Hull complained to Dawson, "Did you have to hit me so hard?"

"I had to get your attention." Dawson handed several greenbacks to the bartender. "Hope this'll cover any damage. And help make you forgetful."

The smiling bartender counted the bills. "For this much money I forget even my name."

Dawson pointed toward the bystanders. "Here's a little more to buy all them other fellers a drink. Won't hurt them to be forgetful either." He stopped at the door and carefully peered up and down the street before he stepped out onto the walk. "You-all come on."

Beau remained addled, but Joey reluctantly guided him by the arm to where Git Out was tied. He had to help Beau get his left foot into the stirrup. Joey untied Taw and mounted, then took Git Out's reins and led the horse into the street. He briefly considered trying to get away from the two outlaws but feared Beau would probably fall out of the saddle before they got halfway started.

Dawson and Hull were arguing. At least, Hull was. "What're we takin' them with us for? Last thing we need is a horse thief and an ear-bitin' kid."

Dawson said, "You got *your* horse awful cheap. Now let's ride out of here in a walk so everybody won't be lookin' at us."

Hull pointed back down the street. "At least we ought to stop in at that little two-by-four bank. We could clean out that place as easy as takin' the poor box in a Mexican church."

Dawson scowled at him. "Even a coyote knows better than to kill too close to its den."

He turned at the first corner to get away from the main thoroughfare, then followed a residential street until they cleared the town. "Now, let's rattle their hocks a little." Watching to be sure Joey and Beau stayed with him, he swung into an easy lope. He cut into a wagon road that trended in a northwesterly direction.

Joey asked apprehensively, "Where we goin'?"

"Llano River country. You could hide half the Confederate army in those mottes and cedarbrakes."

"The Confederate army lost the war, didn't it?"

Joey marveled at the strange turn of fate that had made him a fugitive and suddenly put him to riding with outlaws. Pa would not have understood, nor would Reuben. Joey did not understand, either. The thought was at once frightening and exhilarating. He pictured himself telling the story to wide-eyed friends in school, then realized he could never go back to school, or to his home. Mr. Meacham's unexpected demise had nailed that door shut.

Well, this was an adventure the likes of which he could never have pictured in his wildest dream. He decided to make the best of it for however long it lasted.

Someday he could tell about it in California.

CHAPTER

10

Their direction was westerly, through rough-hewn hills slabbed with brittle limestone outcrops and along narrow valleys where occasional green fields of tall forage and corn reflected the settlers' old-country diligence. The lowland soils were rich and deep, deposited layer upon layer as rainfall through the ages carried them down from the steep slopes where grass was thin and could not bind them.

Deer bounded away in a clatter of tiny hooves and a flash of white tails, disappearing into the dark-shaded protection of live-oak timber and juniper thickets. Wild turkeys, startled by the riders' approach, would gobble in alarm, soar short distances, touch the ground, and soar again. Except for the planted fields, Joey thought the land must still look as it did when the Indians had it. His imagination carried him into a fantasy that Indians might yet be hiding in one of the obscure canyons, that they might be watching him even now.

Dawson made a sweeping gesture with his hand. "See all that game, boy? Long as a man has got plenty of cartridges, salt, and a little coffee, he can live out here for months and never set foot in a store." He glanced at Hull. "Or a bank either."

Hull had said little that Joey could understand since they had left town. He had hung back, mumbling morosely to himself, nursing a grudge over the blow Dawson's pistol had struck him and perhaps over Dawson's refusal to transact business at the bank. Hull's prison-short hair was exposed to wind and sun. His head hurt too much for him to wear the sombrero that hung from the horn of his saddle. He made no reply to Dawson's comment.

Joey had an uncomfortable feeling that if it were left to Hull the man might shoot him and Beau as casually as he would extract a thorn from his flesh. His hostile glare indicated that he regarded them as he might regard such a thorn. He broke his brooding silence once to complain, "For all we know, these two may be rangers."

Dawson gave him the look he might give a puppy that muddied him with its paws. "A boy this age, a ranger? Use your head for somethin' besides a place to put your hat."

Hull withdrew into his prickly shell like a porcupine rolling up into a ball with its bristles out. Beau would probably say he was playing poker with a deck short on aces and long on jokers.

Beau was starting to shed the stupor he had carried out of the dramshop and the first miles from town. His nervous eyes bespoke severe misgivings. He told Dawson, "Me and Joey appreciate your kindness, but we got places of our own to go. If it's all the same to you, we'll be takin' our leave."

Dawson shook his head. "You don't know this country. Like as not you'd stumble into a bunch of rangers."

Hull grumbled, "And you might not remember to forget where we was the last time you seen us."

Joey suspected Beau would be willing to take an oath against whiskey if they could slip away from Dawson and Hull. It might be worth their lives—Beau's, anyway—to try to break loose before the pair was ready to let them go. Joey shared Beau's dread of Hull, but he was instinctively drawn to Miller Dawson. The man fascinated him, especially the contrast between his fierce reputation and the benign look in his eyes. Joey was unable to reconcile the extremes.

He was intrigued by the idea of a life free and unfettered in this wild land where the taming hand of civilization had made so little mark. It was unlike anything he had seen. He asked Dawson, "Do you really live out here in this rough country?"

"I live wherever I happen to be. Home is any place I lay my saddle down, from the Sabine River to the Rio Grande. I'm just a workin' man like anybody else. I go out and take care of business, and then I come back to camp in the Llano River cedarbrakes and rest up from my labors."

To Pa, work had been something a man did with a plow or a hoe or a shovel. He would have a different name for Dawson's version.

"You sure me and Beau won't get caught if we go with you?"

"I ain't never been caught."

"But Hull has, else you wouldn't have had to rescue him."

"Hull gets careless sometimes. I don't."

Dawson's casual self-confidence was reassuring. Joey said, "Maybe we'll stay with you for just a while, then. Me and Beau, we're headed for California."

"Why California? They've already dug up all the gold out there. A feller with ambition can find gold enough around here. You just got to know how to get it."

They camped for the night some distance from the wagon road and built a tiny fire in a ring of rocks that would hide the miserly flames from view. The men made their supper mostly on coffee and brown-paper cigarettes. Joey opened another tin of sardines and finished up with a can of tomatoes. They were a treat because Pa had never indulged much in food that came in airtights. He had said they were wastefully expensive and not nearly so good as a meal cooked fresh.

Joey thought the outlaw life might not be bad at all if he could have canned sardines and tomatoes whenever he felt like it.

Beau seemed to have no appetite except for cigarettes. He smoked several, one soon after another. He did a lot of looking around, as if seeking a place to run.

As the campfire died, Dawson said, "Boy, you sure you ain't just been loadin' me about the two of you bein' on the dodge?"

"It's true. They're lookin' for us."

Dawson's smile was faintly patronizing. "For burglarizin' somebody's barn maybe, or some crossroads store?"

Joey considered long and hard. Perhaps it would ease the tension if Dawson and Hull knew he and Beau had so much in common with them. He blurted, "We killed a man."

That wiped away Dawson's smile. "You're just a boy. Don't you mean your cousin killed a man, and you just happened to be there?"

"I helped him." Joey explained at length about Pa and Reuben, about Dulcie and Mr. Meacham and the fight at the Colorado River. "That's why we've got to keep movin'."

Dawson had turned dead serious. "You're mighty young to be startin' down that trail. It's a narrow one, and hard to quit once you're on it. Believe me, I've tried."

"We didn't mean to. Things just happened."

"Things always do. Ain't many of us set out in life with the notion that we want to be a fugitive. We just kind of stumble into it."

"Is that the way you got started?"

"Pretty much. I had a preacher daddy who gave me a big dose of hellfire and brimstone with a razor strop every time the moon changed. I run off and took up with a rough crowd. Before long I had the devil by the tail, and I couldn't turn him loose."

Joey burned to know more. "They talk like you've killed a lot of men. Sixty or seventy, maybe."

"They've exaggerated a mite. It ain't been that many."

"How many?"

"Well, to tell the truth, not more than three. And they wasn't none of them deacons in the church. Just the same, killin' a man ain't somethin' you feel good about, even when they've got it comin' to them."

Joey remembered Mr. Meacham and felt cold. "Why do they tell such big windies about you?"

"The worse them sheriffs and rangers can make me look, the

better excuse they've got for not catchin' me. Then there's the newspapers. They love a big story whether it's true or not. Somebody gets killed in El Paso and they don't know who done it, they say it was me. Somebody robs a bank the same day in Fort Worth, they say I done that too. I'd have to have my own private express train to get around as fast as they make out." He rolled a cigarette and lighted it with a burning stick from the campfire. "One thing about havin' a reputation: If people are scared enough of you, you don't *have* to kill anybody. They'll help you tote the money out of the bank."

Dawson fell into quiet meditation, not breaking silence for what seemed half an hour. "You remind me of myself when I was about your size, lots of grit and not enough luck. Reformatory ain't no place for you, but that's where they'll send you if you're caught. You and your cousin had better stay with me and Hull. You'll be safe where we're goin'."

"Where is that?"

"You'll know when we get there."

Later, when Dawson was seeing after his horse, Joey told Beau, "I like Mr. Dawson."

"Damn it, boy, he's an outlaw."

"So are we."

"Not like him and that Hull. We ain't robbed no bank or stole any horses. If we stay with them, we'll find ourselves in real trouble."

"I thought we already was."

"First chance we get, we're slippin' away. I am, anyhow. You can suit yourself."

Evidently Dawson sensed Beau's intention, for as they spread their blankets, Dawson casually warned, "Fellers, I wouldn't be gettin' up and movin' around in the dark, was I you. I sleep with a gun by my head. I've got a bad habit of wakin' up sudden and shootin' at whatever moves. I wouldn't want to be the cause of a bad accident."

Given that kind of notice, Beau did not stir from his blankets. Joey knew, for he lay awake all night worrying. He would not move if a rattlesnake crawled into bed with him.

The next morning they did not return to the wagon road. Dawson followed no trail that Joey could see. He picked his way through the hills, through the thickets, and down the centers of spring-fed streams whose clear waters and slab-rock beds would show no tracks. It was obvious why Dawson so easily eluded pursuing officers, especially if they were not eager to catch up to him anyway.

Joey asked, "How much farther is it?"

"Not far," Dawson told him.

"But how can you find it? These hills all look the same. One cedarbrake and one live-oak motte is just like another."

"There's landmarks if you know what to look for. We try not to come and go the same way from one time to the next. We don't want to beat out any trails the rangers can follow."

They came after a time to a wagon road that lay in a generally north-south direction but followed the vagaries of a restless little creek, meandering like a drunk trying to find his way home in the dark. Dawson studied the ruts, which showed recent horse and wagon tracks.

"Boy," he said, "down yonder just past the bend is a small store." He handed Joey a coin. "I want you to go buy you a piece of stick candy and look around. See if there's anybody totin' a badge. If there ain't, ask the storekeeper how long he thinks it might be 'til it rains."

Joey looked up. "There ain't a cloud in the sky."

"Ask him anyway, then come back and tell me what he says."

Joey sensed that the question and the answer were some kind of code between Dawson and the storekeeper. It felt wonderfully mysterious, carrying the message even though he did not understand the meaning of it.

He asked, "You comin' with me, Beau?"

Dawson said, "Beau needs to stay here with us. He might run into a ranger or somebody lookin' for him."

Joey knew what Dawson was thinking, that if the two of them got off alone they might keep riding. Beau was held hostage to guarantee Joey's return. There had been a time when Joey might have left him behind to wiggle off the hook the best way he could, but not now. In a way, he felt that he had become Beau's guardian rather than Beau being his. Joey set Taw into an easy trot along the road.

The store was a crude structure with cedar-picket walls and rough-hewn cypress shingles on the roof. A wagon stood in front, two sleepy-eared mules hip-shot in the harness. One sad-dled horse stood tied to a post in front. Chickens scratched amid fresh droppings, and two hounds came out to meet Joey with deep-throated barking that caused the tied horse to jerk its head up, straining against the leather reins. The mules took no notice. A mule was smart enough to conserve energy any time it could. Joey tied Taw's reins in a cinch ring wired to a post.

It took a minute for his eyes to adjust to the interior darkness and longer for his nose to adjust to the stuffiness. A man stood behind a crowded counter, a dirty apron tied around his middle. A farmer in overalls and a cowboy in high-topped boots gave Joey a long study. Joey was not sure how to tell a ranger from anybody else except by the badge, and he saw no badges here.

"What can I do for you, button?" the storekeeper asked, looking over the top of black-rimmed glasses perched low on his bent-over nose.

Joey showed him the coin Miller Dawson had given him. "I'd like to buy a stick of candy."

The storekeeper opened a large tin and let Joey take his pick. Joey asked, "How soon you reckon it might rain?"

The question startled the storekeeper, who walked to the door and looked out before he attempted an answer. Evidently he saw nothing. He said, "We had a little rain this mornin', but the sky's all clear now."

The farmer remarked, "I didn't see no rain."

"It was just here at the store." The merchant put the lid back on the can and said to Joey, "You tell your friend I don't think he'll need his slicker."

The farmer puzzled, "Ain't needed a slicker around here in quite a spell."

The storekeeper said, "It rains more on some than on others."

Joey returned to the waiting horsemen and told Dawson what the storekeeper had said. Dawson seemed pleased. "Then the way is clear for us to stop by and pick up some supplies before we go on to camp."

The farmer and his wagon were gone. Dawson left Hull and Beau outside to keep watch. Joey perceived that Hull was mainly keeping watch on Beau. Dawson asked Joey, "You like candy, don't you?"

"Yes sir, sure do."

"Well, then, we'd better lay in a supply that'll last you a while." He motioned for Joey to accompany him into the store. The cowboy was still there, drinking a bottle of warm beer. A flicker in his eyes told Joey that he recognized Dawson, and he moved aside to give the man plenty of room.

The four riders left the store with two canvas bags full of goods tied to the horns of Dawson's and Hull's saddles. Joey could hear bottles clinking together in rhythm with the horses' stride. Dawson had bought whiskey before he had bought flour and bacon and beans, salt and tobacco. Joey watched Beau with misgivings. If his cousin ever uncorked one of those bottles, he might not stop until he was flat on his back and oblivious to the world.

Late in the afternoon Dawson pointed to a small bluff that appeared suddenly, as if it had abruptly pushed up out of the earth. "There's a little pocket canyon back in yonder," he said. "Sign shows it used to be a Comanche hideout. The soldiers never found it, and the rangers won't either. Not unless somebody gets careless and leaves a trail they can follow into it." He gave Hull an accusing glance.

Hull turned defensive. "I wasn't careless, I was drunk. Can't blame me for what I do when I'm drunk. Besides, I didn't lead them to anybody but myself."

"If you ever do it again, I'll leave you in that quarry chiselin' rocks. You might learn a useful trade."

Joey caught the quick flash of a mirror from the top of a live-oak-covered hill. Dawson saw it too and reacted with satisfaction. "Somebody's seen us cross this stretch of high ground. Shows they're awake." He waved his hat over his head. "It's too pretty a day for gettin' shot."

Descending from the high ground, the four crossed a narrow

valley and skirted partway around a cedarbrake. Dawson turned into the scrub timber and stopped. "Hull, we're leavin' tracks on that strip of bare ground. Get down and brush them out. There's rangers that can track a buzzard's shadow across a granite rock."

Hull betrayed silent resentment at being ordered around. He complied, though with little grace. Joey had already realized that Hull and Dawson were bound together by mutual need, not by any liking for one another.

Beau had acted anxious all morning, finding himself pushed into a situation from which he might never extract himself. He kept looking westward. "It's not like me and Joey don't appreciate your hospitality, but we need to keep on goin'."

Hull threw aside the cedar limb he had used to brush the tracks. His voice was heavy with threat. "You've seen too much to just ride away."

Beau shook his head vigorously. "I been lost since yesterday. I couldn't find my way back here in a hundred years."

Dawson warned Hull, "Don't you be scarin' Joey now. There ain't nobody goin' to bring the law in here, and there ain't nobody goin' to be hurt."

They came to a limestone ledge where clear water bubbled from between moss-covered layers of rock, forming a small spring that snaked out of sight into a narrow canyon. Above the seeps, clumps of prickly pear clung precariously to thin patches of soil. Joey was startled by the unexpected appearance of a youth on foot, carrying a rifle. His clothes looked as if he had been dragged across the rocks. His shirt sleeves resembled an assortment of ribbons, and his trousers were torn at the knees. Joey suspected he had made a fast ride through thorny brush at some time or other, probably with lawmen shooting at him from behind.

The guard was younger than Beau and not much taller than Joey. His grin was friendly. He seemed delighted to see Dawson. "Miller, you been gone so long we wondered if you'd played out your string." To Hull he showed surprise. "Last we heard, they had you behind the walls."

Hull answered in a low growl. "I busted out." He made it sound as if he had done the whole thing by himself.

Joey was tempted to protest but decided it might be wise to let Dawson speak for himself. The young guard turned his grin toward Joey. "They're weanin' them awful young these days."

Dawson said, "Brought a couple of visitors, Tolley. Their horses need to recruit a few days."

Joey thought Beau perked up a little. By inference, he and Joey would be leaving here after a short rest. Joey hoped that was the truth.

Tolley said, "Farlow may raise hell about strangers in camp."

Dawson's eyes narrowed. "Farlow? Who gave him the big say in things around here?"

"Nobody, he just took it. You know Farlow . . ."

"I know him." Dawson's ironic response told Joey as much as he needed to know about Farlow. He did not look forward to meeting him.

Beau said, "If we ain't welcome, we'll gladly ride on. Just show us whichaway to go."

Hull glowered. "You ain't goin' no place."

The guard said, "I hope you brought some tobacco with you. I'm plumb out, and Farlow won't divide." His face twisted. "Whatever Farlow gets ahold of, he keeps for himself. He don't divide nothin'."

Dawson pitched Tolley a small sack from his shirt pocket. "Don't smoke it all at once. Damned stuff shortens your life."

Dawson seemed troubled as they walked their horses, paralleling the limestone ledge. More seeps and tiny springs yielded modest streams of water that trickled into the little creek, making it wider and deeper as it worked its way farther into the restricted canyon. Joey stared in awe, for he had spent his life in deep-soil farming country where a rise was called a hill and a hill was called a mountain. He had never seen rock formations courthouse high, tilted and buckled and standing aslant.

"I'd hate to've been here the day all this happened," he declared. "Bet there was some awful scared Indians around."

Dawson seemed preoccupied and did not respond. Beau

gloomily studied the high canyon wall as if he were entering a prison. He gave Joey a fleeting look of resentment that said this was all Joey's fault and none of his own.

Joey had been unsure what to expect of the outlaw encampment, but even so he was disappointed. He had thought it might have the appearance of a small town, or at least a decent farmstead. Instead, it was a nondescript scattering of dirty-gray tents and four crude cabins spread haphazardly along the creek. *Cabin* might have been too exalted a term; *shack* would be more like it. One was of traditional construction, live-oak logs laid horizontally, one atop another. Three were picket-style, upright logs and branches forming the walls, the cracks between them chinked with mud. One leaned to the south, buttressed by two bracing logs, all that kept it from lying down like a lazy dog.

Joey did not see a cabin that a competent carpenter would want to carve his name on. He lost the exhilaration he had felt as he entered the canyon; it was gone like a moment of bright sunshine suddenly overwhelmed by dark clouds. In its place came revulsion, dread. Beau had been right; it was a mistake to come into this camp. But Dawson and Hull had allowed them no choice.

Several men emerged from the tents and shacks to stare in curiosity as if Dawson and Hull had returned from the dead. Only a couple extended greetings with any warmth. Most were dressed no better than Tolley. Their clothing for the most part was threadbare and torn and badly in need of a washerwoman's stern attention. Joey saw no one he would call fat. Most of the men had a lank and hungry look, the gaunt ghost of poverty dulling their eyes.

He would have thought the outlaw life should pay better than this. Back home, he had seen field hands show more signs of prosperity. The men and the place repelled him.

Dawson pointed with his chin to the larger of the shacks, south of the others. "Looks like somebody's taken over my cabin. I'll let him finish cookin' supper for us, then throw him out."

Gray smoke curled from a crude rock-and-mud chimney that

leaned precariously against the log structure. Joey was no judge of fireplaces, but he would consider this one a hazard. Whoever had built it was not a stone mason.

A tall, angular man stood in the open front door and anchored his hands on his hips in a way that told the world to go to hell. His thin face, days beyond its last contact with a razor, made Joey think of a hatchet blade. His pant legs were tucked into high boots once black but now mostly the color of the earth around the cabin. Joey's eyes were drawn to the butt of a pistol protruding from the top of the right boot. The man's mouth smiled, his teeth white against heavy black whiskers, but his eyes had the wild, sharp look of a hawk searching for something to attack. Joey suspected he was a little crazy, the same way Hull seemed to be. He had begun to wonder if most outlaws had something loose in their heads.

The usurper leaned back on his heels, giving a false outward appearance of laziness, but he was like a compressed spring, straining to snap free. Joey was instinctively afraid of him. He was glad when Miller Dawson edged forward, setting himself like a buffer in front of the others.

Dawson did not offer a *howdy*. He simply said, "Farlow."

"Miller. Thought they'd throwed you in jail, or maybe even planted you in a graveyard someplace."

"They'll get you long before they get me. That's my cabin. I want it back."

Farlow did not move from the door, nor did he relax his cold smile. "It was empty, and I didn't see your name on it. Besides, I ain't by myself. You wouldn't want to throw a lady out to sleep in the rain."

Dawson stiffened. "We agreed a long time ago that nobody was to bring a woman in here."

"I didn't agree to nothin'. You may cut a big swath outside, but you don't boss this camp. We're all free to do whatever we damn please as long as we're man enough." Farlow glanced back into the cabin. "Woman! Come show yourself!" When she did not appear immediately, his voice hardened. "Alta, I said git yourself out here before I take a quirt to you!"

She hesitated at the door, then came out blinking at the afternoon sunlight and wiping her hands nervously on a flour-sack apron. She was little and thin, as if it had been a long time since she had had enough to eat. Her plain gray dress had been torn down one shoulder and crudely sewn together with black thread that did not match the fabric. Her brown hair was badly in need of a good brushing. Somehow she reminded Joey a bit of Mama, except that Mama used to smile a lot. This woman looked as if she might not know how to smile. By Joey's standards she was middle aged, probably in her midtwenties or edging toward thirty. But her face had nice features, her nose thin, her mouth not overly large, her eyes blue.

He saw fear in those eyes, fear like he had seen in a rabbit trapped and huddling in a fence corner. He noticed a dark bruise on her left cheekbone.

Dawson declared, "Farlow, a woman in a camp like this can cause no end of trouble."

"I can handle any trouble that comes." Farlow turned to the woman. "You've heard of Miller Dawson. Well, yonder he is." He paused, waiting for her reaction, but she showed none beyond her initial fear. He added, "I can see you're disappointed. There ain't much to him."

Dawson seemed to flounder in search of a reply. Joey had thought nothing could catch Dawson on his left foot, but Farlow had, or perhaps it was the surprise of finding a woman in camp.

Dawson directed his question at Farlow. "How long has she been here?"

"Maybe three weeks. I brought her up from San Antone."

"Anybody been killed over her yet?"

"I've bloodied a couple of noses, but I ain't shot nobody."

"You will if you don't take her back where you found her."

Farlow exhibited no intention of following advice. "For a good-lookin' woman, she ain't too bad a cook. Come back for supper and see what she can do with a squirrel stew." He jerked his head toward the door. The woman quickly disappeared inside.

Dawson's hands knotted, braced against the horn of his

saddle. "You'd better get her away from here before she busts the place wide open."

Farlow was defiant. "You may have all the sheriffs and rangers afraid of you, but in this camp you're no bigger than anybody here. Whenever you think you can whip me, you're welcome to come and try."

Dawson turned to the left down the creek, reining his horse a little rougher than was his custom. Joey kicked Taw into motion to follow him. He wanted to be away from Farlow.

Hull muttered, "I see now why Tolley complained about Farlow not sharin'. I'll bet he ain't sharin' *her*." He straightened in the saddle, looking hopeful. "We're goin' to eat supper with them, ain't we? I'd like to see if she's as good a cook as he says she is."

Dawson's voice was gruff. "Ain't her cookin' you're interested in, or what he's keepin' her for. He'd just as well turn a mare loose amongst a dozen stud horses. Sooner or later there'll be blood and hair and strips of hide scattered all over the camp."

There already were, Joey noted, though not in the way Dawson meant. He had never seen a place so unapologetically trashy. Every shack, every tent had a pile of refuse behind it—bottles and tin cans, discarded bones, cattle and deer and rabbit hides, wild-turkey feathers—a perfect picture of sloth as Reuben had described it to him from his understanding of the scriptures. Half-a-dozen mongrel dogs had gathered, some barking at the horses and riders, others nosing futilely at the careless leavings which they had probably worked a hundred times already.

This was nothing like Joey's mental image of Sherwood Forest. He saw his own distaste mirrored in Beau's eyes.

Beau muttered, "Look what you've gotten us into."

"Wasn't anything I could do to help it."

"This is the grubbiest bunch of heathens I ever saw. Horse thieves and holdup men, bunko artists and hog rustlers. Might even be a lawyer in here someplace."

Dawson stopped a short distance below the cabin. "Ain't

slept under roof or canvas for a spell. I can rough it another night or two 'til Farlow decides to clear out."

Perhaps Dawson hoped to outbluff him, but Joey had not seen any indication that Farlow considered vacating.

Beau pointed his chin southward, where the canyon appeared to close tightly. "This place looks like a trap to me. If the rangers ever find the openin', they'll catch everybody in here with no way out."

Dawson dismissed Beau's concern with a motion of his hand. "It only looks like a box canyon. The back door is so narrow you can't see it 'til you're right up on it. This creek runs out the far end and down into a bigger canyon where a hundred men could scatter into the brush and not be found." He paused, reflecting. "If you're thinkin' about ridin' out that way on your own, don't. Those canyons and cedarbrakes could swallow you up and have you wanderin' around in circles like a baby lost in the woods."

Hull added ominously, "Been men never seen or heard of again."

Dawson and Hull untied their gear and unsaddled their horses, turning them loose on green grass along the creek. Downstream Joey could see a crude brush corral, its gate lying open. Several horses were scattered along the canyon, grazing free. It occurred to him that if rangers *did* luck upon this outfit, they might capture the whole bunch before anybody could catch a horse. The fact that the mounts were allowed to run loose reflected the confidence of these men. He wondered where confidence ended and arrogance began.

Dawson seemed to read his thoughts. "There's a brush fence and ropes strung across the bottom end of the canyon to keep the remuda from strayin'. We keep a rustlin' horse staked so we can bring the rest in pretty fast. So don't you worry about the law catchin' us afoot. The guard'd hold them back long enough for everybody to get mounted."

When Dawson had drawn away far enough not to hear him, Beau muttered, "Ain't the law that worries me most, it's the *out*laws. They look like they'd skin their grandmothers if they could sell the hide for two dollars."

"I don't like it here either," Joey said. "But he may be right about us not findin' our own way. Like as not we'd ride all day and end up where we started. I almost wish the rangers *would* come."

"Don't let anybody hear you say that. Hull would gut you like a catfish, and if he didn't, Farlow would. There ain't a one of these old boys that's normal people like me and you."

"Dawson said we'd just be stayin' a few days."

"I don't trust Dawson much further than I'd trust any of these other ginks. But he seems to like you, so stay on his good side. Ain't much else we can do but keep our heads down and watch for any chance that comes our way." He added gloomily, "There's days when old Sheriff Gardner don't seem near as bad as I thought he was."

Joey wondered if Dawson would eventually try to eject Farlow from the cabin. That would be a show worth watching. But Dawson said, "We'll camp down here below the cabin 'til Farlow decides to take that woman out of here."

Hull said wishfully, "If she don't go, Farlow'll have to share sooner or later. The boys'll make him do it."

Dawson's face darkened. "That's when the blood and the hair'll fly. It ain't worth that grief to keep a woman in camp."

Hull said, "Depends on how long it's been since you had one."

"That's no way to be talkin' in front of this boy."

"This boy probably knows more than you think he does." Hull frowned at Joey. "Too much for his own good, and ours."

Joey perceived threat in his voice. Instinctively he pulled closer to Miller Dawson. Dawson laid a reassuring hand on his shoulder. "Don't you fret. Hull knows I'd skin him like a beef if he was to hurt you."

Tolley came down from his guard post and sought out Dawson's camp below the log cabin. He said, "Me and Hank have talked it over. You're welcome to our tent up yonder."

Joey could see respect for Dawson in the youth's eyes.

Dawson looked at the reddening sky. "Thanks, but it wouldn't be big enough for all of us to sleep in. I'll get my cabin back when Farlow takes that woman out of here."

"I don't think he's got any such notion."

"He will. I'll hound him 'til he does."

Tolley's gaze held morosely on Dawson's campfire. "This is the second woman he's brought here since you been away. He told us he was takin' the other one home, but he wasn't gone long enough to've traveled far. We figure he killed her."

Dawson jerked as if a spark had leaped out and burned him. "Killed a woman?"

"A woman don't mean much to Farlow once he gets tired of her. Dead, she'll never tell anybody where this camp is at."

Dawson's eyes were troubled. "Farlow's no Baptist preacher, but I never thought he'd do a thing like that."

"Flora was her name. Saloon woman out of San Antonio, like Alta, only a troublemaker. She got to messin' around with some of the boys, tryin' to set them against Farlow, hopin' they'd kill him. I was glad to see her go, but murderin' her— that curdled my stomach."

"Farlow talked like he's already bloodied a couple of noses over this woman."

"One of them was mine. I told him he was treatin' her mean. He won't hardly let her out of the cabin without he's watchin' her." Tolley placed a chunk of wood on the fire. "Sometimes I hear her cryin'. God knows how he's abusin' her. I'd brace him again, but I know he's crazy enough to kill me. She's not like that other one. Any chance I get, I'm takin' her out of this place."

"Has she asked you to?"

"She hasn't asked me anything, but I can see it in her face. She knows Farlow don't intend to ever take her home."

"I'll talk to him."

"Somebody'll have to kill him sooner or later. I doubt that I can. I don't know anybody here who could except maybe you."

"Killin' is easy to talk about but hard to do. I don't owe this camp anything like that."

"Well, no matter what happens, I don't intend to stand by and let him murder this woman."

Dawson's baleful gaze followed Tolley as the youth walked back toward his tent, his head down.

Hull declared, "Farlow'll chew that kid up and spit him out like a plug of tobacco." He seemed eager to see the show.

Dawson shook his head. "Women sure can complicate a man's life, make him lose it if the cards fall wrong."

Hull said, "I've never seen you interested in one."

"I was once. Even got married."

Hull showed surprise. "How come you went and left her?"

"I didn't. She died givin' birth."

Joey's interest sharpened. "You've got a kid?"

"A boy. He was about your size last time I saw him. Even looked a right smart like you."

"Where's he at?"

"On a farm in Arkansas with his mother's folks. As far as he knows, his daddy's dead. It's better that way."

"How can he not know about you? Everybody's heard of Miller Dawson."

"I wasn't always Miller Dawson. I saw that name on a signboard. It's one thing I took that didn't cost nobody nothin'."

"But how could you have seen your boy if he doesn't know you're alive?"

"Pretended to be a stranger askin' directions. It was a hard thing to ride off and leave him, but I couldn't take him with me, or even let him know. This ain't no life for a kid." Dawson cleared his throat. "It ain't no life for *you*."

"I wish I knew a way out of it." Joey glanced at Beau. "For both of us."

CHAPTER

11

Dawson made no move toward taking up Farlow's invitation to share supper in the cabin. Hull went but was back shortly, disgruntled. "He didn't mean it," he grumbled to Dawson. "He knew you wouldn't go, or he wouldn't have made the invite."

Dawson added, "You just went because you wanted another look at that fancy woman."

Fancy? Joey hadn't seen anything fancy about her. She looked as if she had been dragged through hell and out the far end.

Hull complained, "Farlow acted like he thought I had intentions."

"You did, didn't you? You wished, anyway."

"Maybe, but I ain't goin' to have Farlow kill me on account of a woman. There's women everyplace. Except here."

"I'm afraid Tolley ain't as cautious as you are."

"Tolley's head ain't growed to match the rest of him. If he's got no better sense, then I won't cry over him."

"I don't remember you cryin' over anybody, ever."

"Ain't nobody ever cried over *me*."

That sounded reasonable to Joey, though he deemed it wise to look away so Hull could not read the thought. Beau read it and gave him a frown that warned him to be careful. Even thinking could be dangerous in a place like this.

At dark they rolled out their blankets near the creek. The trickling sound of the water was comforting until Joey heard another sound, a woman's cry of pain from inside the cabin. He raised up on one elbow to listen. He did not hear it again.

He heard Miller Dawson, however. Dawson said quietly, "Best go to sleep, boy. Ain't none of your concern."

"You could do somethin'."

"Ain't my concern either. Farlow didn't kidnap her out of a convent. She left San Antonio of her own will."

"She ain't stayin' here of her own will."

Dawson did not answer. But Beau reached across from his blankets and pinched Joey's arm. "We ain't either," he whispered, "so, damn it, keep still."

Joey got another look at the woman the next morning. He had walked down the canyon, looking for Taw among the horses scattered on the curing grass. He saw several large circles of stones, the blackened remnants of long-dead fires in their centers. He thrilled to the realization that these were tepee rings, that he was leaving tracks where Comanche warriors once had walked.

He saw Farlow coming his way afoot and hurried back toward Dawson's camp, giving the lanky outlaw a wide berth. Farlow scowled at him but said nothing, going on down the canyon to inspect the horses.

Joey saw the woman emerge from the cabin and circle around to a pile of dry wood behind it. Picking up an ax, she began chopping dead branches into short pieces.

Tolley had been seated on a rough stool beside his tent, watching the cabin as though teasing temptation. Seeing the woman, he quickly got to his feet and walked down to join her. After passing a few words with her, he reached for the ax. She glanced anxiously in Farlow's direction, then handed it to him.

Wind carried the broken sound of their voices as Tolley took up the chopping chore, though the pair were too far away for Joey to understand the words. She kept looking nervously down the canyon where Farlow had gone.

Beau's voice startled Joey. His cousin had walked up behind him. "Sometimes it pays not to see too much."

Joey recovered his composure. "I ain't seen nothin'." But he watched Tolley carry an armload of wood into the cabin. The woman followed him. He did not see them come out.

Beau said, "Keep watchin', then, and you're liable to see a hell of a fight. Farlow's comin' back."

Joey could foresee dreadful consequences. "We'd ought to warn them."

"Let them kill one another off. The more the better. Maybe we'd get a chance to sneak out of here."

"But Farlow's apt to hurt her. Maybe bad."

"He could hurt you too. That kind of woman ain't worth it."

Joey held his breath, debating whether to mix in something clearly none of his affair. It did not take him long to decide. He ran to the cabin door and shouted, "Farlow's on his way."

Tolley came out, then turned toward the woman standing at the threshold. "I don't know how, but I'll get you out of this place, Alta. First chance that comes . . ."

Joey moved so that the cabin hid him from Farlow until he reached his tent. Joey took one more look at the woman's desperate face, at the fear in her eyes. He felt compassion, but he knew he had better find business elsewhere too.

Farlow stopped him with a challenge. "Boy, what was you doin' at my cabin?"

Other men in camp made Joey feel ill at ease, but Farlow scared him all the way down to his feet. Even so, he managed to lie with a straight face. "I wasn't at your cabin, Mr. Farlow. I just walked up the creek lookin' for a good place to go fishin'."

Farlow seemed undecided about believing him. He took hold of Joey's shoulders and gave him such a hard shaking that Joey feared his head would come off. "Boy, I'll give you the whippin' of your life if I ever catch you messin' around my cabin again. Ain't nothin' there that's any of your business. You hear me?"

Miller Dawson's voice was stern and loud. "And you better hear *me*, Farlow. You turn a-loose of that boy before I bend a gun barrel over your head."

Farlow eased his hold but did not let go. He turned an angry gaze upon Dawson. "You'd better bring plenty of help."

Dawson drew his pistol, and Farlow turned Joey loose. Joey hurried to Dawson's side.

Farlow pointed a finger in Joey's face. "You mind what I tell you, boy." He turned and entered his cabin. Joey heard a slap and a woman's cry.

He asked Dawson, "Ain't you goin' to do anything about that?"

"I brought you in here, so you're my responsibility. But that woman came of her own accord. Come on, you'd better get away from this place."

As Dawson went to his campfire and poured a cup of coffee, Beau moved close to Joey. "Didn't your daddy ever teach you that a boy who pokes his bill into other people's business ain't got near enough to do?"

"All I done was give them a little warnin'. The law says everybody's got a right to free speech."

"The only law around here is that the meaner you are, the longer you live. And Farlow looks like the meanest man in camp."

That afternoon two horsemen entered the upper end of the canyon, a pair of heavily laden pack mules trailing behind them. Curiosity carried Joey up to the first picket shack, where the riders dismounted. Other men from the camp gathered to greet them, most with more enthusiasm than they had shown Dawson yesterday. Dawson had not brought them anything.

Joey saw Farlow coming and moved far out of his path. Farlow pushed to the front, shoving aside everyone who stood in his way. "Did you bring me my goods?"

One of the new arrivals walked to the nearest mule and untied the diamond hitch that bound a stained tarp over a loaded pack saddle. "Sure did. We cushioned the bottles to where they wouldn't bust."

Farlow grumped, "Last time, you bought the cheapest stuff you could find and kept half of my money."

"This is prime sippin' whiskey. Me and Sim, we sampled it to be sure." He lifted off a burlap bag labeled *beans,* set it gently on the ground, and cut the string. The dry beans rustled as he ran his hand down into them and brought out a bottle. "Try it yourself and see if I ain't right."

Farlow worried out a cork and tipped up the bottle, taking two long swallows. He wiped a dirty sleeve across his mouth and declared, "Maybe this time I won't have to stomp on you."

Some of the men moved close, hoping Farlow would offer them a drink, but he did not. He ordered, "You-all bring the rest of my goods down yonder." He turned on his heel and walked back to his cabin, stopping once for another drink.

It was clear to Joey that the two men had been buying for several in camp. They began dividing up what they had brought. Someone asked, "You hear any news out there?"

Joey moved closer in case they might have heard something about a manhunt for him and Beau. "Not much," the newcomer Sim said. "There was a train robbery up on the T&P day before yesterday. They say it was Miller Dawson, and they've upped the ante on him again."

Day before yesterday. Joey had been with Dawson then, and they had been nowhere near anything called T&P, whatever that was. So Dawson had been right. Once they branded you an outlaw, they blamed you for anything bad that happened. He wondered what mischief he and Beau might be getting credit for. That Bastrop sheriff was probably clearing his books of every unsolved crime on record, pinning them all on him and Beau.

Dawson came up presently to watch the distribution of whiskey and flour, salt and bacon, cartridges and shotgun shells. None of it was for him; he had bought his supplies shortly before reaching the canyon. He inquired about the news, and Sim repeated the report about the train robbery.

Dawson's face twisted in wry acceptance. "I wonder if they'd pay me the reward if I was to turn myself in? It'd be more money than I've ever had at one time in my life."

Sim said, "Let *me* turn you in and I'll split the money with you." Such a statement in earnest could get a man killed in company like this. Clearly he was joking. But just the same, Joey looked quickly at Dawson to see if he took it that way.

Dawson smiled thinly. "They might hang you before the money came in. Then where would I be?"

Joey thought it would be hard to dislike a man who could joke about his own fate.

It did not take long for the newly arrived whiskey to have its effect upon the camp. As darkness fell and campfires began to reflect their glow upon the limestone wall, Joey could hear laughter spilling from one shack, cursing and quarreling from another. Most men in camp were descending into various stages of drunkenness. Hull visited one shack and one campfire after another, sampling the whiskey other men had paid for. He came staggering back, barely able to move one foot in front of the other. He collapsed upon his blankets as if someone had broken an ax handle across his head, which in Joey's opinion would not have been a bad idea.

Dawson drank, but he did it slowly without allowing himself to lose control. Joey was moderately surprised at his self-restraint in view of the lack of it elsewhere in camp, but Beau surprised him more. Though Dawson offered to share his bottle, Beau declined. "Never was one for whiskey," he said.

If lying could get a man sent to hell, Beau was a goner. But Joey realized Beau was trying to keep his wits about him. Should luck provide a chance to take the two of them out of here, Beau intended to be sober and ready.

Tolley came down to Dawson's camp, looking worriedly back over his shoulder. "I'm hearin' ugly talk up yonder. Some of the bunch are tryin' to work up the nerve to come down to Farlow's cabin and take Alta away from him."

Dawson considered the situation, the campfire's flickering light playing over his somber face. "If Farlow gets as drunk as I think he will, it oughtn't to be hard to do. You've been wantin' to see her turned loose."

"Turnin' her loose ain't what they've got in mind."

Dawson scowled. "I knew there would be hell to pay over her, sooner or later. They'll bust up this camp." He pushed to his feet. "I never saw a sportin' woman who was worth this kind of trouble, but do you want her bad enough to take a chance?"

"A chance is all I ask for."

"Catch and saddle a couple of horses for you and her. I'll see that Farlow gets too drunk to know what's happenin'."

Tolley said, "I always knew you had a good heart."

Dawson grunted. "I don't give a damn about that woman; I'm just tryin' to save this camp. Be careful you don't cause any commotion. Drunk or sober, Farlow has got rattlesnake blood in him." He started for Farlow's cabin, carrying two bottles.

Beau whispered to Joey, "Bring our bridles. This is a chance for me and you to get out of here too."

"I don't think Mr. Dawson meant for us to go."

"I don't care what he meant. We're goin'." Beau trotted after Tolley. Joey grabbed their bridles and followed.

Away from the campfire, Joey's eyes rapidly adjusted to the bright light of the full moon. He saw most of the horses farther down the canyon, some standing, some lying down. Tolley welcomed the help. He said, "Let's push them into the corral. They'll be easier to catch."

Several saddles had been left atop the corral fence, along with bridles, blankets, and ropes. Joey began shoving the sagging gate shut behind the horses. Crudely constructed of tree branches tied together with rawhide, it scraped heavily against the ground. Beau hissed for him to be quieter. Joey tried to lift the gate, but it was so heavy he could only drag it.

Beau bridled Taw and Git Out while Tolley saddled two other horses. Beau motioned for Joey to follow him, leading the horses back to Dawson's campfire. They worked quickly, rolling their blankets and tying them onto the saddles with their other meager belongings. Hull stirred and groaned a little. Joey held his breath, watching him, but Hull settled back down and resumed his snoring.

Beau started to mount, then noticed Hull's rolled gun belt with his pistol and holster near the upper corner of his blankets. He stooped to pick them up.

Joey said nothing, but Beau explained in justification, "He borrowed my horse without a by-your-leave. I reckon it's fair for me to borrow his six-shooter."

Joey saw someone running toward them in the shadows. He feared at first that they had been discovered, but the woman emerged into the moonlight. Urgently she told Tolley, "Farlow's pretty far gone. Miller Dawson is drinkin' with him to keep him that way. Said we'd better git while the gittin's good."

Farther up the canyon, the racket of whiskey-driven revelry continued, and the tone of shouting at the farthest shack indicated that there might be a fistfight. Beau said, "I don't see how we can slip past all them heathens without bein' caught."

She pointed southward. "Mr. Dawson said go out the lower end and follow the creek down to where it runs into a bigger canyon. He said Tolley knows the way."

Tolley boosted Alta into a man's saddle, which pushed her long skirt far up her legs. He said, "I've only been out that direction once. We're liable to wander around lost in them cedarbrakes."

Alta replied, "Mr. Dawson said if we travel south long enough we'll strike an old military road that goes east to San Antonio and west to El Paso."

They started in a walk, trying to make as little noise as possible until they were well away from camp. They had gone perhaps two hundred yards when Joey heard a loud commotion from the direction of Farlow's cabin and Farlow's gruff voice shouting into the night. His shout was followed by two gunshots that echoed and re-echoed like a ricochet against the canyon walls.

Joey chilled. For a moment he was unable to move, staring back toward the camp. He heard Farlow's angry voice again.

Beau shouted, "Don't just sit there! We've got to run them horses out ahead of us."

Joey broke free of his trance and grasped what Beau was saying. If they did not drive the horses away, much of the camp could soon be mounted and in pursuit. Some horses remained in the corral. Joey put Taw into a lope, entering the pen and pushing the horses out to join those that Beau had begun herding southward. A couple cut back toward the camp. One was Miller Dawson's. Beau shouted, "Let them go. We ain't got the time."

They reached the short brush fence that had been thrown up across the narrow end of the canyon to keep the camp's mounts from straying beyond easy reach. Exit by the creek had been closed off by a couple of ropes stretched across the water and tied to trees on either side. Beau and Joey held the horses while Tolley stepped down to cut the ropes. The woman rode into the creek and passed through the opening, waiting on the other side while the loose horses spilled past her.

Farlow was chasing after them afoot, shouting, firing in their direction. A bullet ripped through the dry brush that constituted the fence. As Tolley swung into the saddle, Joey heard a thump and knew a bullet had struck something solid. Tolley jerked. Joey wondered if he was hit, but he was reassured when he saw that Tolley was still in the saddle and moving. Joey splashed through the narrow opening. Tolley followed closely behind him.

Beau was last to go through. He jumped to the ground, grabbing a handful of cured grass and twisting it, striking a match on the sole of his boot and holding it until the flame began to crackle through the wad of dry vegetation. Git Out did not like the fire and jerked the reins from Beau's hand. Joey caught him before he could run away. Beau shoved the burning material into a clump of dry grass that had grown up into the dead brush. The flames quickly spread along the fence.

Remounting, Beau declared, "They'll play hell makin' a horse come through there 'til the fire dies down."

Joey marveled. "Beau, how'd you think of that?"

"When you're sober you can think up lots of things."

They kept the horses running for a time, until a couple of the loose ones stumbled and fell on the rough ground. Beau said, "We'd better slow down."

Alta declared, "Farlow don't turn loose of anything easy. Soon as he can catch him a horse, he'll be comin'."

Joey added, "We didn't get them all. There was a couple cut back, and two or three more were staked close to the shacks."

Beau said, "If we cripple our horses we'll be afoot, and then he'll *sure* catch up to us." He frowned at Tolley, hunched in the saddle. "Somethin' wrong?"

"Nothin' as bad as what's behind us. Keep movin'."

From far back, Joey heard a couple more shots.

Beau scattered the riderless horses out into the cedar brush where they would be difficult to find and harder to catch. Joey saw that he had been right about slowing down. The rough terrain prevented the riders from making good time, for gathering clouds were beginning to compromise the moonlight, obscuring the ruts and washouts, the tangles of fallen scrub timber. Joey was gratified that Beau took the lead, seeking the easiest course through the obstacles.

He was amazed at how much Beau had learned during their brief association. There was hope for him yet.

The occasional moments of moonlight and dark shadows cast by the cedar gave the landscape a surreal quality, as in a strange dream Joey occasionally had when he ate something like cucumbers that did not settle quietly in his stomach.

His short stay in the canyon had been bad dream enough to last him the rest of the year, he thought.

By daylight a blanket of gray clouds extended from the eastern horizon all the way to the west, hiding the sunrise. Joey could not even tell for sure in what direction the sun lay. The canyon walls had withdrawn and were not really walls any longer but simply long hills far away. Somehow in the darkness the fugitives had pulled back from the creek that was supposed to point their direction. He was not sure anymore where it was. He turned, but he could see little behind him in the way of landmarks by which he could retrace his steps. He saw no reason he would ever want to.

No one had talked much during the nighttime flight. Now Joey noticed that Tolley was trailing, hunched over so far that the horse's mane was brushing his face. He said, "Beau, somethin's sure enough wrong with Tolley."

Beau turned back, and Joey pulled in beside him. Blood had soaked Tolley's shirt and trouser leg, stained his saddle, and trailed down his horse's left side.

Beau told Tolley, "You should've told us you was hit. You've bled half to death."

Joey saw blood on Tolley's lips. He could hardly hear Tolley's weak voice. "We couldn't stop. We can't stop now."

"You ain't got another mile left in you," Beau said. "Joey, let's help him down." They untied Tolley's blankets from behind the cantle and spread them on the ground, then eased the young man down upon them.

The blood was warm and sticky. Joey tried to wipe it onto his pants, but it would not all come off. The stain on his hands made him want to gag.

Alta had dismounted. She led her horse to where Tolley lay. She choked off a cry as Beau ripped the blood-soaked shirt to reveal a dark and ugly hole still oozing blood. Beau said, "The bullet's in there someplace deep. It never came out."

Tolley's voice was almost too weak to hear. "Keep goin'. You know what they'll do to Alta if they catch her."

Joey did not understand the flush of anger that came over Beau as he glanced up at the woman. "It ain't like she's never had it done to her before."

Alta gave Beau a fleeting look of resentment, then turned her attention back to Tolley. "Can't you take the bullet out?"

Beau's voice was sharp. "What with? A pocketknife?"

Joey did not like the look in Tolley's eyes. He had seen the same look in Pa, just before the end. Alta knelt to take Tolley's hands in her own and hold them. She leaned forward and kissed him on the forehead, tears running down her cheeks.

Tolley tried to smile at her, but the smile was lost in a fit of coughing. When the coughing stopped, his breathing stopped with it. Alta folded Tolley's arms across his chest.

Beau closed the young man's eyes, then cleared his throat and stood up, removing his hat and looking down at the still figure. "He was an outlaw, you can't get around that. But he was a game little rooster."

Joey shivered uncontrollably and turned away so they would not see the tears that burned his eyes. He had watched his father die. He had found Reuben lifeless in the shed that had been his home, and he had watched Mr. Meacham float away facedown in the Colorado River. Lately, life seemed to have become just one death after another.

When he turned back, Alta was still kneeling beside Tolley, her eyes deeply sad. He said, "You must've loved him."

"I didn't even know him, hardly. But he offered to help me get away from Farlow and that camp. I feel like I'm the cause of him dyin'."

Beau said, "You are. If you hadn't been there . . ."

Joey protested, "Wasn't her that shot him, it was Farlow."

Beau said, "We can't afford to stand around here arguin' about whose fault it was. We've got to figure that Farlow's back yonder someplace, catchin' up."

Alta said, "We can't just leave him lyin' here. The coyotes and the buzzards . . ."

Beau said, "We've got nothin' to dig a grave with."

"We can cover him up with rocks," Joey said. "There's aplenty of them around."

Beau stripped Tolley's gun belt, holster, and pistol from the body, hanging them from the horn of his own saddle. "We may need that six-shooter," he said. "And the rifle he carried, too."

The three gathered stones from nearby and stacked them over the blanket-wrapped body, finishing up with several so large that Joey and Beau had to work together to carry them. Beau said, "I don't think there's a coyote in the country big enough to push those away." He placed Tolley's saddle at the head of the grave. "A poor marker, but it's all we got."

Joey said, "Don't you think we'd ought to say some words over him?"

"I never was one to go to church much. I don't know what a man is supposed to say."

Alta said, "Ashes to ashes, and dust to dust." She bowed her head and began to recite the Lord's Prayer. Beau stared at her in amazement until Joey poked him to remind him he was supposed to bow his head too.

When she was done Beau demanded, "Where'd a woman like you learn to pray like that?"

Her voice was defiant. "A woman like me has got a lot to pray about. I doubt that *you're* any candidate for sainthood, or you wouldn't have been in an outlaw camp."

"I wasn't there because I wanted to be."

"Neither was I."

Joey feared they might waste an hour arguing. "We'd better be movin', or we're liable to see Farlow again."

That jarred them into action. Joey gave Alta a boost up into her saddle before he mounted Taw. Beau attached Tolley's scabbard and rifle to his saddle and said, "Joey, you lead Tolley's horse. Might be we'll need it." He began a winding path through and around the cedarbrakes. After a time Joey moved up even with him. "I thought we was supposed to keep ridin' south."

"We *are* ridin' south."

"No, we're goin' east."

"Boy, you've got no sense of direction. If we was goin' east we'd be facin' into the sun."

"We are, only you can't see it for the clouds."

"You're full of prunes." Beau kept riding. Joey burned with frustration but followed him; he saw no choice.

He could only guess how long and how far they had ridden, snaking their way through the thickets and around the hills. Beau finally reined to a stop and took a worried look in all directions. "I believe we've swung too far west."

Joey argued, "We've been goin' east the whole time."

Alta said, "I believe Joey's right."

Beau's face colored. "You think I don't know east from west? If you don't like the way I'm travelin', you're free to go your own way."

Joey looked to Alta for support, then gave up. He followed Beau, though he was convinced the cloudy skies had left his cousin disoriented. Much later, Beau hauled up suddenly and examined the ground. "Here's fresh horse tracks. Farlow must've got ahead of us some way."

Joey dismounted for a close look. He decided the tracks had been made by four horses. One looked familiar. He led Taw a few steps and checked the impressions the hooves had just made. They were identical to one of the other sets.

"That's our own tracks," he said. "We've gone in a circle."

Beau snorted. "That can't be."

"Look at them yourself. There's Taw and Git Out's, and them yonder is from Alta's and Tolley's horses."

Beau declared, "You're wrong." But his eyes betrayed him. He knew. "All right. Just to prove you're mistaken, we'll go your way a while."

Joey pointed in the direction the old tracks led. "That's south." Alta nodded agreement.

Beau did not accept defeat with any grace. "If we wind up back in that canyon with Farlow and them, don't blame me."

Before long they approached the place where they had laid a cairn of rocks over Tolley. Breaking out of a cedar thicket, Joey saw too late that a horse and a man stood beside the grave.

"That damned Farlow!" Beau exclaimed. He seemed paralyzed.

Alta said, "You've got Tolley's rifle. Use it."

Beau made no move toward the weapon.

Alta demanded, "Have you never shot a man before?"

"I've felt like it a few times, but I never did it."

Bitterly she said, "Then give me the rifle. I can shoot him. I'd shoot *myself* before I'd let him get ahold of me again."

Beau said, "Maybe he'll decide to back away."

Joey doubted that. Farlow had seemed the kind who would charge into hell with a bucket of water and challenge the devil to fight. He might not be smart, but he was determined.

The man at the grave had seen them. He mounted and began

moving their way. Reluctantly Beau drew the rifle from its scabbard.

Joey studied the oncoming figure. "Wait a minute, Beau. That looks like Mr. Dawson's roan horse."

Beau lowered the rifle and blinked. "You sure?"

Joey did not reply until he was certain. "It's him. And that's Mr. Dawson ridin' him."

Miller Dawson had come equipped for a long trip, blankets tied behind his saddle, a sack of supplies dangling from the saddle horn. He seemed relieved at the sight of the three riders, especially Joey. He said, "Boy, I'd about given you up. I was afraid you'd ridden off the edge of the earth."

"Seemed like it for a while. Beau got lost."

Joey caught a reproachful glance from Beau.

Dawson said, "I didn't figure on anybody but Tolley and this woman leavin' camp." He fixed an accusing gaze on Beau. "I suppose it was your idea to take Joey and go too."

"You know I never wanted to be there in the first place."

"You could've got this boy killed." He turned back to Joey. "Anyway, I'm glad it's not you in that grave. Everybody's here but Tolley. I suppose it's him?"

Beau replied, "He caught a bullet in his lung leavin' camp. Farlow's doin'."

If Dawson was much moved, he hid it well. "Too bad, but the business he was in, he didn't stand much chance to get a lot older. If it hadn't been Farlow it'd've been some sheriff or ranger." He gave Alta a dark look. "Too bad it couldn't be over somethin' worth dyin' for, like a sackful of silver."

Joey was puzzled. First Beau and now Dawson were acting as if the whole thing had been on account of Alta. Well, he supposed a person could look at it that way. If she had not been in camp in the first place, none of this would have happened. But he figured Farlow must have told her a lot of lies to get her to leave San Antonio with him, and then she was trapped with no way to get out on her own. Helping her escape was the decent thing to do, and to Tolley's credit he had chosen to do it. *Anybody* could have a streak of bad luck. Joey had been having one himself lately, a long one. That wasn't his fault and he couldn't see where this was Alta's.

People kept telling him he would understand things better when he got older. He wished that time would hurry up and get here.

CHAPTER

12

Dawson leaned forward in the saddle, rebuke in the twist of his face. "You-all've been circlin' like a blind goose ever since you left this spot. I gave up tryin' to follow you. Damned poor way to treat this boy, ridin' around lost and hungry."

Beau said defensively, "It's hard to tell directions when the sun's covered up and you've got no landmarks. We ought to've had a compass."

"I never had a compass in my life, and I've been all over this country in fair weather and foul."

Joey pointed. "I kept tryin' to tell him that way is south."

Beau gave him a look that would have meant a paddling if it had come from Pa.

Dawson indicated with his chin, a little off Joey's direction and far from Beau's. "Yonder is south. If you're ready, we'll be gettin' started."

Beau was surprised enough to put aside his pique at Joey. "You're goin' with us?" He did not hide his reservations.

"Only for a while, to get you as far as the road. Then I've got some bankin' business to see about."

Joey could guess the kind of business Dawson intended to transact. "Thought you was stayin' in camp a while to rest."

"Won't be much rest there after last night's ruckus. I'm afraid the camp may be done for."

Beau turned a concerned gaze northward, in the direction of the canyon. "Farlow ain't a man to give up easy. He's probably followin' us."

"He won't be followin' anybody unless it's as a ghost. He sobered up enough to figure out that I was lettin' his woman slip away. He came back on the fight and I had to shoot him."

Alta demanded, "He's dead?"

Dawson gave her another accusing stare. "On account of you, he didn't leave me no choice."

She seemed about to weep but broke into hysterical laughter instead. Beau looked at her askance. "A man bein' dead ain't somethin' to laugh about, even if he *was* a rattlesnake."

Joey realized she was not laughing because something was funny. Her kind of laugh was a form of crying.

Beau was puzzled. "Farlow could go fetch him another woman any time he wanted to. He was probably gettin' tired of this one anyway. We saved him havin' to get rid of her."

Joey did not like Beau's tone. He talked about Alta as if she were not beside him, hearing everything he said.

Dawson said, "You don't understand a man like Farlow and the way he saw things. To him she was property, like his horse. He might sell his property, maybe give it away or even destroy it. But for somebody to take it was like slappin' him in the face." Dawson was grim. "Farlow needed killin', but I never liked puttin' a man in the ground."

Beau said, "The rangers talk like you've done a lot of it."

"Tell a lie often enough and it's as good as the truth." Dawson turned to Alta, his voice severe. "If you hadn't come out to the camp with him, none of this would've happened."

Alta brought her emotions under control. "You've never been where I was. He didn't have to promise much to get me to go."

Beau gave her a look like a preacher confronting an unrepentant sinner. "I doubt that anybody held a gun to your head to make you do what you was doin' in San Antonio."

"They didn't have to. When you've been hungry enough, long enough, you'll do just about anything."

Joey was stirred to anger. "You-all quit pickin' on her. You act like everything's her fault."

Beau glared at him. "You're a boy. When grown men talk, boys listen."

Alta said sharply, "But sometimes men don't know what they're talkin' about. I can go on from here by myself. You men don't need to trouble yourselves about me any longer."

Dawson frowned. "You've got nothin' but the clothes on your back, and they ain't much. No blankets, no grub. Like as not you'd get lost and die, and you wouldn't even have anybody to bury you."

Her blue eyes flashed. "You've made it clear I'm not worth the trouble."

"The trouble's over with. I reckon there's no more damage you can do. So come on, I'll show you-all to where you can find your own way out." His sharp tone brooked no more argument.

Dawson took the lead, Alta following close behind him. Beau and Joey dropped back a little. Joey could tell that Beau was peeved at him for what he had said. Well, that was all right. Joey was a little peeved too. He said, "I don't see why you've got to keep diggin' at Alta so."

"Boy, there's a lot you need to learn about the world and about women like her."

"I already know more than you think I do."

"But not half as much as *you* think. Most of what you know ain't true."

"I just want you to quit bein' so hard on her."

"Looks to me like you're in danger of comin' down with a bad case of puppy love. She's a way too old for you, and the wrong sort of woman at that. I've had my share of experience with her kind. Most of it took on a sour taste before it was over and done with. They ain't got true feelin's like normal people. They're all warped inside, like my mama was when she went off and left me."

"Alta's had a lot of bad luck, is all."

"Bad luck is when people like me and you get in trouble through accident. I expect she walked into hers with both eyes open."

Joey let himself stare at Alta, riding a length behind Dawson with her skirt pushed up and her legs exposed almost to the knees. He would not tell Beau, but she did look pretty good. "All the same, I want you to quit pickin' on her."

"We'll get her to the San Antonio road, and then we'll be shed of her."

Joey knew nothing about the geography of the land they traveled through. Dawson explained that rough terrain prevailed all the way south to the Rio Grande . . . cedarbrakes, broken hills, canyons, and hollows. Cutting through an otherwise dry land were many small creeks and such major rivers as the Guadalupe and the Frio and the Nueces as well as branches of the Llano. The cedar and live oak would prevail most of the way, replaced by cactus and huisache, creosote and other desert vegetation near the Mexican border.

"Ain't good for much except stock raisin'," he said, "especially sheep and Mexican goats. You'll find where people have broke out small farms in some flats and valleys, but most of the land has got too much up and down to it, and solid rock that reaches halfway to China. Lots of deer and turkey and javelina hogs, though. It was a great country for the Indians. They sure hated to give it up."

Joey asked, "How far this way are we goin'?"

"To an old emigrant and army road. When we get there, you and Beau can go west to Fort Stockton, then out to Fort Davis and El Paso. From there you can go to Arizona, California, wherever you want to. And this good lady can go east back to San Antonio." His ironic tone contradicted the term *good lady*.

Alta said nothing.

Joey said, "Mr. Dawson, how about you goin' west with us?"

"I'd like to. I'm tired of lookin' over my shoulder all the time. They say up in Oregon there's the prettiest cropland a man ever saw. Maybe I could go back to usin' my own name and fix a farm up real nice. Then I could send for my boy."

"Go with us then, why don't you? Oregon ain't far from California, the way I remember the map."

"A man's got to have money to buy a farm. I figure if I get real busy I'll have enough before long."

"The rangers might catch you first."

"They talk brave, but they ain't been all that eager to get real close."

They almost got too close while Dawson was talking. Joey's sharp eyes caught a glimpse of horsemen half a mile in front of them. He gave the alarm. Dawson pulled away toward a thick growth of cedar. "You-all keep goin' like you are. I'll catch up to you later."

Beau tensed. "Looks to me like a posse. They could be comin' for me and you, Joey."

Joey's skin prickled. "They might, but they're bound to've seen us already. Taw ain't fast enough to get away."

Beau's jaw set firmly. "We'll have to lie our way out. You've got so good at it, I worry about you." He turned to Alta. "You string along with whatever I say."

"Then you'd better talk like you had good sense."

Joey counted nine men. One wore a ranger badge, another a star that Joey supposed marked him as a sheriff. The rest had no badges that he could see. They were probably sworn in as temporary deputies to legalize whatever they might do.

The men reined into a semicircle around Joey, Beau, and Alta. The ranger moved closest, giving each of the three a hard scrutiny before he spoke. His gaze dwelt longest on Alta. Most women rode sidesaddle, and she was riding astride in a long dress not made for it. Obviously she looked out of place. He demanded of Beau, "Who are you, and what is your business?"

Joey could almost see the wheels of imagination grinding in Beau's head. Beau said, "Name's Smith. Me and my wife and our boy, we're on our way to visit her kinfolks."

"You're travelin' awful light."

"We're not goin' far, just down on the Frio."

The ranger studied Alta critically. "This lady's face is

bruised. Ain't many things I hate worse than a man that beats his wife."

"She fell off of her horse."

Alta backed him with a nod.

The ranger did not appear satisfied, but he seemed to have more pressing business. "We've been informed that there's an outlaw camp somewhere north of here."

"That might be so. Been some hard-lookin' characters come past our place from time to time."

"Where is your place?"

Beau jerked his thumb back over his shoulder. "That way."

"I don't suppose you'd know where their hideout is at?"

"Them canyons look pretty much alike. But if that camp is there, and you keep lookin', I'll bet you find it."

"We intend to do that. We mean to make this a fit country for raisin' families."

"That sure would be an improvement," Beau agreed.

The ranger had not shed all his suspicion. He gave Alta's face another study. "How long you folks been married?"

Beau said, "Since before the boy was born. He's ten."

"Twelve," Joey corrected him. "Goin' on thirteen. You never did learn arithmetic."

The ranger almost smiled. "Honor thy father and mother, son, even when they can't do sums."

The posse rode on northward, and Beau lost no time striking out to the south, looking back often to be sure the ranger did not change his mind. For the next couple of miles Joey kept looking for Dawson but could not see him. Then suddenly Dawson materialized beside him, popping out of a thicket.

He asked, "Them fellers say they was lookin' for anybody in particular?"

Joey said, "They're lookin' for your camp, and they're goin' in the right direction to find it. I suppose you'll want to circle back and warn your friends." He hoped not, for he would hate to see Dawson go.

Dawson gave the question hardly a moment's thought. "Them boys're friends to nobody but themselves. They're a bunch of crooks anyhow."

* * *

They came without much warning upon the wagon road, a pair of twin ruts which iron-rimmed wheels had ground into fine gravel and caliche powder through years of passage. Dawson was gratified at finding no fresh tracks. "Been a while since anybody's passed this way, so maybe you'll have the road to yourselves. I reckon this is where we part company." He lifted off a sack of food hanging from his saddle horn. "Girl, you take enough out of this to carry you a couple of days. The boys can have the rest of it."

Joey argued, "You'll need to eat too."

"I've got some friends to the south a ways. They'll see that I don't go hungry." Dawson took several silver coins from his pocket and offered them to Alta. "You'll strike a crossroads store about half a day east. You can buy enough grub to get you the rest of the way to San Antonio."

She sternly refused the money. "Keep it. I've done nothin' to earn it. If anything, I owe you for puttin' Farlow away. And I ain't left anything in San Antonio that I want to go back for. I'm headin' west."

Joey was pleased, but Beau protested, "You ain't goin' with us!"

"I can travel by myself, in front of you or behind you, whichever way you want it. But I'm goin' west."

Dawson shrugged. "You-all work that out to suit yourselves. I'm headin' on."

Joey pleaded, "I do wish you'd go with us, Mr. Dawson."

"Can't. There's a little bank down south that's gotten a-way too fat on high interest."

"What about Oregon?"

"It'll still be there when I get done. Anyway, I'll probably catch up with you-all long before you get to California." He clamped a firm hand on Joey's shoulder. "You take good care of yourself, young'un. You remind me an awful lot of . . ." He broke off in midsentence and turned away. Joey watched him so long as he was in sight and kept watching a while after Dawson disappeared beyond a green clump of live-oak trees.

Beau and Alta argued over the division of the food Dawson

had left them. Each wanted the other to take more.

Joey said, "If you-all would halfway try to get along, we could all ride together."

Alta said to Beau, "He makes sense. I'm surprised he's kin to you."

"Second cousin, is all."

Joey decided the two would not stop arguing, so he picked up the sack, hung it from his own saddle horn, and turned Taw west. Presently he heard the horses loping up behind him, but he made it a point not to turn and look back. He had heard all the foolishness he wanted to listen to.

Neither Beau nor Alta had anything to say. Their silence was as loud as an angry shout. Beau pulled up beside Joey and gave him a look of recrimination. Joey turned his face away and ignored him. Alta tagged along several paces behind, in no better humor than Beau.

The road meandered, seeking the levelest course among the hills, for heavily laden wagons would have been hard put to climb most of them. It crossed a couple of creeks where Joey would have liked to stop to rest a while, but he figured Beau and Alta would launch another argument if he did. So long as they kept riding, they stayed apart.

For the life of him, he couldn't see what they had against one another. Beau had his faults, but he was not bad company when he stayed sober. Joey didn't know much about Alta except that she was looking better to him all the time. He gathered that her life in San Antonio would not have pleased Preacher Johnson. Dawson had called her a sporting woman, and Joey had a good notion what he meant. But as far as he knew she hadn't killed anybody. That put her a notch or two above him and Beau, so he didn't see any reason for Beau to look down on her.

It was Beau who finally called on Joey to halt. "We rode all night, and we've rode all day. Unless we can ride dead horses all the way to California, we'd better quit a while."

The sun was still an hour or so above the western horizon, but Joey could see another nice creek crossing ahead, with shade and plenty of grass for the mounts. "That place up yonder looks pretty good."

Beau did not offer to help Alta down from her horse. Joey thought about it but feared he might embarrass himself by letting her fall. She dismounted easily enough without help and stood a minute holding onto the saddle, her legs weak from the long ride.

Beau ordered, "Build us a fire, Joey, so she can fix us somethin' to eat."

Joey retorted with sarcasm, "You're back to givin' orders, are you?"

"I'm the only man here."

Alta demanded, "Where is the law written that there always has to be a man in charge?"

"I think it's in the Bible someplace."

Joey doubted that Beau had ever read the Bible past Genesis, if that far. He saw that the situation was about to deteriorate into argument. "All right, I'll build the fire. No use in havin' a fight."

He saw plenty of dry timber lying about, dead limbs broken off by the wind. As he picked it up, a distant movement caught his eye. He discerned a white-tailed doe inching out into the open from a live-oak motte, taking a step and cautiously looking around before she took another. Near where Beau was unsaddling the horses, Joey dropped the wood he had gathered.

"Let me have Tolley's rifle," he said. "I'll get us somethin' fresher than salt pork for supper."

"Boy, you'll just shoot your own toe off or hit one of us."

"I'll bet I'm a better shot than you are. Give me the rifle."

Reluctantly Beau complied. "Be careful where you point that thing. You could kill somebody."

"I don't aim at anything I don't intend to hit."

Beau snorted. "Anything you hit, I'll carry back to camp in one hand."

Joey had never had reason to tell Beau that Pa had taught him how to use a rifle when he was seven, figuring that the earlier a boy learned, the less likely he was to be careless later in life.

He slowly picked his way through a protective thicket, watching his footing so he would not step on a dead limb and break it, startling the doe. He could not see her, but that meant she could not see him either. When the timber began to thin in front of him, he stopped and held still while he located her. She stood just a few yards out into an opening, browsing on a low-growing shrub. She would take a bite, then jerk her head up, wary eyes seeking any excuse to set her bounding back into the wood. Joey measured his steps, moving only when she dropped her head for a bite, stopping as soon as she looked up. She seemed to sense danger, for she turned as if to run. But she stopped to look again.

Joey braced the rifle against a tree. He could only hope its aim was true; he had not had a chance to sight it in. He squeezed the trigger. The doe made a high lêap, then was back in the timber.

Beau had sneaked up behind while Joey was intent on the doe. "Told you you couldn't hit anything."

At another time Joey would have been irked at Beau because he had risked frightening away the deer, but now he was too chagrined over the thought of having missed. "I had my sights set dead on. Ain't no reason not to've hit her. This rifle must be off."

Beau gave him no quarter. "Someday you'll learn not to make a brag you can't back up."

Joey stubbornly refused to concede. He walked to the place where the doe had grazed. Seeing a large blood spot in the grass, he ventured into the motte. There she lay, her open eyes glazing in death.

Joey returned to the edge of the timber, put his fingers in his mouth, and whistled for Beau. Pointing to the carcass, he threw his chest out a little. "Which hand you goin' to carry her in?"

"Lucky shot. Don't let it go to your head."

Joey stood back and let Beau do the bloody work of gutting her. Beau cut into the paunch. It emitted an unpleasant smell.

Joey demanded, "What did you do that for?"

Beau was a little testy over having been proven wrong about Joey's marksmanship. "Wouldn't want to pass up a chance to find a hair ball. The right kind makes a good madstone."

Joey had never seen a madstone, but he had heard of its use to draw out the poison after a bite by a rabid animal. He did not know if there was anything to it or if this was another notion like turning a dead snake onto its back to bring rain. Reuben had always disclaimed superstition, but any time he had killed a snake around the barn or in the field, he had left it belly up. "A farmer grabs ahold of any chance he can get," he had said.

Beau hoisted the doe up onto his shoulder. Joey considered another jibe about his not carrying it in one hand, but the humor would be wasted on Beau. He might throw down the carcass and let Joey carry it.

Movement at the edge of the thicket drew Joey's gaze to two gray doglike animals, watching warily.

"Lobo wolves," Beau said.

Joey felt a tug of fear. He had never seen a wolf before, but he had heard and read many scary stories. "Reckon they're dangerous?"

Beau showed no concern. "They would be if we was sheep."

Alta had started a fire. She made a tentative smile at the sight of Beau carrying the deer. It was the first time Joey had seen any real light in her eyes except for anger. Her voice mocked Beau a bit. "Joey's a better shot than you reckoned him for."

"Just lucky. Probably couldn't do it again if we gave him a week." Beau got a rope and suspended the carcass from an outstretched live-oak limb, just high enough that he could reach it handily. He skinned it partway and cut out the back strap. To Alta he said, "I remember you was cookin' for Farlow, along with whatever else you was doin' for him. Reckon you can do somethin' with this?"

The warmth vanished from Alta's eyes. "I can, but I don't know if you can eat it with your throat cut."

"You've sure got a sour disposition."

"It's the company I've been keepin'." She glanced at Joey. "I didn't mean you. You're a good boy."

Joey was torn between gratification over the compliment and the fact that she called him *boy*. He wondered how long it would be before people stopped doing that.

Beau said, "This'll be enough for supper. I better hoist that carcass up higher. Them wolves might take a notion to come into camp in the night and help theirselves to it." He turned back to Alta, a touch of sarcasm in his voice. "You're not afraid of lobo wolves, are you?"

"Up against some of the men I've known, a wolf is as harmless as a collie pup."

Beau untied the half hitch which had secured the rope and raised the carcass high enough that the hind legs touched the tree limb. Holding the rope taut, he walked to the base of the live oak to secure it.

Joey heard a buzzing sound and saw a flash of movement. Beau cried out and let go the rope. The deer fell, landing with a thump. Beau hopped backward on one leg.

"Rattlesnake!" he shouted.

Joey froze in place. His mind flashed back to his own bedroom encounter with a rattler. He wanted to rush to help Beau, but he could not force his legs to move. For a panicked moment he feared that the snake was coming for him too. A wild notion flashed through his mind that this was the same one, trying to finish a job at which it had failed the first time.

Beau's excited voice broke Joey's trance. Beau sat on the ground, holding his left ankle and shouting, "Kill it! Kill it quick!"

Joey wanted to comply, but his legs felt as if he were bogged to his knees in mud. A movement in the grass drew his attention to a long grayish shape slithering away. He threw a large stone and missed. He followed, picking up the same stone for another try, but the snake vanished down a hole at the base of a rat's nest.

He turned back to see about Beau. Alta was already there, fingers racing to unlace Beau's shoe. In a rushed voice she said, "We've got to get it off before the swellin' starts, or you'll have to cut it loose."

Beau was cursing, partly under his breath, partly aloud. He sucked a sharp breath between his teeth as the venom's fire began taking hold. He demanded of Joey, "Did you get him?"

"He went down a hole."

"Damn it, you've got to kill the snake that bites you or you'll die from the poison."

Alta was examining the bite. Joey could see two tiny blood

drops where the fangs had sunk in. "Superstition," she snapped. "Joey, fetch me his skinnin' knife."

Beau gasped in pain. "What you goin' to do?"

"Cut that wound open and let the blood bring out as much of the poison as it will."

She held the blade over the fire, then made a deep slit across the two fang marks. Beau jerked so hard he almost knocked the knife out of her hands. She grabbed his leg. "Damn you, hold still. If you'd been payin' attention you'd have seen that snake in time to step back. You ought to know this is rattlesnake country." She cut two more slits at right angles to the first. The blood flowed freely at first, then slowed.

"The poison's not all out," she said. She considered the wound as if it were some ugly, crawling thing. "You owe me maybe a hundred dollars for this." She leaned down and pressed her lips over the wound, sucking blood and venom, spitting it out and doing it again. Her face twisted in rebuke. "Don't you ever wash your feet?"

Beau was beginning to break out in cold sweat. "If I only had some whiskey . . ."

"Drinkin' whiskey's the worst thing you could do. Snakebite is just an excuse men use for soakin' their guts in alcohol, like they needed an excuse in the first place."

Despite her efforts, Joey could see that Beau's leg was swelling. Alta's eyes reflected concern. "Joey, run back to where you gutted the deer. Bring me the liver."

"What for?"

"They say raw liver helps draw the poison out. Hurry."

Raw liver . . . madstones . . . probably more superstition, he thought, but this was no time to question anything that might help. He imagined he was running through a gauntlet of snakes, that they lurked beneath every shrub, every weed, striking at him as he passed. His heart felt as if it were swelling to burst. But he forced himself onward to the thicket where the doe had fallen. There the liver should be lying amid the offal.

The two wolves had found it first. They were feeding on the leavings when Joey suddenly burst upon them. They looked up in surprise, then retreated a few steps and faced around, growling protectively over their meal. The nearest had the liver in its mouth, fresh blood dripping from its teeth.

Joey picked up a rock and hurled it, hoping the wolf might drop the liver in its flight. It turned and ran but did not let go of its prize. The two animals disappeared in the timber. Joey ran a few steps after them before stopping in helpless disappointment. He turned and examined the intestines that remained, hoping some of the liver might still be there.

It was gone, all of it.

He trotted back to camp, mindful of the possibility of snakes, and told Alta what had happened.

She said, "Well, then, I reckon we've done all we can."

Beau's face was ashen, something like Pa's and Tolley's had been. It glistened with cold sweat.

Joey shivered. "You think he's goin' to die?"

Alta shrugged. "Snakebite ain't to laugh about, but it doesn't kill as often as folks make out. Your cousin's ornery enough to pull through just to spite the snake. If I was the snake, I'd worry that Beau had poisoned *me*."

Joey pulled a piece of burning wood out of the campfire and carried it to the rat's nest beneath which the snake had disappeared. He poked it into the tangle of dead wood and shoved a rock into the mouth of the hole. He backed away as flames began to lick and crackle through the tinder-dry nest. Two rats skittered away in panic.

Alta asked no questions, but Joey volunteered, "Beau said if we killed the snake the bite wouldn't hurt as bad. So I'm cookin' it."

"It's probably too deep in the hole to feel the heat. Anyway, you can't blame the snake much. It was just doin' what comes to it by nature, like a lot of men swill whiskey and fight and misuse their women."

"Is it nature that makes you and Beau hate each other so much? I keep feelin' like you're about to go to war."

Alta studied Beau's face. His eyes were half open but glazing. In mind and spirit he appeared to have drifted somewhere a long way off. "I don't hate him. It's his high-nosed attitude that makes me so damned mad. But I guess he's not much

different from most of the men I've come up against. They
think all a woman is good for is to cook and sew and go to bed
with them." She studied Joey, her eyes softening. "You're too
young to know about that sort of thing."

"I know more than you think." Joey's eyes burned as he considered the possibility that Beau might not live. "He's hard to
get along with sometimes . . . drinks too much when he gets the
chance. He's talked about leavin' me behind, and I've felt like
leavin' him more than once. But he's all the kin I've got."

"He won't be runnin' off and leavin' you now, not with that
leg angried up so. If the poison doesn't kill him he'll be hob-
blin' around lame for a while."

"I don't want him to die. I guess I need him more than I
thought I would."

"I think he needs you more than you need him. In some ways
you're more grown up than he is. At least you don't condemn a
woman without knowin' her side of the story." She touched
Joey's hand. "Nobody's said, exactly, but it's plain that you two
are runnin' from somethin'."

Joey decided it wouldn't hurt to tell her. He saw no reason
she would go blabbing to the law about it, any more than Miller
Dawson would have. He explained about Pa and Reuben, about
Dulcie and Mr. Meacham. He told how he and Beau had killed
Mr. Meacham in self-defense, but the Bastrop sheriff's prejudice against Beau would keep him from believing the way it
really happened.

A tear glistened in the corner of Alta's eye, and she wiped it
away. "I was an orphan too, time I was seven. A fever epidemic
down in Galveston took my mama and daddy. I was passed
around by aunts and uncles that didn't want the burden or
couldn't afford it, so I ran off when I wasn't much older than
you are. It can be a hard, cruel life when you're all alone."

"I'm not plumb alone. I've got Beau."

"That's not much better than bein' by yourself. There's no
tellin' what's liable to become of you."

"Me and Beau, we'll do all right when we get to California . . .
if he lives through this."

She shook her head. "You're totin' around a lot of trouble for a boy your age."

"I reckon I'm big enough to carry it."

She squeezed his hand, and he warmed in a way that he was not used to. She said, "I believe you are."

CHAPTER

13

Joey watched Beau go into a fever and begin talking in a way that might as well have been German for all the sense he could make of it. He lost interest in supper, but Alta fried a piece of venison and made him eat it.

She said, "If you don't put somethin' in your stomach, you'll wind up as sick as he is."

"Beau needs a doctor."

"It's probably two, three days to where one lives. By the time you could get there and back, he'd either be dead or gettin' better anyway." She patted Joey's hand, trying to calm his fear. "Don't fret so. I'm not goin' to let him die."

Lacking anything more effective, she gathered several juicy prickly-pear pads. She split one and bound it over the wound, sticker side up. "I've heard of people usin' them on gunshot wounds. Can't do any harm on a snakebite, and it might even do him some good. Wish we had that doe's liver."

Joey took the rifle and went out hunting for another deer. All he saw were a few elusive wild turkeys and the two wolves, which kept their distance as if they knew he had the gun. He stayed out until dark, then used the flickering campfire to guide him back, empty-handed and discouraged.

Alta hugged him in an attempt to lighten his burden. "You did the best you could."

The hug was not much comfort. "My best wasn't enough."

"Nobody could ask for more. But of course, sometimes they do. They forget we're only human. We can't always live up to other people's notions." She tried a reassuring smile but couldn't bring it off. "I'm talkin' about me, not you."

"Anything you ever did, I know you had a reason for it."

"You ever been hungry, Joey? I mean hungry for days and days, 'til you hurt all over and couldn't walk straight and your gut was tied in a knot?"

Joey had missed some meals since running away from home, but he knew she was talking about something far more extreme. "I guess I ain't."

"There comes a time when you've got no will of your own anymore. You'll do anything they tell you to, just to stop the hunger. And you'll keep on doin' it so the hunger won't come back."

"I understand."

"I doubt that you do, but you're nearer to it than Beau and most of the other men I've come across." She reached out to touch his cheek. "Don't you grow up to be like them. Hang onto your understandin' ways."

"I think Beau would understand if you told him how it was."

"He'd have to hold still and listen. Right now he's holdin' still, but I'm afraid he wouldn't hear anything I told him." She leaned over Beau and felt his face. From her expression Joey knew she did not like what she found. "This cloth I put over his head has dried out," she said. "Run down to the creek and wet it again, would you?"

Joey brought back the cloth, dripping water. She washed sweat from Beau's face and neck, then folded the cloth and laid it across his forehead. She unwrapped the pear pad and found it almost dry. Beau's fever had drawn the moisture from it. She applied the other half of the pad.

Alta said, "You'd just as well go to sleep. I'll keep a watch on Beau."

Joey tried. He wrapped himself in his blanket, then turned one way and the other, trying to find comfort. He could hear Beau mumbling at times. The faint light from the dwindling fire fell upon Alta, sitting at Beau's side, turning the cloth that covered his forehead. After a long while Joey fell into a fitful slumber and aroused a frightening dream of a snake on his bed, striking at him, sinking its fangs into his flesh. He shouted in imagined pain. He felt something shaking him and thought it was the snake.

Alta's voice was soft. "Joey! You're hollerin' in your sleep."

Joey was suddenly wide awake and trembling, his face covered with cold sweat. "A snake had hold of me," he said, ashamed for his involuntary outburst. He cast the blanket aside and raised up to look toward his cousin. "How is he?"

"No worse that I can see, but no better either."

"I'm awake now. I can watch after him a while." He knew it had been two nights since Alta had slept.

"No, I'm not sleepy. I've got to keep that cloth wet 'til his fever breaks." She remained at Beau's side, fighting the sleep that tugged at her eyelids.

Joey fed the fire to prevent its going out. Beau had assured him the wolves presented no danger, but it didn't hurt to be on the safe side. He made sure the rifle lay within arm's length. Alta had removed Beau's trousers. Joey wondered about the propriety but decided proprieties didn't count for much in an emergency. Alta had split Beau's long underwear from the ankle to the thigh. His left leg had swollen far beyond its normal size.

Joey remembered the times he had considered riding away and leaving Beau to fend for himself. He whispered, "Beau, don't you go off now and leave me."

In spite of his best intentions, Joey dozed just as the black sky began to pale in the east. He awoke with a start as a voice growled, "Where the hell are my pants?"

The voice was Beau's. He found Beau staring at him with wide-open eyes. Joey felt a stinging of tears as he realized his cousin was not only alive but in a quarrelsome mood. That was a good omen for recovery.

Alta had remained at Beau's side, though Joey suspected she

had dozed just as he had. Sleepy-eyed, she retorted, "What do you care? You're not goin' out in company."

Beau turned his attention to her. "It's just you after all."

"Who did you think it was?"

"I halfway woke up a couple of times. Thought I saw an angel sittin' where you're at. She looked a little like you, but you haven't got any wings. Guess I was dreamin'."

"I guess you were. Nobody's called me an angel since I was three years old."

Joey said, "She watched over you all night to make sure you didn't die. An angel couldn't have done any better."

"I'm obliged to you," Beau told her, "but I didn't have any intention of dyin'. I've got my cousin to look out for." He raised up to a sitting position and gingerly lifted the blanket from his leg. It remained badly swollen. He removed the prickly-pear poultice, wincing as some of the tiny needle-sharp spines punched into the tips of his fingers. The entry point of the fangs was angry looking and darkly discolored.

He reverted to complaint. "Look where you cut me with that knife. Probably gave me blood poisonin'."

Alta responded in the same kind of voice. "Your blood's been poisoned since you were old enough to crawl. Keep your dirty fingers away from that cut or you'll probably lose your leg." She split another pear pad and applied its wet side to the still weeping wound. She bound it in place with the same strip of cloth she had used before.

Beau's voice softened with worry. "It don't look any too good, does it?"

"Better than I thought it might. Appears to me the swellin' hasn't got any worse the last few hours. But you won't be walkin' on that leg for a while, or ridin' a horse."

Beau gave the spartan camp a critical look. "We can't just stay here."

"Why not? There's water in the creek. That doe will last us a couple of days, and Joey's a good shot. We oughtn't to lack for meat. This road looks like it's still used once in a while. Somebody might come along."

"That's what I'm afraid of."

"You've already proved you can lie to the law and make them believe it. Just tell them we're a family down on our luck. They might even leave us some provisions." She added, "We're a long ways from Bastrop."

Beau turned his gaze to Joey. "You told her?"

"I didn't see no harm in it. I thought she ought to know who she's travelin' with and have a chance to leave if she didn't like it . . . like you wanted to leave Mr. Dawson."

"If you'll remember, Dawson wouldn't let us."

"But we wouldn't stop Alta if she wanted to go, would we?"

Beau gave her a concerned study. "We've got no hold on her. She's free to do whatever she wants to."

Alta nodded. "Just remember you said that, because if you give me any more fuss I'm liable to leave you sittin' here. And I might take Joey with me."

Joey knew he wouldn't go, but he wouldn't say so. Maybe if Beau had to worry about it he would improve his behavior.

Beau attempted to arise but quickly gave up, sweat breaking out on his face again. It was evident he wasn't going anywhere. "Lady, you never saw a man more meek and mild."

Their departure from the outlaw camp had been too sudden to allow much preparation. Supplies were scant beyond blankets and the food Dawson had given them. Tolley had farsightedly put a hatchet in his war bag along with a coffeepot and a skillet, which Beau had found after Tolley's death. Joey used the hatchet to cut firewood. He smoothed out a spot beneath the heavy shade of a live-oak motte.

Alta told Beau, "Joey and me are goin' to carry you over there where you'll be sheltered from the sun. It's liable to be a rough ride, but at least it'll be a short one."

"I'm too heavy for you-all. You're liable to hurt yourselves. I'll make it by myself if I have to walk on all fours."

It was the first time Joey could remember Beau showing real concern for Alta.

She said, "And maybe cripple yourself for life? You just lie there and be still."

Alta gripped the blankets above Beau's head and Joey those

by his feet. Joey strained hard to lift the weight, but his back
and arms were strong. Farm work had accomplished that. He
and Alta had to set Beau down once to rest a moment. Alta let
her end of the blankets slip enough that Beau dropped the last
foot or so to the ground.

"Sorry," she apologized.

"Didn't hurt a bit," Beau said, though Joey knew from his
expression that it had.

He wished they had a tent to keep Beau out of the rain, but
this did not look like a country where it rained often. With a
little luck perhaps they would dodge that problem. By the way
the smaller trees leaned, Joey judged that the prevailing winds
came from the south. He dug a new fire pit just east of the motte
so the smoke would not likely bother Beau. Joey puzzled as he
watched Alta stretch one of Tolley's blankets between two
trees, forming a screen of sorts. She spread her own blankets
just beyond.

"There's times a woman needs privacy," she explained.

Back home, Joey had always thought it would be fun to go
camping, though Pa never seemed to have the time. The nearest
Joey had come to it had been to spend the day down on the
creek, fishing. Now he had the real thing. All in all, he thought,
this was shaping up to be as comfortable a camp as anybody
could ask for under the circumstances. It would be disloyal to
feel glad Beau had gotten himself snakebitten, but inasmuch as
it had happened anyway, Joey intended to make the most of it.

Other people had camped here over the decades since the military had seen fit to lay out the road. Joey found charred remnants of old campfires along the creek, as well as rusty cans,
some pieces of broken harness, and a blackened pocketknife
with both blades broken off. Walking along the bank, he came
upon a long, thin tree limb leaning against a heavy live oak. It
showed signs of having been trimmed neatly. On closer inspection he found a length of rotten string tied to the end of it and a
fish hook at the end of the string. Up from the hook was a piece
of cork that had been a floater. He could only surmise that
someone had been fishing here and had left it, intending to come
back.

The string was so weathered that it broke apart in his hands. The pole was dried out and too brittle for use. But at least he could salvage the hook and the cork. It would be easy enough to whittle a new pole. The problem would be to find something to serve as a string.

He took his discoveries back to camp and showed them to Alta and Beau. "I'll bet I could catch all the fish we would want to eat if I just had a string."

Alta considered it but came up with no answer. Beau, face still flushed with fever, seemed to have trouble concentrating. "The horses," he said finally.

Joey blinked, thinking Beau might have drifted off into delirium again. "Horses?"

"You ever made a horsehair rope?"

"No."

"I've seen people usin' a rig to twist with, but you can do it by hand. There's four horses yonder, and they can all spare some hair out of their tails. Won't take near as much to make a string as to make a rope."

"You mean I'm supposed to cut part of their tails off?"

"Not all from one place. A little here and a little there. And be careful they don't kick the whey out of you."

Joey thought it wise to begin with Taw because his horse would stand still for almost anything short of a dynamite blast. Like the others, Taw was staked on a long rope. Joey walked up to him, talking softly, patting him on the neck, then along the withers, gradually working around to the rump. He opened his pocketknife and ran his fingers carefully through Taw's tail to gauge the horse's reaction. There was none. Joey crimped a small sampling of tail hair between the fingers of his left hand, then cut them with the blade. The horse turned his head to look back at him but otherwise made no move.

Joey repeated the action several times until he had a sizeable wad of hair lying on the ground. He stepped back to see if the results of his work were visible. Unfortunately they were. Joey remembered once when he had had his hair cut in town by a barber who had been drinking all day.

"Sorry, Taw, but they'll grow back."

He repeated the operation on Git Out, who was a little more skittish about it than Taw. Joey was careful to do most of the cutting from underneath where it would not show quite so much. He had about the same results from Alta's mount. He tried with Tolley's, but that horse tried to kick him. Joey decided he had hair enough to make a line that would hold any fish he might catch in this stream.

With shaky hands Beau showed him how to twist and plat so that the strength of the individual strands was multiplied by the combination of many. It was slow work and clumsy at first, though gradually Joey got the hang of it. The line became increasingly neat as it lengthened. Joey considered doing the first couple of feet over, but what would a fish know about neatness?

Alta came at times to watch Joey's work and to feel Beau's forehead, to remove the poultice and examine the wound.

"I believe a little of the color is startin' to go out of it," she said.

"Still throbs and burns like old Billy Hell. But it'd be a lot worse if you hadn't sucked so much of that poison out. I know it couldn't have tasted very good."

"Between the venom and the blood and your dirty leg . . . no, it didn't."

"Could be you saved my leg. Maybe even my life. I don't know how I could ever pay you anything, but I owe you."

"I'll settle for a little kindness."

"I ain't run onto any excess of kindness in my life, so I don't know much about givin' it."

"Watch Joey. You could learn a lot from him."

It took Joey most of the day to complete what he thought was enough string. It was prickly to the touch, for the ends of each hair were like tiny needles, but it felt strong enough to hold a fish. He found a branch about the right length and thickness, hacked it off with Tolley's hatchet, then trimmed it up with his pocketknife. He attached the string, the cork, and the hook.

"Some little pieces of this raw bacon ought to be all right for bait," Alta suggested, holding up a slab from the sack Dawson had given them. She sliced off a portion.

Joey gave Beau and Alta a moment's study before he started down the creek. "Don't you-all be fightin' while I'm gone."

Alta smiled. "It wouldn't be any fun, whippin' a cripple."

"I won't be a cripple for long," Beau said. "Soon as this swellin' goes down . . ."

Joey had a notion that the fight had gone out of Beau. Perhaps that snakebite had done him some good.

The fish were slow to hit the hook, but Reuben had always said making a catch wasn't the most important element in fishing. The main thing was to get away from the demands of the busy world and hold a long, quiet conversation with one's self and the Lord. Joey was not sure the Lord was answering back, but it was soothing to the soul to sit still and contemplate the pleasant countenance of this land, the long hills, the grass-carpeted valley divided by the clear, cool waters of the narrow creek.

He knew it was not so peaceful as it might appear. A hawk circled overhead, watching for some smaller bird or animal to grab in its sharp talons. He glimpsed the two wolves prowling at the base of a distant hill, trying to scare up a rabbit or a fawn or whatever else they might turn into an evening meal. He saw a fish dart to the top and swallow a surface-running bug that had the poor judgment to put itself at risk. Joey's own fishing venture, however much it might calm the trouble in his soul, meant the end for whatever unfortunate swimmer that happened to impale itself upon his hook. Almost everything preyed upon something else that it might live. Each creature followed its own nature.

Viewing the world in that light, he could almost understand what had motivated Dulcie and Mr. Meacham, even if he could not bring himself to forgiveness. He supposed a tendency toward greed was part of human nature, just as the hunt was nature to all the predatory creatures. Most people managed to keep it bottled up, but there would always be a few who let it take control of them. It was those who caused most of the trouble in the world, outside of natural disasters such as flood and fire.

Watching the water course southward, foaming as it broke around large stones near the bank, he again imagined he could see Mr. Meacham floating along with the current of the Colorado, bobbing as the cork bobbed on Joey's improvised fishing line. He shivered and forced his mind to other matters. He tried to imagine what California must be like. Folks said the sun shone there all the time. It seemed to shine most of the time in this part of Texas, too. He wondered if he and Beau could find work there. Surely there must be farms in California.

But would they be like the farm back home? It hurt, remembering how things used to be. He wished none of this had ever happened, that he could turn around and go back.

Time would cure Beau's snakebite. But Joey wondered if it would ever cure his own homesickness.

He wondered then about Alta. Chances were that she would not go with them all the way. The law was not hunting for her. She might stop when they got to Fort Stockton or Fort Davis or El Paso. He could already feel the hurt of saying goodbye to her.

His luck as an angler was not so good as he had hoped, but he carried three catfish back to camp, one apiece for their supper. He doubted that Beau would have much appetite.

Alta knelt beside Beau, wiping his face with a wet cloth. Joey feared that Beau's fever had worsened, but the calm expression in Alta's face reassured him.

"He's improvin'," she said. "The fever's down a lot."

He noticed that she was holding Beau's hand. Probably just trying to make him feel better, he thought. At least it did not appear that they had fought while he was gone. That was a welcome change.

Beau sat up to eat his supper. He even tried to push to his feet, but he quickly surrendered to the pain. Joey thought the leg's swelling might be starting to lessen a little. In any case, though, Beau wouldn't be walking or riding horseback for a while yet. That did not trouble Joey nearly so much as he thought it should. There were still a lot of fish in the creek that had not sampled his bait. Tomorrow he would take the rifle and see if he might stalk another deer.

He was in no hurry to put home even farther behind him. Let California wait. It wasn't going anywhere.

When he returned to camp before sundown the next day, he found Beau standing, leaning on a makeshift crutch hacked and whittled from a forked live oak. He was wearing his trousers, which told Joey that the swelling had receded considerably. Joey was torn between pleasure that his cousin was recovering and anxiety that Beau would be raring to leave this good camp.

"That leg's still too sore for you to get on your horse, ain't it?" he asked hopefully. The bite was in the left leg. The left foot went into the stirrup first and had to support the body's full weight as a rider mounted.

"I tried to walk up to Git Out on this crutch, but he snorted and ran to the end of the rope. He doesn't know what to make of a three-legged man."

Joey hoped Beau could not see how relieved he felt that recovery was not *too* swift.

Beau said, "I suppose he was afraid I was goin' to hit him with this stick. I've never beaten a horse in my life. Or a woman either." He turned back toward Alta. "No matter how bad she might've needed it."

She grinned, then Beau did. Joey said, "I'm glad you-all have decided to get along."

Beau said, "I have to. She's the cook."

Alta fried the fish. Beau's appetite was better than Joey had expected, for he ate all of his. Beau said, "We've been here too long. No tellin' when some lawman may happen along with our descriptions in his pocket."

Alta touched Beau's good leg. "Don't be in a rush. We can't leave 'til you can ride."

Joey put in hastily, "Don't that fish taste fine? West of here we may not find any fit for eatin'."

Beau gave in reluctantly. "We won't be stayin' any longer than we have to."

The distant sound was slow to penetrate Joey's consciousness and even slower to identify itself. He had hooked his second fish when he became fully aware of animal bleating which rose and fell with the breeze. He turned his ear toward it.

Sheep. He had not seen a domesticated animal except the horses and the outlaw-camp dogs since they had put the German communities behind them. But incongruous as it might seem so far from any settlement, this sound was coming from sheep.

Pa had never kept any on the farm. He always said they were more trouble than they were worth for the small amount of wool he might shear and the mutton the older animals might provide when age diminished their fleeces. A couple of the neighbors had owned small flocks, however, and had fought to keep the lambs alive against the variety of predators attracted to them: foxes, coyotes, stray dogs. Sheep seemed prey also to every ill known to man or animal.

Even so, and despite Pa's low opinion of them, Joey had always wished they had a few around the place. He liked to watch neighbors' young lambs run and jump and play.

He carried his fish and the pole back to camp. Beau was standing, leaning on his crutch, eyes squinched as they searched eastward for the source of the sound. Joey's vision was sharper. He picked out the vanguard of the flock. "Yonder they come. There's an awful big bunch of them."

Alta walked up and stood beside Beau. "I see a dog out to one side, and a wagon bringin' up the rear."

Beau grimaced, then accepted the inevitable. "It's too late to break camp, even if I could ride. It don't seem likely that a lawman would be travelin' with a sheep outfit."

Joey said, "Unless it's to guard against outlaws."

"Who'd want to steal a sheep?"

The sheep kept coming, breaking around the camp, some to one side and some to the other, lining up along the bank of the creek. Ewes bleated for lambs that trailed behind them. They all sounded the same to Joey, but evidently the lambs could sort out their mothers' calls, for they were quick to pair up after they stopped at the edge of the water. Lambs eagerly sought the ewes' udders, dropping to their knees to reach the milk. Most of the ewes shunned the faster current, seeking calmer water where it backed up into the flatter portions of the bank. They lowered their heads and drank.

The dog was a collie, its red and white coat rough and unbrushed, leaves and dry grass clinging to the belly hair. Clearly, this was a working dog, not a pet. As Joey walked toward it, it barked a protective challenge and placed itself between him and the nearest sheep.

Joey tried to speak in a reassuring tone. "I'm not fixin' to hurt them. Come here, boy."

The dog approached him cautiously. Joey extended his hand and held still, letting the animal take its time in appraising him. The collie sniffed tentatively at Joey's fingers and found no threat. It began to wag its tail. Then it looked back toward the wagon as if afraid its master might disapprove.

The driver cut through the flock and came directly toward the camp. The wagon was equipped with hoops so it could be covered in event of wet weather, but the tarp hung loosely over the rear bow and down over the bed. Two mules pulled the wagon. A saddled horse walked along behind, bridle reins tied to the steel rod that held the end gate.

Joey could see that the man was not young, for his short beard was gray. So was the thatch of hair that bushed out beneath the brim of a grimy old felt hat that had the lumpy shape of a half-empty feed sack. He drew up on the lines and shouted at the mules. He took a black pipe from his mouth and studied Joey a moment before he shouted, "I say, my lad, you're not fixing to bite my dog, are you?"

"No sir, I wouldn't do nothin' like that," Joey responded before he realized the sheepman was joking.

The man pulled the brake, then climbed down and tied the reins to the rim of a wheel. The mules did not look as if they had enough ambition to run away.

Joey exclaimed, "I never saw so many sheep in one bunch before. Must be ten thousand of them."

The man's words were crisp and clear but spoken with a bit of an accent that Joey found unfamiliar. "Not quite so many, a couple of thousand not including the lambs. I do not count the lambs until they are raised and ready for market. What the four-legged varmints do not kill, the two-legged ones try to steal."

"I been seein' a couple of wolves around here."

"Well, then, I am afraid Old Rustler may not get much sleep tonight. It is his responsibility to herd the band and protect it." The man shoved his hand forward. It was big and rough, a couple of fingers misshapen from old breaks or perhaps arthritis. Joey's hand disappeared within the enveloping grip. "My name is Alister McIntosh."

"Joey Shipman." Joey heard Beau slowly working his way up from behind, awkward on the crutch. "That's my cousin Beau." Too late he realized he had forgotten their agreed-upon story that their name was Smith and that Beau was his father.

"Beau *Smith*," Beau said, giving Joey a look of silent reproach. He offered McIntosh his hand with poorly disguised reluctance. Joey knew he was uneasy about meeting strangers, at least until they got to California. Beau motioned toward Alta, who was walking out from camp. "That's my wife. Name's Alta. Alta Smith."

McIntosh tipped his hat, giving Alta a moment's special attention. He seemed to accept them all at face value. "You folks appear to have a comfortable camp. I shall move my sheep downstream before dark so they will not be a bother."

Alta said, "I don't see anybody with you. Are you movin' these sheep all by yourself?"

"I had a swamper to drive my wagon and do the cooking. Unfortunately he became ill and had to turn back to Kerrville. I've had no chance to hire anyone else." McIntosh looked at Beau's crutch and the foot held up clear of the ground. Beau still wore only a sock because the swelling had not gone down enough for him to put on his shoe. "Did you break a limb?"

"Rattlesnake. Got me between my ankle and my knee."

McIntosh took a long drag on his pipe. "That is one reason most men wear high-topped boots in this country. The first chance you have, you should buy a pair." He surveyed the camp again. "Are you on the move, or are you settling here?"

Beau said, "We'd be a long ways further west if it hadn't been for that snake. I can't ride a horse yet."

Alta gave the wagon a thoughtful study. "Mr. McIntosh, when you get your sheep settled for the night, why don't you come and eat supper with us? For a change, you won't have to do your own cookin'."

Beau's eyes narrowed with objection, but he did not express it aloud.

"That is most kind of you, young lady. I have subsisted mostly on coffee and smoking tobacco since my swamper turned back. I never quite mastered the art of cooking. Do you have meat in camp?"

The venison was about gone, and Joey had been unable to bag another deer. He said, "We got two fish and some turkey."

"I shall butcher a goat. I always keep a few with the sheep to provide fresh meat." McIntosh turned toward the dog and made a circling motion with his arm, then pointed at the sheep that had moved upstream. "Rustler, round them up."

The dog bounded away, going around until he had passed the last sheep, then moving back, barking. The sheep flushed ahead of him like quail. They skirted past the camp, avoiding the people.

McIntosh said to Alta, "You do not appear to have much in the way of cooking vessels. You will find a keg of sourdough and a couple of Dutch ovens in the wagon, along with flour, coffee, whatever you may need. Please feel free to use all you want, because I have gone hungry for three weeks." He untied the horse from behind the wagon and set off behind the dog and the sheep.

Alta said, "Seems like a nice old man."

"Smart one, too," Beau responded without enthusiasm. "Anybody asks about us later on, he'll remember."

In a while McIntosh returned carrying the freshly skinned and dressed carcass of a goat across his saddle. He hung it from the tree limb beside the remnant of the doe.

Joey had reservations. "I don't think I ever ate a goat."

"Always keep an open mind, my lad, and you will be amazed

at the wonders the world can provide." McIntosh rode off cheerfully in the direction of the sheep.

Joey said, "I think I'll go see if he needs any help." He did not wait for permission or denial but set off in a trot.

McIntosh did not herd the sheep together as Joey expected. He allowed them to spread out and nibble at the vegetation. Seeing Joey watching, he rode over to him, removed his black pipe, and pointed the stem of it. He anticipated Joey's question. "It is in the sheep's nature to group together, so they will not stray far. Rustler will bring back any that may display undue independence."

"I don't see how you can handle a big bunch like this, just you and the dog."

"I let the sheep proceed at their own pace and graze as they walk. Rustler and I have only to keep them pointed in the proper direction. Most of the time I follow in the wagon. When necessary, I stop the wagon and use the horse."

"Where are you goin' with this bunch?"

"I have a ranch southwest of Fort Stockton, where mountains and brushy draws provide winter protection. It has been rested all spring and summer. I am in no hurry to reach it so long as I find feed enough along the trail."

"This land don't belong to anybody, so the grass don't cost you nothin'."

McIntosh smiled. "You are a sharp lad. You have already grasped an essential element of the range livestock industry. Never use your own grass until you must, and never buy a new nail if you can straighten a bent one."

The sheep browsed a while, then began lying down. Those on the outer fringe moved in closer to the main body. Joey wondered if they could smell the wolves. Rustler must have, for he paused periodically to look southward as he patroled the flock's perimeter, bringing back a few of adventuresome spirit. The goats remained to themselves but within the larger group of sheep. Joey wondered if they took any notice of the fact that their number had been reduced by one.

McIntosh said, "All appears to be well. Shall we go back to

camp and see what your cousin's wife has prepared for supper?"

Joey was taken aback by reference to Alta as his cousin's wife, though he realized that was a natural consequence of Beau's lie about their identity. He was not sure what a sporting woman was supposed to look like, but evidently Alta did not fit the pattern, judging by McIntosh's easy acceptance of the story.

McIntosh said, "Your cousin indicated you are on your way west. Have you a definite destination, or are you simply prospecting?"

Joey thought it best to be noncommittal. "We don't have our minds set, exactly."

McIntosh puffed thoughtfully on his pipe but said nothing more until they were in camp. Alta had a coffeepot suspended from a steel bar set between two upright rods that had holding rings on their upper ends. Two Dutch ovens sat on a bed of hot coals. She said, "Tonight, Mr. McIntosh, I'll cook you a pot of beans that you can carry with you tomorrow when you leave."

McIntosh took a pot hook from its resting place beside a pile of dry wood and lifted the lid from one of the ovens. Sourdough biscuits were browning inside. He lifted the other lid and found goat meat roasting. His eyes lighted with pleasure. "Excellent, young lady, excellent. I have not had a proper meal since my swamper left, and even he was barely adequate."

Alta was unaccustomed to compliments and seemed a little flustered. "If you-all would like to go wash in the creek, supper's about ready."

Joey guessed later that McIntosh ate nearly half of the supper by himself. When everyone finished, little remained except some coffee. McIntosh rubbed his stomach, which did not seem large enough to have accommodated as much as he ate. "I am sure kings have fared less well than I did tonight. You are a most lucky man, Mr. Smith, to have such a wife as this."

Beau seemed startled. He was not accustomed to the fiction of Alta being married to him though he had made up the story himself. "Even a blind hog finds an acorn now and then."

McIntosh concentrated on the fire and puffed his pipe. "I understand, Mr. Smith, that you are eager to be on the move but cannot ride a horse until your leg improves. Could you ride in a wagon?"

Beau considered. "Climbin' up might be tough, but once I'm there I ought to be all right."

"Then allow me to offer you a proposition. You and your lady could drive the wagon. The lad and I could handle the sheep. I would pay your lady to cook for us and allow a stipend to the lad for his help as well."

Beau hedged. "I don't know . . ."

"Mind you, it would be slow. A band of sheep takes its own good time about grazing its way along. But I am bound for Fort Stockton, which is on your way west. You will lose a great deal of time in any case, so why not lose it riding in a wagon instead of waiting here until you are able to ride a horse?"

Beau was slow to answer, but Joey was not. He exclaimed, "Sounds like a good idea to me."

Alta said, "We'll do it."

McIntosh smiled. "Done!"

Beau finally spoke. "I didn't say we would." He saw he was out-voted. "But I reckon we will."

CHAPTER

14

McIntosh was out of his blankets before daybreak, so the rest of the camp was awakened by his stirring around. With daylight the sheep began to stand up and start moving, grazing hungrily after a night's rest. McIntosh had breakfast, allowing them ample time to take their fill of water from the creek. When he saw that no more were drinking, he spoke quietly to the dog. "Rustler, get them started."

The collie trotted along the edge of the band, barking, feinting at them. The ewes and lambs moved away from him.

Joey marveled. "Does he understand everything you tell him?"

"He knows the routine of the trail, and a dog learns to understand many words if you speak them to him often enough. He never questions an order, and he never complains. I find the company of a good dog preferable to that of many people."

"My stepmother wouldn't let me have a dog, said they were useless. But I never saw a dog help like Rustler."

"I take it you have never herded sheep, lad?"

"No sir. I don't know the first thing about them."

"No matter. The principal requirement is to be smarter than the sheep. And the village idiot is smarter than a sheep."

Alta supported Beau while he carefully and painfully climbed up the wagon wheel and onto the seat. Then Beau reached down for her. It seemed to Joey that Beau held her longer than was necessary to get her safely into place on the wagon seat. She gave Beau a smile that seemed almost as bright as the sunrise.

Joey had not seen her smile much until now.

On horseback, and with the dog's help, McIntosh and Joey put the band across the narrow creek, starting them in a westerly direction. Joey looked back to be sure the wagon was following. Beau and Alta sat close together, Beau holding the lines. The wagon adhered to the trail, but the sheep spread out south of it, browsing on the vegetation as they moved leisurely along.

Joey asked, "How far will we go today?"

"Perhaps three or four miles, sometimes as much as five. I let the sheep set their own pace. Ewes with lambs are not to be rushed."

"What if you don't find water?"

"Sheep can subsist a long time on moisture from the morning dew and from the plants they eat. Their needs in that respect are less than for cattle. On the other hand they require more protection and care. Cattle can endure in the wild. If domestic sheep were deserted and left on their own, in time they would perish."

"Herdin' sheep looks like an important job, then."

"Yes, to any man who understands the business. Many cattlemen hold a much lower opinion, however. If we should encounter any of those gentlemen along the way, you will find that they do not rate us very highly."

Joey felt uneasy. "You mean we might have trouble?"

"If I expected physical harm I would not let you go with me. But I hope you have a high tolerance for insult."

"My stepmother talked awful hard to me sometimes."

"These gentlemen have expressions your stepmother never heard of. Just remember that dollar for dollar invested, these sheep will probably return twice as much revenue as their cattle. Have pity for the poor and misguided."

Joey decided after a time that there was no great challenge in trailing sheep beyond the simple tiresomeness of it. McIntosh allowed them a high degree of freedom in setting their own course, riding around the far edges and turning those that might drift too far north or south. Most of the time he and Joey stayed behind the band, prompting any that might fall back too far. The dog worked much harder than McIntosh or Joey, patroling one outer perimeter, then the other. Now and then a ewe would defy him, standing to face him and stamping a forefoot. She would turn and retreat when he pressed her. Joey thought Rustler seemed to be having a great time, for after each small victory he wagged his tail vigorously and turned toward McIntosh as if asking for praise. Usually, he got it.

McIntosh explained, "Sheep have an instinctive fear of the wolf, and to them the dog represents a wolf. That is why a dog can control a flock better than a man. The old highlanders depended heavily upon their dogs."

"Highlanders? What's that?"

"My father came from the highlands of Scotland to this country when he was not much older than you. My family has been with the sheep for more generations than I know."

"My teacher talked a lot about England, but she didn't say much about Scotland."

"A beautiful country, my father said. But it had many troubles, and hunger among the common people. The old country was like a mother to him, and a man never forgets his mother, but he found this land to be like a good wife. It was a happy marriage."

"You got a wife of your own?"

"I did. She rests in a churchyard back in Kendall County."

"I oughtn't to've asked you."

"The time for mourning is long since past. The memories give me comfort on a dark night, and I take pleasure in watching other couples like your cousin and his wife. I hope they have a strong marriage."

Joey was careful in his answer. "They've had their differences."

"I noticed last night that they did not share their blankets. I trust that any problem they have will be temporary."

Joey suspected that Alta would go her own way when they reached Fort Stockton. "I imagine it will."

Toward midday the flock stopped moving. McIntosh said, "They are used to a noontime rest through the worst of the day's heat." Many of the sheep found shade beneath the scattered trees. The rest formed small circles and hid their heads in the shadows of each other's bodies.

Sitting so close to one another on the wagon seat must have had a healing effect upon the relationship between Beau and Alta. Joey noticed when they stopped to make evening camp that Alta was very solicitous of Beau as he climbed down the wagon wheel, leaning over and maintaining a strong grip on his left arm to keep him steady until he was on the ground and had the crutch tucked snugly beneath his arm. Beau reciprocated by holding her tightly as she followed him. Beau hobbled to a shallow blackened pit where someone had had a campfire in the not-too-distant past.

"I'll dig this out a little deeper for you," he told her.

Alta gently vetoed his offer. "How could you use a shovel when you can't put but one foot on the ground? You'd just aggravate that leg and be longer in gettin' well." She brought a three-legged stool from the wagon and set it down. "Now, you sit there and be still. Won't take me any time to set up camp."

She could have spoken harshly and made it an order, but her voice was soft, so that it sounded like a polite request.

Joey fetched her several armloads of dry wood, enough to cook both supper and breakfast. He lifted down the Dutch ovens and the steel rods from which she would suspend the coffeepot. Then he stood beside Beau, watching as Alta built a fire in the shallow pit. "You're treatin' her better. Maybe you've decided she couldn't help what she did in San Antonio."

"I reckon her reasons were better than mine were for spendin' half my life drunk."

"You've been sober for a long time now."

"I ain't had any choice. I was afraid if I got drunk in that outlaw camp I might not live long enough to sober up again. Since then, I ain't even seen a bottle." He held out his hand to see if it might shake. It did not. "There was a time I thought it'd kill me to go a week without a drink, but I ain't died yet."

"Not even a rattlesnake was able to kill you."

"Sheriff Gardner could still do it, him and his rope. I just wish these sheep would move along faster."

"I like it here with Mr. McIntosh and his dog and the sheep. Reminds me of the good days back home with Pa and Reuben."

"By the time we get to Fort Stockton my leg ought to be well enough to where I can ride again. Then we'll go our own way."

"What if Alta don't go with us?"

Sadness came into Beau's eyes as he studied the woman kneading dough to make bread. "I couldn't wait to get shed of her at first. Now I've got used to her bein' around."

"Then ask her to stay with us."

"And be on the run like we are? That wouldn't be fair to her. Wouldn't be fair to any woman."

"In a way she's on the run herself from all the bad stuff that's behind her."

Beau had no reply. He kept staring at Alta.

McIntosh came to camp after seeing that the band was scattered enough to graze but not enough for any of the sheep to become lost. He filled and lighted his pipe, then glanced around with contentment. "There is a lot to be said for the tranquility of the solitary life, but it is a blessing at times to have company to share the road. Are you enjoying the trip, lad?"

"Yes sir." It felt good to be doing something constructive, something of worth.

"Do you like to read, Joey?"

"I do. Ain't had any chance lately, though."

"You have a chance now. If you'll look in the wagon, up near the seat, you'll find a box of books I am carrying to the ranch. There are none that will do you harm, and they may do you some good. Reading fires the imagination and broadens the mind."

Joey climbed up and sought out the box. McIntosh said, "Have you read *Tom Sawyer*?"

"I don't think I even heard of it."

"It tells of a lad about your age, the troubles he gets himself into and the ways he confronts them. I would not advise you to emulate him, but you could learn from his mistakes."

Joey was not sure what *emulate* meant, though he did not want to reveal his ignorance by asking. He found the book and slouched on the wagon seat, flipping through it to see how many pictures it had, then starting to read about Aunt Polly calling for Tom. He became so absorbed that Alta's first summons to supper did not penetrate his consciousness. McIntosh had to walk over and shake his leg to bring him out of the spell Tom Sawyer had cast over him.

McIntosh said, "Books nourish the soul, but you need nourishment for the body as well. One beauty about books is that when the world calls you away, everything remains suspended in place until you return. Tom will be waiting for you, right where you left him."

Joey rushed his supper so he could read more of the book before darkness forced him to quit. He remembered studying a little about the Mississippi River. From what the teacher had said, and this book, it must be at least as wide as the Llano, and maybe even the Brazos.

When Joey saw the horsemen, his first thought was of sheriffs and rangers. His heart tripped a bit faster. He looked toward the wagon on the beaten trail two or three hundred yards north of the sheep. Beau did not have time to hide, and his game leg would not allow him to run even if the brush had been dense enough to conceal him.

McIntosh had been riding south of the band, where some of the sheep were trying to drift off into a brushy draw, responding to the strong attraction of grass and weeds made lush by runoff from some recent rain. He circled back around, his horse moving in a brisk trot. He appeared as eager as if he had just been invited to a party. "Let us go and meet our company, Joey.

I believe I recognize a cattleman whose acquaintance I have made before."

Maybe they weren't sheriffs or rangers after all. Joey's relief lasted only until he recalled what McIntosh had said about cattlemen sometimes making sheepmen decidedly unwelcome. Some party! But McIntosh showed no concern, so Joey rode alongside him, steeling himself for whatever verbal abuse might come.

The riders, obviously cowboys, had stopped at the wagon. Beau and Alta had halted the mules but remained on the wagon seat, silently waiting for McIntosh.

Joey quickly picked the leader of the group, broad-shouldered, about McIntosh's age, heavy-browed, and wearing a dirty-gray moustache almost as large as Miller Dawson's. He greeted McIntosh in a deep bass voice. "Howdy, Scotchman. I thought this looked like your outfit."

"You're an observant man, Tol Evers. It is an unusual cattleman who can tell one sheep outfit from another."

"Your sheep smell the same as everybody else's. But I thought I recognized that mangy dog of yours from the last time you passed this way. I hope you're just travelin' through, not figurin' on stoppin' a while and sheepin' off my grass."

"I would not do such a thing to a man who has offered me so many kindnesses in the past." McIntosh's voice carried a tinge of good-natured sarcasm.

"The kindest thing I could do for me and you both would be to run all them sheep off of a cliff. But I ain't got a cliff. Best I can offer is a fair-sized ditch. They'd probably just break a leg or two. Wouldn't hardly be worth the sweat."

"Then I suppose we are each doomed to continue in our misguided ways, me with my sheep and you with your cattle."

"Looks like."

Joey sensed that beneath the bantering lay a mutual respect, even if the two men were adversaries on the subject of sheep.

McIntosh said, "You should put aside your prejudice and buy some sheep. They would fare better than cattle on this stingy type of range. You would find that they are certified mortgage lifters."

"I'm not a prideful man, but I have more pride than that." The rancher turned to one of the cowboys. "Look under that wagon bed. See if maybe he's got a broken wheel tied there amongst his trappins."

That took McIntosh by surprise. "Now, by the eternal, why would any reasonable man be carrying a broken wheel when he has four good ones?"

"Why would any reasonable man want to saddle himself down with a bunch of stinkin' sheep?"

The cowboy reported that he found no such wheel. The rancher told McIntosh, "There was a sheepman came through here a while back and stopped at one of my best waterin's. Had a broken wheel and said he had sent to San Angelo for a new one. A week later he was still there. We found out he had a good wheel hidden under a pile of wood. He was carryin' a broken wheel to put on whenever he found a place he wanted to camp."

"An ingenious man. I must get acquainted with him sometime. Or did you kill him?"

"I don't go around killin' human bein's, or even sheepmen. We just gave him a quick escort onto the Bar Seven and warned Old Man Carrington about the feller's tricks. He hates sheep a lot worse than I do."

"I have made Mr. Carrington's acquaintance."

"He eats barbed wire for breakfast and washes it down with lye water. I'd tell you to go way around and avoid his place, but you'd stay that much longer on mine. So you'll just have to take your chances with him."

"He has no right to stop anyone from using the trail."

"Your wagon is on the trail, but your sheep ain't." The rancher began turning his horse away. "Good luck to you, Scotchman."

"I don't suppose you would know where I might find a broken wheel?"

The rancher laughed and rode away, his cowboys spread out on either side of him. McIntosh watched them, then discovered that his pipe had burned out. He refilled it and struck a match on the horn of his saddle. "Not a bad sort, that Evers, but too stubborn to recognize an opportunity that fairly pounds on his door." He drew on the pipe until the tobacco caught. "You'll see the day, lad, when there'll be sheep all over western Texas. The climate fits them well, and economics favors them too. Pride may hold the line for a while, but economics always triumphs in the end."

Joey had noticed that each day they traveled west the land took on more aspects of a desert, vegetation increasingly sparse and much of it prickly. Across the hill country, live oak had dominated for a long time, slowly giving way to smaller and shorter cedar trees, or juniper. Now cedar gave way to grease-wood and occasional stands of mesquite in the draws where water collected when it rained. Joey had not known mesquite before. Most of the trees were much smaller than live oaks, though now and again he came across a huge old mesquite that had survived drought and prairie fires and had grown to be a foot or more in diameter.

"This has been a good year for the bean crop," McIntosh observed. The tree had thin, lacy leaves that yielded a spotty shade, but it bore an abundance of long bean pods that were drying and browning now in summer's heat. "I have seen lambs fatten on them in the fall. Horses like them, but they can be dangerous if they have lain on the ground and molded."

"I suppose every part of the country has somethin' good about it."

"In this western country you have to search harder to find it, but it is there. The sheep by its nature is a dry-weather animal. It fares better here than in the eastern part of the state where rainfall makes the grass grow rank and tall and where all manner of parasites thrive. Out here most parasites dry up and blow away." He looked across the flock, and alarm widened his eyes. "Except the coyote."

McIntosh drew a saddle gun from a scabbard beneath his leg. "Stay here, lad." He pulled away to the south. There, beyond the edge of the flock, Joey saw a coyote slinking along watching the sheep. Rustler was on the other side, near the wagon, or the coyote would never have been allowed so close.

McIntosh set his horse into a run, the rifle at his shoulder. He fired, and the bullet kicked up dirt two feet from the coyote. The animal bounded away, its bushy tail tucked in tightly. McIntosh pursued it relentlessly, firing repeatedly even though his chance of hitting it from a running horse was akin to his chance of being struck by lightning. He was still riding hard and firing when he vanished over the hill. Joey could hear more shots in the distance.

McIntosh returned after perhaps half an hour, his horse lathered with sweat but his face aglow with satisfaction. "Finally got the bugger. It will kill no sheep of mine."

"Is the coyote really that bad?"

"When you've found as many of your flock dead as I have, when you've seen a lamb half eaten but still alive, stepping on its own entrails as they drag along the ground, you'll have no love for the coyote."

Not only the vegetation had changed, but the face of the land as well. No longer did Joey ride among high round-top limestone hills as in the Llano River country. Now the land was flat or sloped gently westward toward the Pecos River. The hills were mostly long and gray and stony-sided with broad, flat mesa tops. Dry yucca stalks suggested Indian lances on the rough hillsides. Clumps of prickly pear protruded through the short, thin, summer-brown grass. Small cactus plants with domed tops lay in ambush, waiting for the unwary to step on them and risk crippling themselves on barbs as ungiving as steel blades. In almost every way this resembled the deserts Joey had read about in school except for the lack of sand dunes. McIntosh assured him there were plenty of those too, farther north and west.

Once when McIntosh was on the far side of the band, Joey noticed something odd about the rocks through which Taw was gingerly picking his way. Dismounting, he dislodged one from its resting place in the dried earth. Imbedded in it were what appeared to be small seashells like his teacher had brought back once from a trip to the Galveston seaside. He found snail shells as well, and an imprint of a fish skeleton. They seemed grossly out of place in this desert environment. He stuck the rock in his pocket.

In camp that evening he showed it to McIntosh. "Looks to me like there was a time when fish lived on dry land. Or else this country got covered up in Noah's flood."

Beau snorted. "At the time of Noah's flood it probably didn't rain a quarter of an inch here. Hasn't rained much since, either."

The sheepman studied the rock but a moment. "Imagine if you will, lad, the look of this region a million years ago. All this land was at the bottom of an immense sea. Gradually it was lifted up out of the water, and the sea retreated back to the Gulf of Mexico. But it left pockets that evaporated to give us salt beds and heavy deposits of gypsum. You will find the history of the earth written in these stones."

McIntosh left to take a last look at the sheep as they bedded down for the night. Beau watched McIntosh riding away. "Books are all right if you're careful which ones you read. But some of them'll fill your head with crazy notions like he's got."

The trail they had followed combined with other trails more heavily used, and the McIntosh outfit began encountering occasional travelers bound either east or west. Unable to escape, Beau would pull his hat brim down low over his eyes, and if anyone asked, Alta would say their name was Smith. Most people did not ask. Too many questions were considered impolite in this western country, and occasionally even dangerous.

They watered the sheep at a place McIntosh called China Pond. Beyond, Joey could see a broad, flat-topped mountain and what appeared to be a scallop cut out of its center.

"That," McIntosh said, "is Castle Gap. It is the gateway to the Pecos River. Gold hunters passed through it on their way to California almost forty years ago. The Butterfield stage used it, and many a westbound wagon train. Past it lies Horsehead Crossing on the Pecos."

"Is that where we take the flock over?"

"No, it is usually too deep and swift there for sheep. The weight of their wet wool would drag them under. We will follow the river up to the grand falls. There is a place where the water is usually shallow enough for sheep to wade across."

"That's a lot of extra miles, seems like."

"Time means but little to a sheep."

Next morning McIntosh and Joey rode away after breakfast to catch up to the flock, already off the bed ground at sunup and drifting westward. The stockman looked back toward the wagon, where Alta was helping Beau climb up onto the seat. "Your cousin and his wife are still not sharing blankets like most married couples."

"Beau's leg is givin' him a right smart of trouble yet." Joey felt guilty about perpetuating all this deception. The sheepman had been so generous to them that it seemed unfair. Joey had felt safe enough in telling the truth to Miller Dawson, for Dawson himself was on the dodge. McIntosh was unlikely to betray them to the authorities, but he was so scrupulously honest that he would probably experience remorse over harboring fugitives. All things considered, it was better to spare him that.

Honesty was not always the best policy.

The approach to the Pecos from Castle Gap was down a long desolate slope where grass was scarce and greasewood or tarbush plentiful. Joey had noticed that sheep did not eat greasewood, though they browsed on other shrubs and the tough weeds that pushed up through the hard ground. The goats ate almost anything that held still long enough for them to nip at it.

McIntosh worked hard to keep the band hazed away from a scattering of alkali waterholes. Skeletons of cattle bleached in the sun, mute testimony to the deadliness of these inviting pools.

McIntosh said, "A man named Charles Goodnight brought one of the first herds of cattle through this way. He called the Pecos River the grave of a cowman's hopes."

Joey could understand why. This looked like the dreary kind of place where a sick animal might instinctively go to die.

He rode with McIntosh ahead of the flock to find a spot where the edge water was calm enough for the sheep to drink. Sight of the river reminded Joey that he was thirsty. He stepped down to allow Taw to take the water first. The horse dipped its nose three times before it reluctantly decided to drink. Joey walked a couple of paces upstream and dropped to his stomach, cupping his hand to catch the current. The first sip made him raise up, sputtering. This was the worst water he had ever sampled.

McIntosh chuckled. "Not quite like new wine, is it, lad?"

"Not like anything I ever drank before."

"It grows on you after you have lived here a while and have eaten your peck of alkali. One needs to buy but little medicine when he lives on the Pecos. It is already in the water."

The band spread out in a wide arc. One lamb ventured too far and was caught up in the current. On command from McIntosh, Rustler plunged in after it, grabbing its throat wool in his teeth and fighting his way back to the bank. The lamb scrambled out, bleating for its mother, more frightened of the dog than of the water.

Joey saw deep wagon ruts where the trail dropped down a sloping bank on the east side and others where it came out on the opposite side. He could understand how horses and cattle might swim it. The river was not particularly wide, though its current was swift. But it would be a challenge for sheep.

Once the ewes and lambs had taken their fill, McIntosh and Joey pushed them northward, moving them back away from the river far enough that its sometimes steep banks were not a hazard. Joey had considered the country they had passed in the last few days to be dry and desolate, but this along the Pecos was more so. Grass was thin compared even to the drier portions of the hill country. The sheep seemed to find enough weeds and low shrubs to feed upon, however.

To the east he could see the long blue mountain and the scallop marking the pass through which they had come. To the west, across the river, he saw open terrain that seemed almost flat at first glance, though on closer study he perceived that the land rolled gently with a gradual climb toward the west. More blue hills lay in the distance, topped by long mesas. It seemed an unlikely place for people to live. McIntosh had said thousands had passed through here on their way to somewhere else.

Joey could imagine that the challenging nature of the land made most of them want to hurry.

He contrasted it to the farm he had left behind, and homesickness swept over him anew. Every day was carrying him farther away from what he had known and loved.

"I hope your ranch is better than this," he told McIntosh.

"It is. But do not judge this land too harshly. The good Lord placed it here for a purpose."

"It's hard to see what. Makes me wish I was back home, with things like they used to be."

"Perhaps one purpose is to make you re-examine the reason you left that home. I suspect you have not chosen to tell me all of it."

"I've told you that my mother died, and Pa too."

"Yes, and you have also mentioned a stepmother. I take it that you are running away from her."

"You would too, if she was yours."

"And what of Beau? Is he really your cousin?"

"Yes sir. Second cousin, anyway."

"But the young lady . . . I do not believe she is really his wife."

Joey felt warmth rising into his face. "No sir, that just seemed like the best thing to say."

McIntosh waited for more. When Joey did not volunteer it, the sheepman said, "I am not given to judging others, and I do not mean to pry into business that is none of my own. But any time you feel the need to unburden yourself, I will offer a sympathetic ear."

CHAPTER

15

McIntosh warned Joey not to expect the grand falls to be as grand as their name implied. "When you live in a land where water is scarce, a creek becomes a river and a small drop in the riverbed is called a fall."

Joey had been watching a dark cloud to the west and north-west, wondering if it meant rain. This thirsty land could make good use of whatever moisture it might receive. But the prospect brought no cheer to McIntosh. He said, "I would hope we could cross the river before it rains."

The precipitation, when it came, was little more than a dust-settling shower, though it was enough to make the sheep stop moving and huddle up. McIntosh said, "It looks as if rain is heavier to the north and west. Stay with the sheep while I ride ahead and survey the crossing."

Joey rode to the nearby bank and saw for himself that the river level had risen. Muddy runoff water from the rangelands had turned the Pecos brown. Dead wood, bits of old vegetation and other debris floated on top. Sheep ventured to the edge and sniffed at the moving current but refused to drink.

They drank instead from rainwater collected in a hundred small potholes.

McIntosh returned disappointed. "The river is up a couple of feet at the crossing. We cannot wade the band over until the water goes down."

Joey shrugged. "We weren't in a hurry anyway, were we?"

"I encountered one of Carrington's cowboys. As soon as he recognized me he changed his course and struck a beeline for the ranch headquarters."

"I didn't think you were afraid of Carrington."

"No, but he is a most unpleasant old man. I would have liked to avoid any confrontation with him."

"That other rancher, Mr. Evers, didn't seem bad. Long as they don't do anything more than cuss you a little . . ."

"Carrington claims this side of the river as his own. I doubt that he has ever paid the state a nickel for its use, but I never enjoy arguing with an angry and unreasonable man, even when I know I am right."

The usually talkative sheepman rode along in silence, much of the time watching toward the east. Joey knew he wished to move faster, but it would be of no use if they could not cross the river right away.

They reached the place where McIntosh said the water was usually shallow enough for sheep to wade. Flotsam deposited along the bank showed that the river had dropped a foot from the highest point of its rise, but it was still too deep and too swift to risk putting the flock into it.

Joey said, "Too bad nobody's built a bridge."

"No one has seen a profit in it yet. Most of civilization's great advancements have resulted from the search for a profit. So have some of its greatest disasters."

Joey followed McIntosh to the wagon, where the sheepman soberly told Alta that she may as well build a fire and get the noon meal started. It would be hours—possibly even the next day—before it would be safe to put the sheep into the water. Beau climbed down from the wagon first. He moved without the crutch, though he still walked carefully and with a pronounced limp. He reached up to help Alta.

A warm smile passed between them. Joey could not shake off a nagging feeling of jealousy, though he knew Alta was too old for him. He could see that the nurse-and-patient relationship had overcome the initial antagonism between the two. She had developed a strong interest in Beau, which kept it in the family, sort of. Beau's luck seemed to be changing for the better since the snakebite, Joey thought. Perhaps Alta would not be leaving them when they reached Fort Stockton. And maybe Beau would not be getting drunk.

Joey saw the horsemen as he returned to the Dutch oven for a third sourdough biscuit to wipe up thick molasses he had poured into his tin plate. His appetite vanished, apprehension taking its place. He let the plate tip downward and the biscuit tumble over its edge onto the muddy ground as he counted the horses. "We got company comin', Mr. McIntosh."

"I see them. Just go on with your meal and try to look as innocent as a newborn. The last thing we want is to let Carrington see fear. The man's darker nature feeds on it."

Beau limped to the wagon and fetched down his rifle.

McIntosh said, "Keep it in hand, but make no threatening move with it. We will offer Carrington no excuse for violence."

Beau stepped in front of Alta, shielding her. He said, "Joey, get over here. If they start anything I want you and Alta to be back of me where I can take care of you."

Joey was surprised by Beau's protective attitude toward him. Up to now he had seen little such inclination. "They ain't goin' to hurt me."

"Damn it, do what I tell you." Beau's voice softened. "I ain't got enough cousins that I want to lose one."

Rustler trotted forward to intercept the visitors, barking a challenge and making some of their horses skittish. A cowboy spurred toward Rustler. Joey feared he might shoot the dog, but the rider tried instead to whip him with a doubled rope. Rustler retreated to one side but kept barking.

Joey had no difficulty in deciding which man was Carrington. The rancher rode a full length out in front, a tall, skinny, stoop-shouldered old man with a long white beard that would reach halfway down to his belt buckle if the strong north wind were not tugging it sideways. His bushy white eyebrows reminded Joey of piled-up snow about to slide off the edge of a roof. Beneath those brows two dark gray eyes burned as fiercely as a hawk's.

Joey counted seven cowboys, four on one side of Carrington, three on the other. Each carried a pistol, either in a holster, a belt, or the pocket in a pair of leather chaps.

"McIntosh," Carrington shouted, "what the hell are you doin' here? Didn't I give you warnin' enough the last time?"

McIntosh appeared as calm as if he were in church, though Joey suspected it took a lot of inner strength to cover up his apprehension. "You did, Mr. Carrington, and I remind you of what I told you then. I am following the river. The river belongs to everyone and to no one."

"The river, maybe, but not the land to the side of it. This land is mine."

"By what right, sir? Do you have title?"

"I got the title from the Comanches. It was theirs, and I ran them off, so now it's mine."

"The army and the rangers were the ones who subdued the Comanches. But no matter who did it, if you do not have title duly registered at the county courthouse, you have no right to prevent a traveler from using a recognized trail. Tens of thousands of cattle have been driven up this side of the river, across this very land."

"Cattle yes, but not them woolly locusts that foul everything they touch and grub my grass plumb down to the roots."

"If you will examine our back trail, sir, you will see that these sheep have grubbed up nothing. We have kept them spread out enough to avoid that. As for grass, there was precious little of it in the first place."

"And even less of it now. I doubt that my cows will go down to the river to drink because they'll smell where your damned woollies have been."

"That is an old wives' tale, long since discredited."

"My old wife still believes it, and so do I. Now, McIntosh, I've come to see that you put them sheep across the river."

"I plan to do that, but I have to wait until the water goes

down. You can see for yourself that it is too high. It would
drown a lot of my flock."

"And good riddance that would be. Put them across, now!"

"I cannot."

"Then we will."

"I'll sue you for every sheep that drowns."

Carrington gave him a mirthless grin. "In this county? There
ain't a jury in a hundred miles that'd give you a Mexican peso
for the whole damned bunch." He turned to the cowboys on his
left. "You know what we came to do. Let's be movin' these
sheep."

The cowboys charged in among the band, shouting, slapping
coiled ropes against their legs. The nearest sheep broke away
from them, pushing into the interior of the grazing flock. Some
of the cowboys rode around the sides, yelling, trying to put the
sheep into a run. The outer sheep ran, but not in the direction of
the river. They pushed toward the center. Alarm rippled across
the flock like wind rippling the surface of a lake.

Old Carrington cursed and drew his pistol. Joey gasped,
thinking he was about to start shooting sheep. He turned fear-
fully toward McIntosh. Whatever emotions the sheepman
might be feeling remained hidden from his face. He stood with
arms folded defiantly, not resisting but not pleading, either.

Alta moved closer to Beau. He put a protective arm around
her and motioned to Joey. "Stay back of me. They'll have to
ride over me to get to you two."

Joey obeyed, but he doubted that the cowboys meant the
people any harm. The animals were their target.

Carrington triggered his pistol at the sky and spurred his
horse into the sheep, trying to make them run. The cowboys
took his action as a cue and began firing into the air.

Joey surmised that their intention was to stampede the sheep,
to run them into the river so fast that momentum and pressure
from behind would push them across before they could slow
down. But the swift current was sure to carry many away. Once
their wool became soaked, its weight would drag them under.

Joey exclaimed, "Mr. McIntosh, they'll drown half of your
flock."

McIntosh still appeared calmer than he had any right to be under the circumstances. "Perhaps, perhaps not. Cowboys know cattle. They do not know sheep."

His meaning soon became clear. The sheep did not stampede, as cattle might, and plunge headlong into whatever hazard lay in front of them. Instead, their panic carried them into a compact mass, all trying to reach the relative safety of its center. The more the cowboys shouted and fired their weapons, the tighter and more immovable the mass became.

The horsemen kept trying for what Joey thought must have been half an hour, but they made no progress. Wherever they pressed against the outer rim of the band, the sheep there simply circled, trying to move out of their way.

Carrington shouted and cursed and shook his fist, but nothing changed. The flock was wound up tighter than the spring in a clock. At length the old rancher called his men together. They sat on their horses, Carrington in the center of the gathering. He cursed and they argued. Joey saw much waving of hands and heard a lot of loud talk, most of the words undecipherable at the distance.

Carrington broke away and rode toward the wagon, his face so red that Joey half expected him to go into some kind of spasm. Beau raised the rifle, which he had held at arm's length, but the old man ignored it if he saw it at all. His wrath was focused on the unmoving McIntosh. The cowboys trailed at a respectful distance, having suffered a brutal chastisement for their ineffectiveness.

"What's the matter with these stupid sheep, McIntosh?" the old man raged. "If they had any sense they'd all be on the other side of the river by now or drowned and gone to hell, and you with them."

A slight smile lifted the gray ends of McIntosh's moustache. "You stated it correctly. They are stupid. You boogered them. When you booger a sheep it loses what little sense it ever had."

Carrington grumbled, "Only thing dumber than a sheep is the man that owns it. The minute the water goes down, you put them woollies across the river."

"That I shall."

"And I don't want to see you here ever again."

"Ah, but you will. I have not finished stocking my ranch. I intend to come this way with another band next spring."

If a stare could kill, Joey thought, McIntosh would fall dead on the spot. Carrington turned his horse and rode eastward, muttering to himself. His men followed, careful not to crowd him.

McIntosh abandoned his show of stoicism and revealed the anxiety he had kept tightly corked. "We have to go in there and scatter them or we will have a lot of smothered sheep. I am afraid we have lost some lambs already."

It took a while to break up the tightly knotted band. As McIntosh had feared, several grown ewes and twenty or so lambs lay dead, suffocated in their massing together. The rest of the sheep got over their scare and spread out looking for browse, their memories mercifully short.

McIntosh accepted his loss philosophically. "A sheep is born looking for a place to die. We would have lost far more had Carrington been able to drive them into the river."

"Looks to me like he owes you for these sheep."

"I will settle with Mr. Carrington in my own way and my own good time. Land here is cheap because no one wants it badly enough to pay for it. I intend to buy this strip from the state and make him pay me or discontinue his use of it. The law will have no choice but to support me."

Joey suspected the lease price would not be cheap.

One of the smothered ewes was fat. McIntosh said she had probably lost her lamb weeks ago, so the energy that would have been required to produce milk had gone to her own flesh instead. "She will provide meat enough to feed us the rest of the way to Fort Stockton."

That evening Joey noticed that Alta kept watching the east as if she thought Carrington and his cowboys might return. She remained close to Beau.

McIntosh sought to reassure her. "Carrington has suffered all the indignity he can tolerate for now. We'll not see him again, not this time."

Joey suspected it was not fear that made Alta stay so near to Beau. She smiled too much to be frightened. The two kept touching one another at every opportunity that arose and at some they contrived.

In the middle of the night Joey awoke to the sound of someone moving around. Beau rolled up his blankets and hobbled off to the far side of the wagon where Alta slept. He did not come back.

Joey no longer worried that she would be leaving them at Fort Stockton.

The Pecos River at that point meandered in a generally southeasterly direction. From where the sheep forded, Fort Stockton lay almost due south on a trail worn deeply by years of wagon traffic. The course crossed an irrigation canal that diverted some of the river's flow to nearby Mexican farms. McIntosh watered the flock at a large spring which poured forth what Joey considered a tremendous body of water despite the desert terrain's dry nature.

McIntosh said Fort Stockton was home to possibly a thousand people, a substantial number for a difficult land which demanded a hard and continuous struggle to produce even a modest living. The town owed its original existence to the huge Comanche Springs and the creek to which they gave birth, an oasis in a broad expanse of greasewood and mesquite and cactus, distant blue mountains and tabletop mesas edged by broken rimrock.

McIntosh explained, "Nobody knows how much water flows out of the ground, water sweet as a man ever tasted. Indians have come here since yon mountains were but anthills. All the old trails passed this way. The army built the fort to intercept the hostiles that were accustomed to using the springs.

"There are not many towns in this part of Texas, and those few exist for some good reason. The land would not support them if they had sprung up willy-nilly as in the East."

Joey was torn. On the one hand it was good to see a town again after so many weeks. On the other, he saw a strong chance someone might recognize him and Beau if word had reached this far west. He decided to avoid the settlement if possible.

McIntosh made camp on the creek east of the springs, where grass was far better than on most of the land they had traversed in the last hundred and fifty miles. Regret was in his eyes as he ate the supper Alta had prepared. "I suppose you folks will want to continue your journey."

Beau said solemnly, "We need to move on."

"I can find help here to take the sheep on down to my ranch, but I shall miss this lady's good cooking." He turned to Joey. "And I shall miss you too, lad. With your patience and your diligence you could become a real sheepman."

"I wouldn't mind that at all." Joey had taken a liking to the flock. He supposed part of the reason was their dependence. They made him feel wanted, necessary. If ever he were able to return to the farm, he would get him some sheep.

McIntosh said, "Were you to stay with me, Joey, I would give you sheep in return for your help. By the time you are grown you could have a flock of your own."

Temptation exerted a strong tug. Joey looked toward Beau and Alta. Beau shook his head, and Joey knew he was right. Though they had come far from Bastrop, it was not yet far enough. Sooner or later someone was likely to come looking for them. Huge though this Pecos River country was, the sparseness of its population meant that no one was likely to go unnoticed for long unless he hid out and became a hermit. There was no crowd in which you could lose yourself.

Joey said, "Beau's got his plans, and he's the only kin I know."

"At least I shall see that you are well provisioned. It is a long way to Fort Davis, and even farther from there to El Paso."

After supper McIntosh prepared to ride to town, saying he planned to inquire about hiring help. "Beau, if you will come to the Gray Mule after a while, I shall be glad to buy you a drink."

Joey and Alta both looked apprehensively at Beau. He caught the worry in their eyes. "Well, maybe just a beer."

A number of townspeople came out to look at the band and

indulge their curiosity. Sheep had not yet become common-place west of the Pecos. Fort Stockton was still considered cattle country.

At dusk Joey became conscious of a lone rider approaching from the direction of the fort. He assumed McIntosh was returning, until he recognized the horse.

"Beau," he said in a loud whisper, as if he feared somebody might hear him in town, "don't that look like Miller Dawson?"

"Damned if it don't. How'd he get here ahead of us?"

"These sheep don't move very fast."

Alta shrank back toward the wagon. "I hoped we'd never see him again. His kind bring nothin' but bad luck."

Dawson reined up short of camp and surveyed it cautiously. Remaining in the saddle, ready to spur away in an instant, the outlaw asked, "Anybody else here?"

Joey walked out to greet him. "Nobody but us. Mr. McIntosh went to town."

Dawson dismounted and gripped Joey's shoulder, shaking it hard. "It's good to see you, young'un. I wondered what became of you-all 'til I heard talk about this bunch of sheep. By description I figured out you was with it." He shook hands with Beau and turned back to Joey. "I'm afraid you've come down in the world, playin' shepherd to woollies."

"Ain't nothin' wrong with herdin' sheep. They're kind of helpless and need takin' care of. I'm pretty good at that."

"What about your pardner, Beau? You still takin' care of him too?"

"Somebody else has been doin' that lately."

Dawson's gaze touched Alta, who remained at the wagon. He seemed surprised to see her. "The way Beau and her argued, I figured she'd gone off and left you-all long before now."

Beau said, "We got tired of fightin'. It's easier on the diges-tion if we get along." Beau regarded the town with some appre-hension. "Ain't you afraid somebody here'll know you?"

"This desert dried me plumb out. Had to get some grub and some whiskey. I never was in this part of the country before, so nobody recognized me. Been campin' close to the spring and waitin' for you-all to show up."

Disturbed, Alta moved out from the wagon. "Why? What do you want with us?"

"Me and Joey and Beau, we talked about goin' to California, and then on up to Oregon. I was afraid if I didn't find them here we might never get together again."

She took Beau's arm. "We'd all be better off that way."

Realization came into Dawson's eyes. "You two *did* get tired of fightin'." He seemed disappointed. "That could change the complexion of things a right smart. With a woman on your arm, you're apt to get tired of travelin', too."

"I already am," Beau replied. "But I don't see I've got any choice unless I turn back and give myself up to the law." He turned to Alta. "To tell you the truth, I been thinkin' some about that. This runnin' ain't no life for me, and it sure ain't any good for you."

Dawson's gaze shifted from Beau to Alta, then to Joey. "The law ain't much on forgivin'. Many a time I've thought what you're thinkin', but I knew what'd happen to me. Runnin' ain't a good way to live, but hangin' ain't a good way to die."

Joey could not take his eyes from Beau. This was the first indication Beau had given that he entertained some thought about going back.

Dawson asked, "What about you, Joey? You got any of the same notions?"

Joey found it difficult to answer. "Yes sir, I get to thinkin' about home, and . . . well, I been doin' a lot of thinkin' about home."

"They've probably got a hard cot waitin' for you in a reformatory."

"I know. Me and Beau have got to talk it over. Me and Beau and Alta."

Dawson squatted and poked absently at the fire, thinking. "Well, I've got no business tryin' to tell you-all what to do, but I'm goin' to Oregon, with or without you. Goin' to make me a new start and send for my son. Who knows? Might even take up preachin'."

Joey marveled. "You, preachin'?"

"Why not? I know my Maker. I've been mighty close to Him several times."

"You have enough money to buy that farm you talked about?"

"No. I got a pretty good contribution from a little bank down south after I parted company with you, but it wasn't all I hoped for. Thought I'd make a touch on a bank here in Fort Stockton, only they ain't got one yet. You'd think a town with a thousand people would have a good bank, wouldn't you?"

Joey didn't know. Banks had played no part in his life so far.

Dawson said, "There's a saloon that's got a safe, though. And I happen to know that a cattle buyer hit town this mornin' and put a sackful of money in it. So I figure to make a little withdrawal tonight after everybody's gone home."

Joey's jaw dropped. "You mean to rob the safe?"

"It ain't much of one. It'll be like openin' a can of sardines. Anyhow, let's call it a loan. Might even pay them some interest someday when I'm able."

Alta said dryly, "And you wanted us to be a party to it."

"I don't need any help for a simple job like this. But if you-all decide to make the trip to Oregon with me, cross over to the Mexican side at El Paso del Norte and look in the cantinas. I'll rest there for a week or two."

Joey said, "I wish you wouldn't do this, Mr. Dawson. There's other ways to get money."

"I'm too old to break broncs and too lazy to punch cows. I'd have a gray beard down to my knees before I'd ever earn enough. I ain't got that kind of time." He shook hands with Joey and Beau. To Joey's surprise he nodded at Alta and touched the brim of his hat, showing her a respect he had not exhibited before. "Whatever you-all decide, the best of luck to you."

As Dawson mounted his horse, Joey trotted after him. "I wish you wouldn't go."

Dawson waved his hand. "El Paso del Norte," he shouted back, and rode off into the gathering darkness.

CHAPTER

16

McIntosh was grim as death, riding into camp. Dismounting, he called, "Beau, we shall have to forget about that beer. There is a good chance for a shooting in town tonight."

Beau stepped away from the campfire to meet him. "I wasn't thirsty noway. But a shootin'?"

"You would never guess who I saw as I started to leave town. The outlaw Miller Dawson."

Joey swallowed hard. Beau did a good job of covering any reaction. Joey did not even look at Alta.

McIntosh said, "Evidently he has been around for two or three days. Some people in town have suspected he was up to no good, but they did not know who he was. I knew him because I saw him once in Kerrville. So I rode back and confirmed his identity to the sheriff."

Joey had trouble finding voice. "You told them who he is?"

"As citizens we all have a duty to help uphold the law. It is common knowledge that a considerable amount of money was placed in a saloon safe this morning. The supposition is that Dawson may have designs upon it. The sheriff has removed it to a locked cell in the jail, and they have set up an ambush at the saloon in event Dawson makes a try."

An icy chill gripped Joey. "They'll kill him."

McIntosh nodded. "The choice is his own. If he leaves town peaceably the sheriff has no wish to confront him for crimes committed elsewhere. But if he tries to rob the saloon he may not see another sunrise." The sheepman mounted his horse again. "I promised the sheriff I would be back to make positive identification if need be. It is best that all of you remain here. Should there be gunfire, this camp is out of effective range."

Beau watched McIntosh fade off into the darkness. "Poor old Miller Dawson. I wish we could warn him that he's drawin' into a stacked deck." He appeared to consider going.

Alta took Beau's arm as if to hold him back. "He said he intended to reform, but he had just one more job to do. They always have one more job to do. And that one gets them killed."

Joey protested, "He saved your life, Alta. If he hadn't shot Farlow, we might all be dead."

She argued, "He didn't kill Farlow for us. He did it because Farlow was tryin' to kill *him*."

Joey fought down the urge to cry. "You heard what Mr. McIntosh said. They won't bother him if he doesn't try to rob that place. I've got to find him and tell him."

Alta reached out to Joey. "It's too dangerous to go in to town, and it'd make no difference in the long run. If we stop him here he'll just try it somewhere else . . . Fort Davis or El Paso or farther west. Luck always runs out for his kind. He'll never see Oregon."

"Maybe he can change. I've got to give him that chance." Joey grabbed his bridle and moved quickly toward the spot where Taw and Git Out were staked on grass beside the creek.

Beau hobbled awkwardly after him, grabbing his arm and stopping him. "Alta's right. If it doesn't happen here it'll happen somewhere else. We can't watch out for him forever."

Joey jerked free of Beau's grip. "I ain't fixin' to let him die without I try to help him."

"And maybe catch a stray bullet. Damn it, boy, he's of age to pick his own road, but you're not. It's goin' to be dangerous out there."

"Everything we've done since Bastrop has been dangerous." Joey slipped the bit into Taw's mouth and the headstall over his ears. Beau grabbed for him, but Joey swung Taw around to block him. He grasped Taw's mane and pulled himself up bareback.

Beau caught the bridle reins near the bit. "Joey, wait."

Joey beat his heels against Taw's ribs. The horse moved forward, jerking the reins from Beau's hand. Beau's weak leg gave way and he fell. "Damn it, Joey, you come back here. I don't want nothin' happenin' to you."

Joey put Taw into a lope. He could hear Beau hollering after him, and Alta as well, but he made it a point not to look back.

He did not know just where Dawson was camped except that it was somewhere near the springs. He could see the dim glow of lamps in town windows and lanterns hanging on open porches. Ahead and to his right lay the parade ground and the dark square walls of stone buildings on the military post.

He heard the sound of rushing water but could not see the springs. A rising moon cast a silver glow on the creek created by the artesian flow. Seeing two campfires, he rode to the first and called softly. "Mr. Dawson!"

A dark shape moved toward him, silhouetted in the fire's soft light. A voice spoke in a language he recognized as Spanish, though he did not know the words. He was disappointed to see that the camp was not Dawson's. It belonged to a Mexican family, their team of small mules tied to the wheels of their wagon, munching grain from a short wooden trough attached to the sideboard. Joey said to the man who walked out to meet him, "I'm lookin' for somebody else. Sorry I bothered you."

"No le hace."

Joey did not know what the words meant, but the shrug said enough.

He rode toward the other fire. He felt disappointment again even before he reached it, for he saw a peddler's wagon, all manner of sale goods stacked on shelves and suspended from its sides. The owner said, "I am closed for the night. Come back in the morning."

"I'm lookin' for a feller that was supposed to be camped close by. Maybe you saw him. Large man with a big black moustache. Rode a blue roan horse."

"Yes, he was over that way." The peddler pointed. "But he has broken camp. He came by here a while ago, riding toward town. He had all his belongings tied on his saddle."

Joey began to burn with anxiety. He did not know where to look. Fearing recognition, he had purposely avoided riding into town before. He had no idea how many saloons it supported or which was Dawson's target. He rode aimlessly down one street, then another, hoping chance might carry him to Dawson.

This was a quiet kind of country town where most people believed nightfall should find them at home. Most of the store buildings were already dark. Joey saw a saloonkeeper close a front door behind him, lifting down a lantern suspended beneath the porch roof. The light shone full in the man's dark face.

Joey did not ask for advice, but he received it free of charge in an accent heavily Spanish. "*Muchacho,* is best you go home now. Is too late for a boy to be on the street. I bet your mother looks for you."

Joey wondered how much the man knew about what was planned here tonight, and could this be the saloon? He doubted it. The small adobe building had the word *Cantina* crudely painted on the plaster above the door, marking it as a Mexican saloon. He thought it was unlikely to attract many gringo customers. A cattle buyer who carried large sums of money would probably look for a larger and fancier place.

He asked, "How many more saloons has this town got?"

The Mexican shook his head disapprovingly. "Now, what business has a young boy to talk of saloons? You go home now, or I tell the *cherife.*"

Joey pulled away to avoid calling more attention to himself. On another street he saw a larger structure which bore a sign reading *Liquors—Billiards—Beer.* That was another way, he guessed, of saying *Saloon.* The door was closed, the stone building dark. This, he thought, was a more likely prospect. He held Taw to the shadows and watched a few minutes but saw no sign of life. He reasoned that if they had set up an ambush here they would not be moving around and risking discovery.

He saw the dim figure of a horseman coming up the street, all but lost in the dark shadow of the buildings. He put Taw into a rough trot, which felt as if it would bounce Joey's innards up into his throat. "Mr. Dawson!" he called. "Mr. Dawson!"

The horseman rode out into the moonlit center of the street. Joey saw that he was not Miller Dawson.

Beau said, "Joey, I done everything but hold a gun on you to stop you from comin' into town." The words were of reproach, but the tone was of apprehension. "Come on, let me take you back to camp. This place is trigger-happy tonight."

Joey was amazed that Beau was sitting on Git Out, his bad leg extended awkwardly, the foot out of the stirrup. It must be causing him agony. "I didn't think you could ride yet."

"I oughtn't to be, but you didn't give me no choice. I couldn't stand by and see you get hurt, maybe killed."

Joey's throat was so tight that it pained him to speak. "I can't find Mr. Dawson. I don't know where he's at."

"I ain't seen him either, but I ran into a bunch of men with guns. They acted like they thought I was him, and I came damned near gettin' shot. Let's quit these streets before they make targets of us."

"We can't just turn our backs on him."

From a block down the street Joey saw the flash of a pistol, followed a split second later by the report. A man was running, afoot. He saw several more flashes, then heard a fusillade of shots. The man went down. The shots continued several seconds more, then stopped. The echoes reverberated against the buildings.

Joey froze, unable to breathe.

Beau's voice was strained. "Looks like we're too late."

Joey put Taw into his long, rough trot again. Beau spurred to catch up. Several men boiled out of a building, and three others emerged from around the sides. Indoors, someone lighted a lantern and brought it out. As Joey and Beau approached, the man carrying the lantern lifted it high over the body in the street.

The voice was McIntosh's. "That is your man, sheriff."

Joey was sick, bile rising in his throat. Miller Dawson lay twisted as he had fallen, a pool of blood spreading around him.

"My God," someone declared in awe, "we shot him to pieces."

"Well," said a man with a star on his shirt, "he won't be holdin' up any banks or robbin' any safes where he's gone. Like as not they'll have him shovelin' coal."

Beau rode up close beside Joey and placed his arm around Joey's shoulder. "Ain't nothin' we can do here. Come on, let's go back to camp."

Joey rode with him, his head down, his throat aching. His eyes burned, but no tears came. There had been too many tears already, and he was getting too big for them.

After a couple of hours Joey gave up trying to sleep. He laid back his blankets and went to the campfire, which had died down to a few glowing coals. He built it up with small pieces of dead mesquite. The night was not particularly chilly, but he found comfort in watching the play of the flames, listening to the crackle of burning wood. He thought about Miller Dawson and, in an effort to keep from dwelling on Dawson's violent death, forced himself to think about home. That awakened an ache of a different kind.

Long before daylight McIntosh seated himself by Joey's side. "Too much excitement," he said. "It has been a poor night for sleeping." He lighted his pipe with a blazing stick from the fire. "You're carrying the world on your shoulders, lad, and they are not broad enough to support the weight."

"Never got a wink of sleep."

"Perhaps you have never been so close to a shooting before. The man they killed was an outlaw. The world is better off without him."

Joey considered the propriety of confession and decided it

was time to level with the man who had been kind to him and Beau and Alta. "I knew him. I knew Miller Dawson."

McIntosh took the pipe from his mouth and studied it as if its taste had suddenly soured. "How would a lad like you come to know such a man?"

"There's a lot we never told you about, Mr. McIntosh. Me and Beau, we're wanted back in Bastrop."

"Now, what could *you* be wanted for?"

"For murder." Joey was not surprised by the strong look of disbelief. He had seen it before. He told it all, from the deaths of Pa and Reuben to his own narrow escapes, to the fight with Mr. Meacham and the accident of fate which had thrown him and Beau into the company of Miller Dawson.

McIntosh drew thoughtfully on the pipe. "I had a feeling you were running away from something, but I assumed it was nothing more than a strict stepmother. I had no idea you had endured so much."

"I know Mr. Dawson did some bad things in his life, but he was good to me."

"Very few men are totally bad."

"Farlow was, but not Mr. Dawson. You'd have liked him."

"Perhaps. He was a predator, however, like the coyote. He took from other men the fruits of their labor instead of working for his own."

"He might've changed."

"My dog Rustler is smart, but his ways are set. It is difficult to teach him something new. Miller Dawson was too old to change. You are young and still have time to make your choices. I believe you will make the right ones. You have a good heart."

Beau and Alta arose at dawn. Beau was surprised to find McIntosh and Joey seated together near the fire. "How long you-all been up?"

McIntosh said, "Quite a long time, long enough for Joey to tell me many things."

Beau gave Joey a quizzical look. Joey said, "No use tellin' him any more lies. He knows all of it."

Joey had feared Beau would be upset, but if anything he

seemed relieved. Beau told McIntosh, "You can turn me in if you want to. For all I know, there may be a reward."

"I did not turn Dawson in for a reward, nor would I do that to you. I know you are not an outlaw at heart."

"It wouldn't matter. I laid awake a long time last night, thinkin'. I've decided to go back and turn myself in. I don't want to spend the rest of my life runnin', lookin' back like Miller Dawson did, waitin' for the law to reach out and take me."

"But what of Joey?"

"I'll tell them he had nothin' to do with it. I think he'd like to stay here with you. You could teach him to be a sheepman."

Joey said, "That wouldn't be fair. I'm goin' back with you. Maybe they'll listen when I tell them how it was. Mr. Dawson did, and Mr. McIntosh too."

"Sheriff Gardner ain't like Mr. McIntosh. He'll gladly dance at my funeral." Beau jerked his head toward Alta. "I'd appreciate it if you could help her someway. Maybe you could hire her to cook for you or find her somethin' decent to do here in Fort Stockton."

Alta declared, "I'll stay with you, Beau, wherever you go."

"You can't. There's no tellin' what they may do to me."

"Whatever it is, I'll be there. I'll stay as close as the law will allow."

"You'd be lettin' yourself in for a lot of hell."

"I've already been through more hell than you can know. I'm stayin' with you. There's just one thing, Beau. I want you to marry me."

"You'd marry me, knowin' what's ahead?"

"I would, and I will."

Beau turned to McIntosh. "What can you say to a woman like that?"

McIntosh gave them a look of pride, and of sadness. "You say *yes*, and thank God you have her."

Joey and Beau and Alta attended two religious ceremonies that day, both conducted by the same minister. The first was a graveside funeral service for Miller Dawson. It drew few mourners but a large crowd of the curious to see a famous outlaw put into the ground. Joey's throat was so tight he could not speak, but he shed no tears.

The second was a wedding, performed in an almost empty church. The minister asked Beau and Alta their religious preference. Beau said, "I ain't got one, so pick any that the Lord'll approve of. About the only times I ever been in church was for somebody's funeral."

The minister smiled. "Fortunately none of them was your own. You might have been ill-prepared to pass through the Holy Gates."

"Anything you can do to get me ready would be appreciated, preacher. We never know what lies ahead."

"Marrying this young lady is a long step in the right direction. The Lord looks kindly upon the marriage sacrament. Now, who will give the bride away?"

McIntosh said, "The lady's father is no longer living, so that would be for me to do."

"And the best man?"

Beau turned his eyes to Joey. "My cousin here. He's a little short in years, but he's grown up considerable since we've been together."

We both have, Joey thought.

The only outside witnesses were the minister's pregnant young wife and a couple of neighbors who had gotten dressed up for the funeral and thought they might as well make a day of it.

The minister said, "What God has joined together, let no man put asunder."

No man except maybe Sheriff Gardner, Joey thought glumly.

Beau kissed the bride, then McIntosh did. Joey held back. The bride kissed *him.*

In gratitude for helping him with his sheep, McIntosh bought provisions for their trip eastward and provided a pack mule to carry the load. When he had said his good-byes to Beau and Alta he rested his big hands on Joey's thin shoulders.

"You'll write me a letter and let me know what's happened, won't you?"

"I sure will."

"I'll contact a good lawyer I know in Austin. I'll ask him to do whatever he can."

"The preacher said he'll pray for us."

"Sometimes a lawyer can do you more good than a minister. A minister talks to the Lord, but a lawyer can talk to the judge."

Joey said, "I wish you'd had a chance to know my pa. You-all would've liked one another."

"If the father was like the son, I am sure we would."

Beau and Alta struck out upon the trail toward Horsehead Crossing. Joey followed, leading the pack mule. He looked back once at Alister McIntosh and the collie, then turned his gaze eastward. He was going home.

Leaves were turning yellow and red and gold as they rode back through the hill country and picked up a familiar trail into Fredericksburg. Stopping there for flour and coffee, they heard about rangers finding the entrance to a hidden canyon and discovering a nearly deserted outlaw camp. The lawmen had set fire to the place and brought in six men who fitted descriptions in their "wanted" books. One was an escapee from a stone quarry near Austin.

The road led the three past the quarry, where Joey could imagine Hull back at work chiseling limestone, and into Austin, where it appeared that little progress had been made on construction of the new capitol.

"Government job," Beau said.

Joey dared not speak of it, but it pleased him that Beau passed through both Fredericksburg and Austin without mentioning need for a drink. Joey would have understood had he gotten himself staggering drunk, for the nearer they came to Bastrop the deeper was his own sense of foreboding.

They camped just outside of town the final evening, postponing the confrontation with Sheriff Gardner. Beau and Alta clung together after supper as they stared unhappily into the campfire. They went to bed early. Joey dragged his own blankets far to the other side of camp to give them privacy. They would be borrowing tonight against a long, dark, and lonely future.

He did not sleep much, and from the tired looks on Beau's and Alta's faces the next morning, he sensed they had not either. They talked little, soberly packing the mule and saddling their horses for the short ride into town. Joey's heart pounded hard as they rode up to the jail. He blinked away a burning in his eyes while Beau and Alta embraced one another before walking the final short distance.

Beau knocked. Gardner's wife came to the door and invited them inside. The sheriff sat at the kitchen table, sipping from a cup. Surprise made him arise too quickly, sloshing hot coffee on his hand.

Beau said, "I've come to give myself up."

Gardner blinked, confused and none too pleased. He wiped his hand against his shirt. "Thought you'd left the country for good." He gave Alta a long, curious study.

Beau said, "You remember my cousin Joey."

"I do. I'm surprised you ain't quit the boy someplace long before now. Or him you. Well, don't just stand there with the door open. It's drafty in here."

Gardner's wife closed the door. Beau moved farther into the room and motioned toward Alta. "This here is my wife."

"Wife? I never thought that would happen. You must've caught the poor woman on her blind side." Gardner set the cup down and came around the table toward the visitors. Joey could not take his eyes from the set of handcuffs swinging loose from the sheriff's belt. Gardner said, "The air's startin' to get a little fall nip. You-all want some coffee to warm you up before we get down to cases?"

Beau said, "No sir, it'd only rile my stomach worse than it already is. I just want to get this over with. I'm givin' myself up."

"On which charge? There's so many to pick from . . ."

"For the killin' of Joey's stepdaddy, Blair Meacham."

The sheriff's mouth dropped open, but no sound came from it. He looked at his wife as if she might know what Beau was talking about. He demanded, "When did this killin' take place?"

"When you sent him out to Casper Tatum's farm to fetch

Joey. He did his best to drown the boy, and he tried to pistol-whip me. I stove his head in with a chunk of wood. Last we seen of him, he was floatin' off down the river."

"And that's when you decided to quit the country?"

"Didn't seem like we had much choice. I didn't figure you'd believe anything we told you."

"You were right. I wouldn't have, and I still don't."

"But it wasn't murder. It was self-defense."

"It wasn't murder because there wasn't nobody killed. Meacham's head must've been harder than you thought. He managed to crawl out of the river after you left him to drown."

This time it was Joey's and Beau's mouths that fell open. Joey's skin tingled with realization. "Then we've been runnin' all this time from somethin' that never happened."

Beau was stunned. "He looked awful dead."

"You rearranged his face some . . . broke his nose and cracked his jaw. He came in here lookin' like a horse had fallen on him. Said the boy fell in the river, and he was tryin' to save him. Claimed you were drunk, and you were mad because he wouldn't pay you anything for takin' Joey. Said you tried your damnedest to kill him."

Joey protested, "It wasn't that way at all. Mr. Meacham pulled me off of my horse and tried to drown me so him and Dulcie could have the farm. When Beau drug me out of the river, Mr. Meacham tried to kill him too."

Joey could not tell if he was making any impression.

Gardner frowned at Beau. "I've got a warrant for you on a charge of attempted murder."

Beau said, "And I want to file charges on Meacham for the same thing."

The sheriff grunted. "Looks to me like the two of you have canceled one another out. I don't expect Meacham will ever come back here again, and I'd be obliged if you'd do me the same favor. The county's bill for feedin' prisoners has been a lot cheaper since you've been gone."

Beau was incredulous. "You ain't puttin' me in jail?"

"And have you eat off of the county 'til God knows when? Hell no!"

Beau and Alta threw their arms around one another. Alta sobbed a little.

Gardner frowned. "You ain't figurin' on stayin' around Bastrop, are you?"

Beau held onto Alta. "I was so sure you'd throw me in jail that I hadn't made any plans."

"Your shack ain't there anymore. Couple of tramps took it over after you left. They got drunk and burned it down, so you've got no place to live." The sheriff's eyes lighted with hope. "I reckon you'll be movin' on?"

Joey felt that a hundred pounds of dead weight had been lifted from his shoulders. He wanted to jump and shout, but he kept a discreet rein on himself. "I wish you'd go home with me, Beau. I'll need you to help me with the farm." He chose not to say so, but he also needed somebody grown to help him stand his ground against Dulcie. Beau should be able to, and if he couldn't, Joey would bet that Alta could.

Guardian or not, Dulcie had to leave . . . and take Meacham with her.

Beau seemed ready to collapse. He looked at Gardner, still not quite believing. "I'm free to go anywhere I want to?"

"Yes. And I wish to hell you would, someplace besides here."

Beau embraced Alta again. "Come on, Mrs. Shipman. Joey is fixin' to make farmers out of me and you."

CHAPTER
17

Joey felt a rising excitement when he reached territory he had known as far back as he could remember. Athens seemed no different from the last time he had been there. Riding by the schoolhouse, he could hear the teacher's voice and hoped she did not look out the window. She would likely come running and demand to know why he had not been there at resumption of classes in the fall. He intended to start again soon. Reading Kipling and Scott and Dickens from Mr. McIntosh's box of books had reawakened his interest in learning. But first he must get everything straightened out at home. There was a reckoning to be made with Dulcie and Mr. Meacham.

Joey said, "I'd like to talk to Sheriff Lawton before we go to the farm. He was always a good friend of Pa's. He'll know what we ought to do."

Beau was dubious. "A friendly sheriff? That's somebody I'd like to meet."

Lawton leaped from the chair in his courthouse office as Joey walked in the door. "Joey Shipman?" The sheriff's face glowed like a new lantern. Eagerly, he grabbed Joey's hand. "My God, boy, I was afraid you might be layin' dead some-place." He backed off at arm's length to give Joey's face an intense scrutiny. "You've changed. I believe you've grown a little, and you're startin' to look like a man."

Beau said, "He's seen the elephant and bucked the tiger."

Joey introduced Alta and Beau. The sheriff offered Alta a chair, then turned back to Joey. "Dulcie came and told me you'd run away. I helped her and Blair Meacham write letters to officers all over this part of the state."

"They worked," Joey told him. "The sheriff over at Bastrop made sure I stayed around 'til Mr. Meacham could come after me."

Beau said, "He came, all right. Tried to kill Joey and me both."

The sheriff frowned. "That's not exactly the way Meacham told it when he came back. I'd like to hear your version."

Joey and Beau took turns telling what had happened. Beau said, "I'm surprised he had the nerve to come back here. He ought to've known the truth would come out someday if Joey ever showed up again."

Lawton shook his head. "It would be his word against that of a boy who had already told several wild stories about his step-mother tryin' to kill him. And, bad as I hate to say this, Mr. Shipman, I gather that your reputation around Bastrop didn't shine very bright either."

Beau admitted, "No, I suppose not."

Joey feared that the prospects were dim. "So you don't believe us."

"At this point I'm not sure what to believe. I'm leanin' toward you, but Meacham sounded convincin'. Could it be that all of you misunderstood each other's intentions?"

Joey said firmly, "There wasn't any misunderstandin'. Mr. Meacham meant to drown me. Told me straight out that there wasn't no use in me fightin' him."

The sheriff walked to the window and stared out onto the street, thinking. "He would say you were in such a panic that you didn't hear him right. He told me he was tryin' to rescue you, and your cousin attacked him."

"I know what I heard, and I know what he tried to do. If it hadn't been for Beau, I'd be dead."

"I want to believe you, but I'm afraid a court might not accept your word." He reached for his hat, hanging on a peg near the door. "I'll get my horse from the wagon yard and ride out to the farm with you. I want to see if Meacham changes his story any when you're standin' there lookin' him in the face."

"If he doesn't, what can I do? I don't want Dulcie to be my guardian anymore. I don't see where I need one anyway. I can take care of myself."

"The judge won't see it that way. You're under age."

The afternoon sun was a long way down toward the horizon by the time they came in sight of the farm. Joey rode out a bit ahead of the sheriff, Beau, and Alta. He wanted to put Taw into a run, but he feared such a show of impatience would make him look like a kid.

There was no dog to bark at the new arrivals, but a peacock set up a shrill cry. So far as Joey could see, everything looked the same . . . the white frame house, the barn and windmill, the old shack where Reuben had slept. The sight of them filled him with joy, quickly dampened by an invasive sense of melancholy. They *appeared* the same, but they would never *be* the same, for Pa was no longer there, nor was Reuben.

The cotton field was white as if a winter storm had passed, leaving a spotting of snow. Joey could see that it had been picked over once already. The white bolls would yield a good second picking after frost dropped the leaves. Only stubble remained in the field where the corn had been harvested. The milk cow grazed there, salvaging the stalks. The calf was not with her, nor did Joey see it in the milking pen. He guessed Dulcie had sold it. But the mean Jersey bull was wrapping a long tongue around dried corn leaves and pulling them into his mouth.

Me and you, we're going to have us a little head-butting, Joey thought. *You're going to learn who's in charge here.*

But the bull could wait. The first order of business would be to settle things with Dulcie and Mr. Meacham.

The peacock's cry brought Dulcie out onto the front porch. One hand gripping a post for support, the other at her throat, she fastened a dismayed gaze on Joey. He saw no welcome in her gray eyes. He saw fear.

Well, he thought, she had something to be fearful about. If he had his way, she would soon be hunting a new home. It might be that Sheriff Lawton would provide one in jail for her and Mr. Meacham. Being man and wife now, they might even share a cell.

The sheriff said, "I've brought the prodigal home."

She did not answer.

Lawton stepped down from his horse and led it to the edge of the porch. He said again, "I've brought Joey home."

She bit her thin, pinched lower lip. "So I see." To Joey she said accusingly, "I didn't know but what you were dead."

You're not that lucky, Joey thought.

The sheriff waited in vain for her to say more or to move. He said, "Aren't you even goin' to ask the boy into the house?"

Tightly she replied, "He'll do pretty much as he pleases. He always did." She turned abruptly and retreated back inside, closing the door.

Joey had half expected her to hug him as a show for the others, though he would have shrunk from her if she had tried. He thought most women under the circumstances would at least have made the pretense. He had to give her credit for being honest after her fashion.

Confounded, Lawton said, "Odd woman." He nodded toward the barn. "Joey, you'd better put our horses and the pack mule in the corral. Then we'll go in the house. It's chilly out here."

Joey thought it would be chilly in the house too, though not in the same way.

When he and Beau returned from taking care of the horses, the sheriff knocked on the door, then pushed it open. "Dulcie, we're comin' in." He paused, waiting for a reply but not receiving it. He motioned for the others to follow him. Joey held back until last, not wanting to be in the house alone with Dulcie even for a moment.

Dulcie stood near the rear door, looking out a window toward the backyard and the chicken pen.

Lawton said, "Dulcie, you and Blair put me to a lot of trouble huntin' this boy. Now you act like you don't want to see him."

Dulcie turned, her face severe. "I didn't tell him to run away, and I didn't tell him to try to kill Mr. Meacham."

Joey figured she knew it anyway, but he said, "It was Mr. Meacham that tried to kill *me.*"

Lawton said, "I want to talk to Blair. Where's he at?"

She was slow and reluctant in answering. "He's gone to town."

"I didn't see him. How long's he been gone?"

"A while. I don't know when he'll be back."

He could not have been gone long, Joey thought, for he smelled tobacco smoke. He doubted Dulcie had taken up the habit.

The sheriff tried to overlook her defensive manner. He introduced Beau and Alta. "Joey and his cousin tell things considerably different than Blair did. I'd like to hear his story again."

"He wouldn't change it none."

"I'd like to hear it anyway."

She turned hostile eyes on Joey. "You know what kind of lies Joey's told before. Why would you believe him now over the word of a grown man?"

"I'm not sayin' what I believe or disbelieve, not yet. But somebody's wrong, and I want to know the truth. So I'll wait."

"Then wait. It's liable to be a long evenin'. Sometimes Blair forgets to come home at all." Chin high, she strode into her bedroom and closed the door behind her.

Lawton gave Alta and Beau an apologetic look. "I've never seen her like this before."

Joey said, "I have. She was like this most of the time when there wasn't any company around."

The sheriff opened the back door and peered outside. Joey and Beau took chairs and sat at the kitchen table. Alta went to the stove but found the coffeepot sitting on the edge, empty and cold. "Show me where the coffee beans are, Joey."

The sheriff eyed the closed bedroom door. "It could be a long evenin', like Dulcie said. She may not know about it, but it didn't take long for her honeymoon to be over with. Blair Meacham's seein' a widow lady over in town."

Joey supposed he should feel sorry for Dulcie, but it was possible she had plotted with Mr. Meacham to get Pa and Reuben and himself out of the way so she could have the farm. Now Mr. Meacham was playing Romeo with another Juliet. He could see a certain rude justice in that.

A new idea almost took his breath. "The only way Dulcie could own the farm would be if I was to die, ain't that right?"

The sheriff agreed. "That's the way the will was set up."

"Say somethin' did happen to me, and Dulcie got the farm. What if somethin' happened to her then? Who would get the place?"

"Meacham's her husband." The sheriff's eyes widened as he grasped what Joey was thinking.

Beau caught on too. "That widow in town . . . is she better lookin' than Dulcie?"

"Some would say so. And she inherited a fair amount of money from her husband. That helps her looks a right smart."

Beau asked, "How did her husband die?"

"An accident. A horse drug him to death." He swallowed. The look that passed between him and Beau indicated they were both thinking the same thing.

Joey was already ahead of them. He said, "I wonder if Dulcie has thought of it."

They waited in silence. Fidgety, tired of sitting around, Joey poked wood into the stove to keep the kitchen warm. Seeing that the woodbox was nearly empty, he went outside and brought in enough to fill it.

Not until daylight faded into dusk did Dulcie emerge from the bedroom, her mood subdued. "If he was comin', he'd be here by now. I'll fix you-all some supper."

The sheriff arose from the table. "I hadn't figured on spendin' the night. I'll be gettin' back home. Maybe I'll meet Blair on the road or find him in town." He beckoned for Beau to walk out onto the porch with him.

Joey became uneasy. He had counted on the sheriff's remaining until the situation was resolved. It would be awkward, he and Beau and Alta staying here with Dulcie. And what if the sheriff missed Mr. Meacham and the man showed up without the law on hand to preserve the peace? There was apt to be one hell of a fight.

After supper Dulcie sat in the chair that had once been Mama's. The creaking of the floor beneath the rocker emphasized the cold and painful silence. It was if she had shut everyone else out, pretending to herself that she was alone.

Joey wished she were. He thought back to the pleasant nights in Alister McIntosh's sheep camp and wondered if he might have been better off staying in the Fort Stockton country. But he had made up his mind to see this thing through to conclusion, whatever that might be.

He did not want to sleep in the house, not with Dulcie there. He chose to bunk in Reuben's shack. He told Beau and Alta they could use his old room for the night. When Dulcie left— and one way or another she was going to—they could have the room where she and Pa had slept.

Beau was concerned about Joey's leaving the house. "I'd feel better if you stayed under the same roof with us."

"That'd mean bein' under the same roof as Dulcie. I can't do that any more."

Alta seemed inclined to argue the matter further, but Beau said, "He's old enough to make up his own mind. Let him do what he wants to."

The moon was rising as Joey walked to the corral to untie his blankets from the saddle he had removed from Taw's back and placed on a rack beneath a shed. He could see the outlines of the milk cow and the Jersey bull at the edge of the corn field. It was in his mind that he would sell the bull at his first opportunity, but not before a settlement of their differences.

The bull saw or sensed him and slung its head. It began pawing dirt and made a threatening bellow. Joey picked up a rock and sailed it, missing by a yard.

He felt a chill as he approached the shack, carrying his

blanket roll. The night air carried a hint of coming frost, but his reaction was not due entirely to the cold. He felt as if Reuben might be awaiting him inside.

He pushed the door open and lighted a match so he could find the lamp. He lifted off the glass chimney and touched the flame to the wick. It caught just as the match curled black and its flame burned his fingers. He turned the wick back a little so the lamp would not smoke, then replaced the chimney. It was dusty and streaked, in need of cleaning, but it would do for now.

He shivered again and considered starting a fire in the little stove. He picked up the iron poker and stirred the old cold ashes but decided against wasting wood that he would have to replace later. He would soon be warm in the blankets anyway. He closed the stove and propped the poker against it.

He lay awake awhile, stirring through old memories as he had stirred the ashes. He remembered happy times with Mama and Pa, with Reuben. He wished he had gone up to the cemetery to visit their graves, but night had overtaken him before he got to it. Tomorrow he would, he promised himself.

Sleepiness began to burn his eyes. He blew out the lamp and crawled under the blankets. They warmed quickly, and the monotonous creaking of the windmill carried him away like a lullaby.

He awakened suddenly in great fear, unable to breathe. He struggled for breath, but something pressed down against his face, closing off his nose and mouth. His hands came up fighting against the obstruction, and he realized it was a pillow. He kicked and squirmed and choked.

"Best hold still, damn you. Ain't nobody goin' to help you this time."

He knew that gruff voice. It was Meacham's.

Joey's lungs blazed like a runaway fire, begging for breath. His hands fought against the pillow that pushed upon his face. He managed to twist his neck and caught a little air before the pillow pressed down again.

Meacham's voice was angry. "How many times have I got to kill you before you stay dead?"

Joey squirmed and kicked as calves did when he tried to hold them down. He managed a kick that made Meacham curse and loosen his grip on the pillow. In an instant Joey was out from under him and on his feet.

The poker! He remembered he had propped it against the stove. He could not see it in the darkness, but he knew where it must be. He groped in desperation, his fingers closing around the cold iron handle. He swung it at the dark shape that lunged at him. From the impact he knew he had struck Meacham on the side of the head. Meacham staggered, then came at Joey again before Joey was able to raise the poker high. He swung it from just above the floor and struck the man across the shin.

Meacham screeched and hopped on one leg. Before he could recover, Joey threw himself toward the door and burst out into the nippy night air. He could hear Meacham just behind him, almost within arm's length. He stopped and swung the poker a third time. It connected with Meacham's knee. The man stumbled, then sprawled on the ground.

Joey did not wait to strike him again. He dropped the poker and ran toward the house, shouting. "Beau! It's Mr. Meacham!"

He was aware of two other figures moving in the night. Sheriff Lawton's voice commanded, "Meacham! Stop or I'll shoot!"

Meacham was limping, but he did not stop. He headed for the cotton patch. Lawton's pistol blazed. Meacham shouted, stumbled, and fell. He pushed to his feet again, turning to fire a pistol shot in the sheriff's general direction. He crawled through the wire fence and was lost in the darkness.

Beau threw his arms around Joey. "God, boy, you scared me all the way down to my toenails."

"He tried to kill me."

Sheriff Lawton cautiously advanced most of the way to the fence, then retreated. Meacham had shown himself to be armed.

"It's too dangerous to go in there after him in the dark," Lawton told Beau. "He ain't apt to travel far afoot. We'll find him at daylight." He put a hand on Joey's shoulder. "Sorry, boy. We were hid in the barn, watchin' that shack, but Meacham slipped by us someway."

"I thought you went back to town."

"That's what I wanted Meacham to think. I knew Dulcie lied about him bein' gone. He must've seen us comin' and lit out the back door, but he'd been smokin' tobacco. I smelled it when we first went into the house."

"He tried to smother me with a pillow."

The sheriff nodded, understanding. "A pillow wouldn't leave any trace to prove that murder was done. I reckon we know now how Old Reuben died."

Joey had been too frightened to think of that for himself.

Alta and Dulcie came out onto the porch as Joey and the two men returned to the house. The sheriff faced Dulcie. "You lied to me about him goin' to town."

Dulcie offered no answer.

Lawton said, "We'll get him come daylight, and he can talk for himself. Things might go easier with you if you talk to me first."

"A woman doesn't go tellin' the law about her husband."

"She does when there's been murder, and when there might be another. Otherwise she's an accessory." He looked sternly into Dulcie's eyes. "She might even become a victim."

Dulcie trembled. "What do you mean?"

"I'll bet you've already thought about it. And I'll bet you know about that widow Blair's been seein' in Athens."

Dulcie was slow to reply. "I know about her."

"Blair tried to kill this boy with a pillow so there wouldn't be any proof of murder. What if he'd got it done, and you inherited this farm? Knowin' what you know, how long do you think he'd let *you* live?"

Dulcie hung her head. Joey thought it would not take much to make her break down and cry.

The sheriff pressed, "You ought to've known Joey would show up sooner or later and the truth would all come out."

Dulcie sobbed a moment, then regained control. "I was afraid of Blair, sore afraid. He wanted this land. I didn't know 'til afterward, but he caused John's accident, and he killed Reuben. I dreaded the day Joey might come home because Blair would try to kill him and make it look like an accident.

Once I had title to the farm I was as good as dead too. All I meant to him was a way to get hold of this place."

"If you'll testify to that, I'll recommend that the judge give you probation. But there's one condition. I'll want you to leave Henderson County and never come back."

"I've got no place to go."

"You've got kinfolks, haven't you?"

"None I get along with."

"It's your problem. You'll just have to work it out the best way you can."

She will survive, Joey thought. *She still has her looks, sort of. She can find herself another lonely widower, the same way she found Pa. At least then she'll be somebody else's problem; she won't be mine.*

Sheriff Lawton stayed at the barn the rest of the night in case Meacham circled back and made a try for one of the horses. Beau wrapped himself in a blanket and took up a post on the front porch. Dulcie retreated into her bedroom and closed the door. Alta sat in the rocking chair, holding Beau's pistol in her lap. It was the one that had been Tolley's. She said, "You try to get some sleep, Joey. He ain't fixin' to hurt you anymore."

Joey said, "The only way I could sleep would be if you hit me across the head with that six-shooter."

At daylight Beau and the sheriff came in for breakfast. Dulcie never ventured out of her room. The sheriff became concerned that she might have done something to herself, so Alta went in to check on her. She came out reassured. "Dulcie's all right. Scared as she was that her husband might kill her, she's not about to do it to herself."

Alta fixed breakfast, then the two men started outside to look for Meacham. The sheriff admonished, "Joey, you stay in this house 'til he's caught. He's got nothin' to gain now by killin' you, but he might take it in his head to do it just out of spite."

"I'd like to go and help you find him."

Beau commanded, "You do what the sheriff tells you, boy. Stay in the house."

Joey's temper flared. There was Beau, ordering him around again like he was a kid. He had thought they had gotten that sort of thing all straightened out.

Dulcie did not emerge from her room until the men had gone. She looked haggard, as if she had not slept. Alta offered to fix breakfast for her, but Dulcie demurred. "All I want is some coffee. I'm cold, awful cold."

She filled her cup and walked to the door, staring out through the oval glass. "Looks like they'd've found him by now."

Joey said, "They ain't been gone that long."

"What if they don't catch him at all? There won't none of us be safe around here."

Alta sat down again, the pistol in her lap. "They'll catch him. That sheriff looks like a determined man. And so is Beau when he sets his mind to somethin'."

Joey had put aside the fleeting resentment against his cousin. "Like not drinkin' the way he used to. I reckon he found somethin' he wants more than whiskey."

Alta smiled.

Dulcie turned to Joey. "I know you've got cause enough to doubt me, but I never meant you any harm. When I married your father I intended to be a good wife to him and a real mother to you. But nothin' seemed to work out like we wanted it to. Wasn't your fault, it was mine and your father's. I suppose we were both lookin' for somethin' the other didn't have."

"After he was gone, it didn't take you long to marry Mr. Meacham."

"Another mistake. When it comes to marryin', I ain't done much good for myself."

She returned to the door and gasped. "My God! It's him!"

Joey ran to the window. He saw Meacham in the front yard, moving toward the porch. He carried a pistol.

Dulcie's face drained white. "He's come to kill us all." She retreated into the bedroom.

Alta came quickly to Joey's side, drawing back the hammer on the pistol Beau had left her. She raised the weapon, extending it in front of her, gripping it in both hands. Joey heard heavy footsteps on the porch.

Dulcie came out of the bedroom carrying a rifle that had been Pa's. "Step aside, Alta. I'm not lettin' him get me." She moved near the door and shouted, "Blair, do you hear me?"

The answer from the porch was plain. "I hear you. Send that boy outside."

"What for? You've lost any chance of takin' this farm. They're out yonder now, lookin' for you."

"That boy's goin' to get me away from here. Long as I've got him, they ain't goin' to push me. Open that door, Dulcie, and send him out or I'm comin' in."

Joey saw a dark form through the oval glass. The door burst open and Meacham stood at the threshold, pistol in his hand.

Dulcie pulled the trigger. The explosion of the rifle seemed to shake the walls. Meacham screeched and fired the pistol. Dulcie jerked as if a horse had kicked her. Alta's six-shooter blasted, the recoil almost kicking the weapon out of her hands. Meacham screamed and staggered, dropping his pistol as he fell from the porch.

Dulcie slumped, the rifle clattering upon the floor. Joey grabbed it up and ran out onto the porch, levering a new cartridge into the chamber. He raised the rifle and aimed at Meacham, lying on the ground and gripping his bleeding leg. He bled too from a wound in his shoulder.

Meacham screamed, "No, boy, no! Don't shoot. For God's sake, don't kill me!"

Joey's blood was cold. His finger tightened on the trigger. Here was the man responsible for Pa's death, and Reuben's. Joey leveled the sights on the bridge of Meacham's broken nose.

Alta's voice was calm but firm behind him. "Ain't we seen enough of killin', Joey? Wasn't Tolley and Farlow and Miller Dawson enough? And Dulcie?"

Joey eased his grip on the rifle. "Dulcie's dead?"

"Yes."

Meacham pleaded, "Boy, don't do it. For God's sake, I'm a wounded man."

Joey lowered the rifle only a little. "Don't you move. Don't you move an inch."

Meacham's voice was shrill with pain and fear. "I think Dulcie shot my leg off. I'm bleedin' to death."

"Then lay there and bleed, but don't you move."

Blinking away a mist that clouded his eyes, Joey saw Beau and the sheriff spurring in from the pasture. He stepped down from the porch and picked up Meacham's fallen pistol. Meacham saw the two riders coming. He begged, "Please, they'll be wantin' to shoot me. Don't let them. For the love of God, I'm not ready to die."

"Neither were Pa and Reuben and Dulcie."

Joey knew Beau and the sheriff weren't going to kill Meacham. They would let him live a while. They would let him soak in cold sweat, dreading the rope that would strangle him. They would probably have to drag him kicking and screaming up those thirteen steps, but that was the way it should be.

Joey stood with Alta and Beau outside the small family cemetery, looking at the headstones. Dulcie never had put up one for Pa. Joey said, "First thing I'll do when we finish the cotton will be to get a marker carved for him." Pa wouldn't mind waiting that long. As a farmer he would have understood the necessity of finishing the harvest.

Pa was buried beside Mama, but there was a space on the other side of him, still within the stone fence. "I don't guess Mama would mind all that much. After all, Dulcie was Pa's wife too, for a little while."

Beau asked, "Are you sure you want her here? The sheriff said the county would provide a buryin' place in town."

Joey had given it a good deal of thought. "Me and her didn't get along, but I won't fight her all the way to the cemetery. We'll bury her by Pa."

Alta clasped Joey's arm. "That's a grownup way of lookin' at it. A lot of grown folks wouldn't be so forgivin'."

Beau said, "I don't know what your pa would say about me livin' in his house. Me and him didn't see eye to eye about much."

"You haven't had a drink in quite a spell now."

"Wait 'til we get the last of the cotton in."

Alta gave Beau a look that said he had better be joshing. Beau gave her a look that assured her he was. Alta was a small woman, but she was strong enough to drag Beau up against the snubbing post.

They started back down the slope toward the house. In the field the Jersey bull was feeding on stubble left from the corn crop. He and the milk cow had just about finished it.

Beau said, "We ought to turn them out into the pasture. There ain't much left for them in the corn patch."

"Good idea," Joey said.

They walked together to the gate. The bull saw Joey coming and began to paw dirt, bawling a challenge. Joey stopped. "You-all stay out here. I want to do this myself."

Beau warned, "That bull is spoilin' for a fight."

"It's time he got one." Joey looked for the iron poker he had dropped last night. He found it, entered the field, and walked around to the wire gate that opened into the pasture. He unfastened it and laid it back.

The bull pawed again, then came running, head down, its nose so near the ground that its breath raised puffs of dust. Joey stood his ground.

Reuben had always said a bull on the fight would close its eyes just before it made contact. Joey had never built the nerve to test that theory, but now he held still and waited. Just a few feet away the bull shut its eyes and came rushing with a belligerent snort.

Joey stepped to one side and swung the poker with all his strength, bringing it down across the bridge of the bull's nose.

The bull moved past him, shaking its head. An angry bellow trailed into painful protest. The Jersey pawed dirt and charged again. Once more Joey stepped aside and brought the poker down with all the force in his arms and back.

The bull kept running until it was a dozen yards away, then turned and faced around, slinging its head, trying to shake free of the hurting. Gone was the bluster, the challenge.

Joey made a run at it, waving the poker and shouting. "*Hyahh!* Git, you son of a bitch!"

The bull turned and ran, blindly bumping the gate post as it fled into the pasture.

Beau and Alta waited outside the field gate. Beau grinned. "Boy, don't you know you oughtn't to be usin' that kind of language?"

Joey closed the gate behind him and watched in satisfaction as the Jersey bull trotted farther away, slinging its head in confusion and fear and pain.

"And don't you know it's time you quit callin' me *boy?*"

Available by mail from

TOR FORGE

1812 • David Nevin
The War of 1812 would either make America a global power sweeping to the pacific or break it into small pieces bound to mighty England. Only the courage of James Madison, Andrew Jackson, and their wives could determine the nation's fate.

PRIDE OF LIONS • Morgan Llywelyn
Pride of Lions, the sequel to the immensely popular *Lion of Ireland,* is a stunningly realistic novel of the dreams and bloodshed, passion and treachery, of eleventh-century Ireland and its lusty people.

WALTZING IN RAGTIME • Eileen Charbonneau
The daughter of a lumber baron is struggling to make it as a journalist in turn-of-the-century San Francisco when she meets ranger Matthew Hart, whose passion for nature challenges her deepest held beliefs.

BUFFALO SOLDIERS • Tom Willard
Former slaves had proven they could fight valiantly for their freedom, but in the West they were to fight for the freedom and security of the white settlers who often despised them.

THIN MOON AND COLD MIST • Kathleen O'Neal Gear
Robin Heatherton, a spy for the Confederacy, flees with her son to the Colorado Territory, hoping to escape from Union Army Major Corley, obsessed with her ever since her espionage work led to the death of his brother.

SEMINOLE SONG • Vella Munn
"As the U.S. Army surrounds their reservation in the Florida Everglades, a Seminole warrior chief clings to the slave girl who once saved his life after fleeing from her master, a wife-murderer who is out for blood." —*Hot Picks*

THE OVERLAND TRAIL • Wendi Lee
Based on the authentic diaries of the women who crossed the country in the late 1840s. America, a widowed pioneer, and Dancing Feather, a young Paiute, set out to recover America's kidnapped infant daughter—and to forge a bridge between their two worlds.

Westerns available from

TOR FORGE

TRAPPER'S MOON • Jory Sherman
"Jory Sherman takes us on an exhilarating journey of discovery with a colorful group of trappers and Indians. It is quite a ride."—Elmer Kelton

CASHBOX • Richard S. Wheeler
"A vivid portrait of the life and death of a frontier town."—*Kirkus Reviews*

SHORTGRASS SONG • Mike Blakely
"*Shortgrass Song* leaves me a bit stunned by its epic scope and the power of the writing. Excellent!"—Elmer Kelton

CITY OF WIDOWS • Loren Estleman
"Prose as picturesque as the painted desert..."—*The New York Times*

BIG HORN LEGACY • W. Michael Gear
Abriel Catton receives the last will and testament of his father, Web, and must reassemble his family to search for his father's legacy, all the while pursued by the murdering Braxton Bragg and desire for revenge and gold.

SAVAGE WHISPER • Earl Murray
When Austin Well's raid is foiled by beautiful Indian warrior Eagle's Shadow Woman, he cannot forget the beauty and ferocity of the woman who almost killed him or figure out a way to see her again.